MURDER ON ROUTE 66

MORE MYSTERIES FROM THE
BERKLEY PUBLISHING GROUP . . .

CAT CALIBAN MYSTERIES: She was married for thirty-eight years. Raised three kids. Compared to that, tracking down killers is easy . . .

by D. B. Borton

ONE FOR THE MONEY	TWO POINTS FOR MURDER
THREE IS A CROWD	FOUR ELEMENTS OF MURDER
FIVE ALARM FIRE	SIX FEET UNDER

ELENA JARVIS MYSTERIES: There are some pretty bizarre crimes deep in the heart of Texas—and a pretty gutsy police detective who rounds up the unusual suspects . . .

by Nancy Herndon

ACID BATH	WIDOWS' WATCH
LETHAL STATUES	HUNTING GAME
TIME BOMBS	C.O.P OUT
CASANOVA CRIMES	

FREDDIE O'NEAL, P.I., MYSTERIES: You can bet that this appealing Reno private investigator will get her man . . . "A winner."   —Linda Grant

by Catherine Dain

LAY IT ON THE LINE	SING A SONG OF DEATH
WALK A CROOKED MILE	LAMENT FOR A DEAD COWBOY
BET AGAINST THE HOUSE	THE LUCK OF THE DRAW
DEAD MAN'S HAND	

BENNI HARPER MYSTERIES: Meet Benni Harper—a quilter and folk-art expert with an eye for murderous designs . . .

by Earlene Fowler

FOOL'S PUZZLE	IRISH CHAIN
KANSAS TROUBLES	GOOSE IN THE POND
DOVE IN THE WINDOW	MARINER'S COMPASS

HANNAH BARLOW MYSTERIES: For ex-cop and law student Hannah Barlow, justice isn't just a word in a textbook. Sometimes, it's a matter of life and death . . .

by Carroll Lachnit

MURDER IN BRIEF	A BLESSED DEATH
AKIN TO DEATH	

PEACHES DANN MYSTERIES: Peaches has never had a very good memory. But she's learned to cope with it over the years . . . Fortunately, though, when it comes to murder, this absentminded amateur sleuth doesn't forgive and forget!

by Elizabeth Daniels Squire

WHO KILLED WHAT'S-HER-NAME?	REMEMBER THE ALIBI
MEMORY CAN BE MURDER	WHOSE DEATH IS IT ANYWAY?
IS THERE A DEAD MAN IN THE HOUSE?	

MURDER ON ROUTE
66

EDITED BY
CAROLYN WHEAT

BERKLEY PRIME CRIME, NEW YORK

MURDER ON ROUTE 66

A Berkley Prime Crime Book / published by arrangement with
the editor

PRINTING HISTORY
Berkley Prime Crime edition / July 1999

The Penguin Putnam Inc. World Wide Web site address is
http://www.penguinputnam.com

ISBN: 0-425-17064-0

Berkley Prime Crime Books are published
by The Berkley Publishing Group,
a division of Penguin Putnam Inc.,
375 Hudson Street, New York, New York 10014.
The name BERKLEY PRIME CRIME and the BERKLEY PRIME CRIME
design are trademarks belonging to Penguin Putnam Inc.

PRINTED IN THE UNITED STATES OF AMERICA

10 9 8 7 6 5 4 3 2 1

ACKNOWLEDGMENTS

CONTENTS

MURDER ON THE MOTHER ROAD

We got our kicks on Route 66. Officially opened in 1926 as the first federal highway, it became the main street of America, taking intrepid travelers all the way from Chicago to Los Angeles. Bootleggers and jazz musicians drove Model As from Cicero to Joplin, Missouri. Those same Model As, loaded with washtubs and handmade quilts and hungry children, ferried dustbowl refugees from the farms they'd lost in Oklahoma to the orange groves of the San Fernando Valley. When war came, jeeps filled with soldiers took the road from McLean, Texas, to the Kingman Army Air Base in Arizona.

In the fifties, the former GIs piled their baby-boomer kids into station wagons and saw the U.S.A. in their Chevrolets—fins and all. The sixties saw Day-Glo–splashed VW buses with curtains made of Indian cotton whizzing through small rural towns before the road meandered into history, replaced by an eight-lane interstate superslab with a new number and no personality.

All those people, all those stories. Surely the highway John Steinbeck christened the Mother Road saw more than its share of murder.

This was the thought that struck me as I made the trip from Edmond, Oklahoma, where I was living and teaching, to Tulsa on what Oklahomans call the Old Road. I was in

Sapulpa, a lovely little town that still serves chocolate sodas at a real soda fountain, when I realized there were untold stories waiting to be collected, celebrating the most famous highway in the world.

The mystery writers who contributed to this anthology are uniquely qualified to tell these stories, living as they do in towns and cities all along the route. Each writer chose not only a locale (sometimes more than one; the road is essentially about movement, after all), but a time period, so that the reader of this collection travels not only between Chicago and Los Angeles, but from the 1920s to the present day.

Route 66 closed officially in 1985, but it lives on in the hearts of auto-loving Americans. Each of the eight states along the route boasts its own Route 66 Association, complete with museums. There are coffee-table books, guidebooks for the driver who wants to travel down memory lane, reproduction postcards, souvenir mugs and T-shirts, and documentary videos of the way things were.

This book is a loving tribute to the Mother Road and the people who traveled it, searching for a better tomorrow, or escaping an intolerable present. Several of the travelers in this book are running away from their crimes, others from themselves. Some of the stories involve the people who live along the route, providing food and shelter for the travelers, and sometimes becoming, to their eternal regret, entangled in their secrets. Cops solve crimes, private detectives ask too many questions of the wrong people, children learn lessons they'll never forget, and people make decisions that will haunt their lives forever.

And the road, like Old Man River, just keeps rolling along.

SHADES OF 66

Michael Allen Dymmoch

Michael Allen Dymmoch's first book, *The Man Who Understood Cats*, won the St. Martin's Press Malice Domestic Award and received enthusiastic reviews. *Incendiary Designs* is the third book in the series, which features Chicago police detective John Thinnes and psychiatrist Jack Caleb.

"**What's** next?" Thinnes put the carton he was lugging on the tailgate of the rental truck and shoved it inside the sixteen-foot box. Toward Rhonda.

She gave him a little smile. "Is this the last?"

"One more." He leaned on the tailgate and watched her drag the box toward the wall of cartons she'd built in the front of the truck. She shoved it up against the others, then wiped sweat from her face with the back of her hand. Thinnes added, "Maggie's bringing it."

Margaret Chandler, Rhonda's cousin. Rhonda had volunteered to help her move out of the old Berwyn tavern she'd grown up in on Ogden Avenue, Drover's on 66. It had been a stagecoach stop on the road to Springfield after the Chicago fire, and a going concern in the days when Ogden was part of America's Main Street. Truckers from as far away as California stopped in for a hot meal or a friendly drink. When the old Route 66 signs came down, Drover's became a neighborhood restaurant and bar. Soon it would be salvage.

Thinnes had been volunteered to drive the U-Haul. He didn't mind. He'd have offered to oil the hinges on the gates of Hell if it meant working with Rhonda. And it was a nice change from looking at dead bodies.

Rhonda said, "The basement, I think. Better ask."

He nodded and headed back inside.

He figured the basement would make an antique buff hyperventilate. It was dimly lit by naked bulbs hanging at intervals from BX cable strung along the ceiling beams. The twelve-by-eight beams bristled with nails holding up odds and ends: old horseshoes and harness parts, the first electric wires ever strung—complete with ceramic insulators and vintage light fixtures. The basement walls were brick, patched and retucked, looking like they were laid soon after the suburb's incorporation. The floor was poured concrete, cracked and crumbling in places, showing old brick pavers underneath. A pool table that looked like it had been disassembled with a chain saw leaned against one wall. An old enameled metal kitchen table held an assortment of canning jars, a smashed Tiffany lamp, hubcaps from a Checker cab, and the hood ornament from a Rolls. The peeling DROVER'S ON 66 sign, which had hung out front until the IL ROUTE 34 signs went up, brought to mind vacations out west when Thinnes was a kid. He'd never driven it. By the time he got his license, they'd closed the old road down.

Maggie's stuff was neatly packed in boxes, labeled CHANDLER with black marker. As he hefted the first—books by the weight—he heard a cat cry. There was no sign of it, though, and a dozen cats could have been hiding among the junk, so he started up the stairs.

The cat cried again when he returned. This time he called, "Here, kitty." Nothing.

He kept the boxes moving; the unseen cat kept up its complaints. Each time it sounded more like Thinnes's own cat stuck on the wrong side of a door.

When he was down to the last two boxes, Thinnes detoured past the kitchen where Rhonda and Maggie were packing up. "Your cat's yowling his head off downstairs," he told Maggie.

"There hasn't been a cat here since my mother died."

"Well *somebody's* cat's down there."

"It must've sneaked in. Just chase it out."

"It sounds like it's stuck somewhere."

"I'd better get a light."

By the time Thinnes returned from putting the last box in the truck, Maggie had located an industrial-strength flashlight, and she and Rhonda were prowling through the clutter.

"Are you sure it didn't follow you out, John?" Rhonda asked.

As if to argue the point, the invisible cat let out a feeble "meow" that seemed to come from behind a newer stretch of brick, to the right of the stairs. Thinnes wasn't sure the women heard it. "Maggie," he asked, pointing. "What's behind there?"

"Nothing. Why?"

"It sounded like the cat's behind the wall."

"Maybe it's just outside *near* the wall," Rhonda offered. "I'll look."

Maggie said, "I'll check up in the kitchen."

While they were gone, Thinnes used the flashlight to go over the room again.

None of them found so much as a whisker.

• • •

It took twenty minutes to knock a hole in the wall big enough to get the flashlight and Thinnes's head through. The cat he found in the bricked-over coal cellar beyond the wall wasn't the one he was looking for. He backed away from the opening and told Rhonda, "You and Maggie go call the police. Tell them we've got a dead body, but there's no rush. It's been dead a long time."

Maggie said, "Who . . . ?" at the same time Rhonda said, "How . . . ?" They both laughed. Nerves. If they'd been cops, they would've cracked a joke.

Once they were gone, Thinnes took another look at the remains. Professional curiosity. He couldn't help himself.

The cat was an orange and black and white calico that looked like a hunk of fur pulled over a wire frame. It was stretched out on its side, on the dirty skirt of a blond woman dead long enough to be black from age and post mortem changes. She lay face up, arms and legs splayed out, as if she'd died elsewhere and been dumped. Her dress was fifties-style, something his mother might've worn. A purse was half-hidden under an edge of her skirt. He itched to get his hands on it and the information it contained, but it would wait 'til Evidence was through.

After he'd given his statement to Berwyn's finest, and helped enlarge the hole to admit the evidence technician, Thinnes joined the women upstairs. They gravitated to the dark old bar, Maggie behind it, Thinnes and Rhonda perched on stools opposite. Maggie lined up three shot glasses—from habit, it seemed—and filled them from one of the few remaining bottles. Jack Daniels.

"When did your mother die?" Thinnes asked her.

She seemed surprised. "That's an odd question."

"You said there hasn't been a cat here since then."

"Oh. Well, I must've been five. That'd make it forty years ago."

Rhonda slipped her hand under Thinnes's arm. Leaning her head against him, she asked Maggie. "*How* did she die?"

"Funny you should ask," Maggie said. Like a robot, she topped off the glasses and stared past them while she thought about it. "I don't remember my mom's funeral. I guess I've blanked it out. I remember going into her room one morning and she wasn't there. And when I asked my grandpa where she was, he told me God took her to heaven to be with Daddy. I couldn't find Queenie either. Our cat. Grandpa told me she must've gone looking for Mama and got lost."

"What did Queenie look like?"

"I've got a picture somewhere."

She went out and came back with an old album, and they adjourned to one of the tables to study it. The stained glass fixture above shed a circle of warm light on the old book; the rest of the room was in near darkness. Maggie flipped the pages until she found the black and white photo of a calico cat. It looked to Thinnes like the one downstairs, but he didn't say so.

Other images caught their attention. The pictures went back to horse-drawn days—Drover's when Ogden was a wagon rut through swampy prairie; Drover's with various owners down the years; Drover's with the last owner before Maggie.

"This one was taken just before my mom died," she said.

It was a long shot from Ogden, with the DROVER'S ON 66 sign still new and shiny. Vintage fifties cars were parked on either side of the entrance, and the Drover's staff were posed out front.

"This is my grandpa, Walter Chandler," Maggie said, pointing to an older man who held a blond child in the center of the group, staring at her with obvious adoration. "And me."

She pointed to the others, naming them. "My mom, Kathryn Chandler," the blond woman to Walter's right; "Cousin Jake, our cook," a dark-haired man with an arm hooked around Kathryn's neck, gazing intently at her as she smiled into the camera. Maggie identified the man and woman on Walter's left as Russ and Evie, bartender and barmaid. "Drover's was a family business back then. And we were all family."

"What were they like?" Rhonda asked. She'd have made a fine detective.

"Evie was like my mom after Mama died. She was down-to-earth and funny. Russ was a great listener—I guess you have to be to be a good bartender. Jake was serious. Evie said Mama's death hit him the hardest, but he was her cousin so I guess it would. And Jake and Russ were like my uncles. When I got old enough for men to notice me, it was like I had *three* fathers all giving my dates the once-over."

"What did they tell you about your mother's death?"

"Just that they missed her and that she had to be in heaven. I think Grandpa told them not to say much."

"What do you know about the brick work in the basement?" Thinnes asked.

"Russ and Grandpa did it. I don't know when or why, but they did all the fix-up work around the place. Jake helped sometimes, and Evie." She glanced around, seeming sad. "We had some great times. I never really missed my parents."

"Your dad died in Korea?" Rhonda said.

Maggie nodded. "Before I was born. And Mama came to live with Grandpa."

"She worked in the tavern?" Thinnes asked.

"Oh, yes. Grandpa used to tell me how beautiful she was.

So did Evie. All the truckers used to leave her great tips and ask her to marry them."

Rhonda said, "How did the others feel about that?"

"I think they were proud of her."

"Where are they now? Have you kept in touch?"

"With Evie. I can give you her address. Russ and Jake have died. They were both smokers." Her mind must have traveled the same path as Thinnes's because she said, "The police won't just blow this off, will they? They'll follow it up?"

"There'll be an autopsy. If the woman was murdered, which is pretty likely considering the circumstances, they'll do what they can to find out who did it. And if he's still alive . . . There's no statute of limitations on murder."

There was a scraping sound—a chair being moved aside—and a Berwyn patrol officer materialized in the gloom near the outside door. "We're about to remove the remains," he said. "The detective would like a word with you before he goes."

"We'll be right there," Thinnes told him. To Maggie he said, "Did you ever ask what your mother died of?"

"Oh, yes. When I was older. Grandpa told me she died of heart trouble."

Tuesday morning. On the northeast corner of Wesley Avenue and Twenty-sixth Street, the Berwyn cop shop was a yellow brick building with panels the color of dark chocolate above and below the windows. All the parking by the entrance on Wesley was reserved for police vehicles, but Thinnes found a space in the municipal building lot diagonally across the intersection. Inside the station, he was directed to the detectives' office, which had its own photocopy machine and heavy duty printer, and a PC on every desk.

The detective on duty wasn't the one who'd been out to Drover's on Saturday.

Thinnes held his hand out. "I'm John Thinnes, Chicago, Violent Crimes."

The detective came around his desk to shake. "Matt Holbrook. What can I do for you, Thinnes?" He waved at a chair opposite the desk. "Have a seat."

Thinnes sat.

Holbrook perched on a corner of his desk. He was about Thinnes's age but heavier. He reminded Thinnes of an overweight cat.

"You finished the death investigation on the body from Drover's?" Thinnes asked him. "Kathryn Chandler, wasn't it?"

"Yeah. Off the record—'til we tell the next of kin—she was strangled. The cat died of starvation. Looks like whoever did it dumped Chandler in the coal bin and threw the cat in after her." Holbrook shrugged. "Or maybe the cat sneaked in before the killer got done bricking it up and got itself buried alive for its trouble. It tracked coal dust all over before it croaked."

Holbrook leaned back and laced his fingers together behind his head. "You'd a been just a gleam in your daddy's eye when she died, so you didn't kill her. What's your interest?"

"My wife's family," Thinnes said. He repeated the story Maggie'd told him, including Walter Chandler's version of the cause of death.

"Well, he coulda been right," Holbrook said. He flipped open a file folder on the desk and pulled out a yellowed paper in a plastic sleeve. As he handed it to Thinnes, he added, "It wouldn't be stretching it *too* much to say she had heart trouble."

The paper was a love letter written to Kathryn Chandler

by a man named Dan, asking her to run away and marry him the next time he came through Chicago. There was a stained envelope with Kathryn's name and the Drover's' address, and a return address in Tulsa, Oklahoma. Dan's surname was McLean.

"She had that tucked in her pocket along with ten fifty-dollar bills," Holbrook said. "Back then you could run pretty far on five hundred dollars."

Thinnes nodded. "So it looks like Walter killed her to keep her from running away with Dan."

"Or somebody Walter cared about killed her to keep her from running away with Dan, and Walter covered it up."

"*Or* someone else killed her and hid the body so Walter would *think* she ran off with Dan." Thinnes shook his head. "The one thing wrong with all of the above is why didn't Dan come looking when she dropped out of sight."

Holbrook shrugged. "Maybe he did. Maybe there's a missing persons report somewhere. Say, you want in on this investigation? I can arrange it."

"I'm on vacation."

"Yeah, well just between you and me it doesn't look like this old case is gonna get much attention." He got up and carried the letter to the photocopy machine. As he put it under the cover, he said, "For sure, *I* don't have time to track down people who disappeared forty years ago." He punched the button.

"I see."

The machine did its thing and spit out a copy; Holbrook removed the original. "Hey, feel free to poke around. You can even come in and use my phone."

Thinnes stood up. "I'll think about it."

Holbrook handed him the photocopy. "Keep me posted." Thinnes was halfway to the door when the detective added, "You ever find that cat?"

• • •

Evie Williams remembered. Thinnes found her at the address Maggie'd given him—a retirement home, not a bad place. She was white-haired and thin, but spry as a squirrel, and delighted to have a visitor. When they were seated in the lounge, Evie said, "Kate ran off with a trucker. Thought Walter would blow a fuse. She was his daughter by marriage only, and I think he was a little in love with her. I thought it was strange at the time, *and* afterwards. When we never heard from her. I thought that she'd come back for Maggie 'cause the sun rose and set on the child.

"And Walter worshipped Maggie. He told her her ma died, and she was living with him so we didn't tell her different. I think Walter eventually had Kate declared dead, 'bout ten years after that. And Walter's been dead, must be, fifteen years now."

"If he thought Kathryn had run away, why did he tell Maggie she'd died?"

"I asked him that. He said no child should have to grow up thinking she'd been abandoned."

"And you *never* told her the truth?"

"She never asked." Evie made a face. "I guess it's best to let sleeping dogs lie. But I often wondered. . . ."

With luck and the help of a Chicago detective who'd retired to Tulsa, Thinnes got a line on Dan McLean. "Small world," the ex-cop told him a week after they first talked. "When he hung up his CDL, he moved to Berwyn."

"Illinois?"

"Yeah." He gave Thinnes the rest of the address. "How's things in the city of big shoulders? Homicide rate still up?"

Thinnes thought he sounded nostalgic.

"Same old same old," Thinnes told him. "We do what we can."

• • •

Thinnes brought Rhonda along when he went to interview Dan McLean's sister. She lived in one of the neat, brick Chicago-style bungalows on Oak Park Avenue. He knocked on the door and they waited.

After a minute or so a woman called out, "Who's there?" She studied Thinnes's star a long time through the peephole, then demanded to see it again when she opened the door with the security chain. "*Chicago* police? This isn't Chicago."

"Yes, ma'am. We're looking into an old murder." He didn't mention that it hadn't happened in Chicago. "We think your brother may have known the victim."

"He didn't do it!"

"He's not a suspect, but we'd like to know something about him. May we come in?"

She closed the door and reopened it without the chain. "Just for a minute." Female Caucasian. Five-two. Thin white hair. Cloudy blue eyes. And a sour expression on a face as pudgy as bread dough and wrinkled as old white leather. She stood aside to let them pass. She didn't offer them a seat. "Who're you?" she demanded of Rhonda.

"I'm John's wife."

"You a cop too?"

"No," Thinnes said, "but she's helping with the investigation."

"Could you tell us about Dan?" Rhonda asked.

"He was a good man. Drove a truck all his life. Thirty years without a ticket. He never married. He only loved once—a barmaid—and she ran off and left him for another trucker. He never got over that."

"Do you know her name?"

"Kathryn Chandler. He deserved better, but he loved her—even kept her picture all the years. He wanted to be buried with it, but I said, enough's enough. Couldn't bring myself to throw it out, though. Not the letters either. Guess you could have 'em. Don't guess Dan'd care now."

She shuffled into the next room, closing the door behind her, and she was gone a long time. Thinnes forced himself to be patient. After forty years, another five minutes wouldn't matter. Rhonda spent the time looking around.

When McLean returned, she had an eight-by-ten color photo of Kathryn that had turned orange with age, and a packet of yellowed envelopes held together with a cracked rubber band. The handwriting on five unopened envelopes was the same as on the photocopied letter. Same return address in Tulsa, same addressee. The postmarks were from Springfield, Illinois; St. Louis, Missouri; Arcadia, Oklahoma; Vega, Texas; and Seligman, Arizona; all towns on Route 66. All of them had RETURN TO SENDER stamped on them, and MOVED—NO FWD ADDR scribbled by the same hand. All the opened envelopes were addressed to Dan McLean by "K. Chandler."

It was Rhonda who asked, "Would you mind if we read these?"

"Go ahead. Take 'em with you. Throw 'em all out when you're done." She walked over and opened the door. "Take the picture, too."

Interview over.

Outside, on the porch, Rhonda said, "Now what?"

"We go somewhere nice for lunch while we study the evidence."

When they were seated side by side, waiting for their orders at Maggiano's, Thinnes handed Rhonda the letters. She pushed the table set aside and sorted them—first Kathryn Chandler's, then those sent to her by Dan—into chronological order. Then, starting with the first, she read them.

Thinnes rested his arm on the back of her chair and leaned toward her to read along. He noticed, as she turned the pages over, Rhonda shifted her weight toward him, then her chair.

The letters told a love story. Two years before her disappearance, Kathryn had answered, "Yes" to a lonely trucker's question, "Will you write to me?" Each page showed her growing closer to the man, more impressed by him, more infatuated. His responses were missing, of course, but they could be inferred from the answers they evoked. Dan had been in love from the first moment he set eyes on her.

By the time she'd turned over the last of Kathryn's letters, the one in which she'd accepted his proposal, Rhonda was biting her lip and reaching for a napkin to wipe her eyes and blow her nose. Thinnes slipped his arm off the chair back and around Rhonda's shoulders. She reached up to stroke his hand.

Then she opened Dan's first letter, mailed in Springfield.

Dearest Kathryn,
  It has taken me nearly 200 miles to pull myself together enough to write this, to realize you could not have been so cruel. I know something terrible must have happened or you'd have told me to my face that you'd changed your mind. If you did. I was just so numb with pain when that guy you work for told me you'd run off with someone else, I couldn't think straight. I should have asked him for details, or at least a name and address.
  Maybe you wrote to me about it. Maybe there's a letter waiting for me in Tulsa. I can only hope. . . .
  In the meantime I remain yours. Always. Dan.

The rest of the letters were similar. There had been nothing from Kathryn waiting in Tulsa; the letter postmarked Vega,

Texas, expressed his disappointment. The letter he'd sent
from Seligman said he wouldn't write again until he heard
from her. Rhonda put the letters back in their envelopes.
"Walter killed her, didn't he? To keep her from leaving."

That guy you work for.

"It looks that way."

"Will you have to tell Maggie?"

That her grandfather killed her mother? It didn't seem
likely.

"Not just yet. Do you know if Russ or Jake left any family?"

"I could call Maggie and find out."

After they'd finished, Thinnes paid the bill while Rhonda
made the call. When she came back, she said, "Maggie
thinks Russ may have been gay. He liked women well
enough, but as she recalls, he never had a girlfriend. And he
never married. Jake's widow lives in Rogers Park. I called
her. She'll see us today."

"You're here about Kathryn." Jake's widow was a tiny
woman, not much older than Maggie, Thinnes judged, with
hair an amazing shade of gold. "You're the police? Jake said
you'd come one day. To ask about Kathryn."

Thinnes just nodded. Rhonda slipped her hand in his and
squeezed.

"Well, come in," the widow said.

In was a neat, uncomplicated living room with a couch
and two chairs, coffee table, and sideboard with pictures of
Maggie, Walter, and Jake.

"Might as well sit," their hostess told them. She pointed
to the couch. "Jake left you something. Just a minute." She
went out of the room and closed the door behind her. *Déja
vu.*

She came back with a letter. *All over again.*

"Don't get me wrong," she said, taking the chair next to Rhonda. "Jake loved me well enough, but he never got over Kathryn. Here." She reached the letter toward Thinnes. "He said to say 'It's all in here.' Whatever that means."

Thinnes opened it and read, then read again, aloud:

To whom it may concern:

If you are reading this, you must have found Kathryn. I'm glad. She deserves a decent burial.

I never meant to kill her. She asked me to give Walt a note saying she was leaving to get married. She was afraid to tell him herself, afraid he'd try to stop her. Instead I did. And when she started yelling, I tried to quiet her. I silenced her forever.

Not a day has gone by since, that I haven't remembered. And regretted it. I hope this letter will appease her spirit. I hope she's forgiven me. God may. I cannot. Jacob Chandler.

Thinnes looked up. Both women were in tears.

"All these years," the widow said, "I thought he was just carrying a torch. He was a good husband. I thought he was a good man." She sounded unsure.

Rhonda reached over and patted her arm. "One horrible mistake doesn't undo a lifetime of goodness."

The widow wiped at her eyes. "That's kind of you to say." That was Rhonda.

Thinnes said, "The police will want to see this, Mrs. Chandler."

"Of course."

"And we appreciate you talking to us."

Sitting in the car, afterward, Rhonda said, "How did you know?"

"The picture in Maggie's album. The way he had his arm around her, the way he stared is like the photographic memory of an obsession." Thinnes started the engine. "There's one thing I haven't figured out. We never found the cat."

Rhonda smiled though tears were streaming down her cheeks. "I think Queenie found *us*."

Thinnes had seen plenty of dead bodies. He'd even seen some of them *become* bodies; he'd never seen a spirit or a ghost. But he couldn't rule it out.

He put the car in gear and pulled onto the road.

MOTEL 66

Barbara D'Amato

Barbara D'Amato is the author of the series starring
Chicago freelance reporter Cat Marsala and the Suze
Figueroa/Norm Bennis Chicago cop series. She has
been nominated for mystery awards for short stories,
true crime, and novels, and has won both the Anthony
and the Agatha.

June 11, 1971

About eight miles south of Bloomington-Normal, June finally convinced Donald to let her drive. At that point they
were a hundred and thirty miles away from Chicago. A hundred and thirty miles from home. Donald had crossed the
middle line too often, and she was worried about the amount
of champagne he had drunk. The secondhand Packard that
was her grandfather's wedding gift held the road through
sheer weight, tacking slowly like a working sailboat and not
much less hefty than a Packard hearse, but there were giant
produce trucks with vertical wooden pickets holding loads
of asparagus coming the other way, bound to Chicago prob-

ably, and June was terrified about what would happen if Donald steered into one head-on.

Once relieved of driving, David picked a champagne bottle off the floor of the back seat and swigged some of it. Donald's brother had put six of the bottles of champagne that had not been drunk into the car, saying "Celebrate!"

"Do you think you should have all that?" she asked, very cautiously, not wanting to start off their marriage sounding like a nag.

"Why, sure, Juney. If I can't drink champagne today, what day can I ever drink it?"

"Well, that's true."

It was getting late and the sun was low. A noon wedding had been followed by the wedding lunch, then the bouquet-throwing, and finally she had changed into this peach-colored suit and matching little hat, and her new wedding hairstyle. She felt glamorous, but the straight skirt was too tight for comfortable driving. She wondered if she should hike it up, but she would feel brazen to have her thighs exposed. Then she thought, "How silly. We're married." But she still didn't hike it up. Somehow it just didn't seem right.

Her mother had insisted on June and Donald having a good solid snack before they left, and it turned out, much as June hated to admit it, her mother had been right. They would really have been hungry by now otherwise. The woman had also put a package of sandwiches wrapped in wax paper in a bag in the back seat and June had eaten a sandwich while Donald drove. He only seemed to want champagne.

They had passed three or four Motel 66s along Route 66 as they headed south. But they had no connection with each other, Donald said. She said, "Maybe they're a chain, like Howard Johnson's."

But Donald said, "No. Howard Johnson's is restaurants. There aren't any motel chains."

She was sure she'd heard of some, but she didn't want to contradict Donald, because he didn't like being contradicted. And anyway it wasn't important.

Motel 66 Motor Court was nice looking, a dozen separate little cabins painted white with navy blue trim. The cabins were plunked down in a horseshoe shape in the middle of open land. Young trees had been planted between each cabin and the next, but they were saplings and didn't soften the flat, featureless landscape much. June thought that the trees were copper beeches. Donald pulled up to a tiny cabin in the center that had an OFFICE sign in front.

"Do you think we need our marriage license?" June said, as she smoothed her skirt before getting out of the car. She had never checked into a motel before—the idea still made her quite nervous—and she had heard bad things.

"No," Donald said.

"But people say they'll wonder if you're really married, and they check to see if you have luggage—"

By then Donald had entered the door of the office and she followed right away, suddenly feeling alone. As she closed the car door, a little rice blew out. Well, if they don't believe it, she thought, there's the proof.

June heard angry voices, quickly cut off. The office was not more than ten feet by ten feet, with a counter topped with linoleum in the center. The same linoleum covered the floor. The office was spotlessly clean, and in fact a teen-aged girl with a dust pan and broom was digging dust out of the corner where the two far walls came together.

A cash register sat on a card table against the rear wall. A man sat cranking the handle of an adding machine, holding small sheets of paper in his left hand.

"Welcome to Motel 66," said a pink, plump woman in a pink dress sprigged with blue carnations.

Donald said, "Thanks. We'd like a room."

"How many nights?"

"One."

"That'll be six dollars."

June saw Donald wince, thinking this was more than he had expected to pay. She hoped he wouldn't make a fuss.

The woman seemed to want to gloss over the price too, and talked on breezily. "I'm Bertine, and this is Pete. You're lucky you stopped now. We're full up except for two units."

Pete stood up, saying, "Soon as the sign goes on, people start coming off the highway."

Donald peeled six ones from his roll of wedding money. Pete was very handsome, June noticed, and he smiled at her, then actually winked. Immediately she told herself loyally that Donald was a good-looking man too.

Donald reached out for the key, a big brass key attached to a piece of wood into which the number three had been burned with a wood-burning tool. June patted her hair, unfamiliar and somewhat uncomfortable in its new style. Rice flew out onto the counter.

"Oh, gee!" she said.

Bertine said, "Why you're just married!"

June blushed. "That's right."

"That's so exciting. Isn't that exciting, Pete?"

"Sure is. Congratulations."

"On your wedding trip?" Bertine said.

"Yes. My uncle has a house near Los Angeles he's lending us for two weeks. And we're seeing the country, the Painted Desert and the Petrified Forest and everything, as we go."

"Well, isn't that the best!"

June ducked her head, still embarrassed because these people would know it was her wedding night.

The cleaning girl tipped up her dustpan to hold the dust and headed for the side door of the office. As she passed behind Pete and Bertine, Pete casually reached his left hand back and patted her bottom. Donald noticed, but June did not, and Bertine was standing to Pete's right and could not have seen.

Donald seized the key and headed for the door. June followed him quickly, afraid somebody might embarrass her with wedding night jokes.

As the screen door closed behind them, June heard Bertine say cheerily, "There. There's another car turning in. We're full."

"Oh, yeah. That's swell, isn't it?"

"It is, Pete."

June stopped to listen. She was interested in people.

"It is *now*," Pete said. "How about in a couple of years? Once the interstate is in. Huh?"

"Maybe it won't be so bad. You know the government. It could be years before they even get started. Prob'ly will be. Decades, maybe."

"I heard they started a section near Bloomington."

"Well, that's there. This is here."

"I told you we should never've bought here. Goddamn President Eisenhower anyhow!"

His hand on the car door, Donald said, "Come on, Juney."

As Donald drove the car over to cabin three, June whispered, "They've been arguing."

Donald said, "Obviously. But it's not our problem."

"Oh, no. Of course not."

"We're on our honeymoon," Donald said. He didn't say anything about Pete patting the cleaning girl.

It was past eight-thirty P.M. now, and the sun was setting.

• • •

The cabin was as spotless inside as the office had been. The decor was fake rustic, with red and green plaid linoleum, wood-look wallboard, and a white ceiling with wooden beams. June knew the beams were hollow. Her parents had exactly the same thing in their rec room. But she liked it.

The bathroom didn't quite match. All the fixtures were pink.

June said, "This is so exciting. I know I'm just a silly romantic, but here I am getting married in June and my name is June. It's almost like it's *meant*."

"Most people get married in June."

"Yes. That's true." This was not the answer she'd hoped for. She'd rather he'd said something like, "It feels like it was meant for me, too." Not wanting to be argumentative, she said, "Well, not everybody's name is June."

Donald picked up a bottle of champagne and went to the bathroom to get a glass. "Pete and Bertine must've got a real deal on pink porcelain," he said, coming out. He poured the glass full.

"Uh—should we go get dinner?" June asked. "There's the Moon Shot Restaurant across the street. Just behind the Phillips 66."

"I'm not hungry. Are you?"

"No, I ate a sandwich."

"Then let's go to bed."

Timidly, June picked up her overnight case—white leather, a gift from her aunt Nella—and went into the bathroom. She showered, then splashed on lilac-scented body lotion. A gift from her niece Peggy.

Embarrassed, thrilled, and a little giddy all at the same time, she took the top item from the overnight case. It was a beautiful lace nightgown, with ruffles at the hem and neckline. The girls from the Kresge five-and-dime where June worked had pooled their money and bought it for her. There were some other gifts at the shower that were embarrassing, but June had pretended to be too sophisticated to notice, and if she hadn't blushed so hard, it would have worked. One of the girls confessed that she had actually "done it" with her boyfriend, and the others glanced at one another, thinking, but not saying, that she was a fallen woman.

The nightgown was a lovely orchid color. There had been much laughing at the shower, when two of the girls insisted it was lilac and would "go" with Peggy's lilac scent. Three of them said the color was orchid, and June herself kept saying lavender, and they all giggled. A satin ribbon in darker orchid was threaded through eyelets around the neckline and tied in a bow in front. June wondered briefly if she would look like a candy box, but then thought, no, it was beautiful, and it went well with her dark hair. She slipped it down over her shoulders, wiggled it over her hips, smoothed everything into place with nervous hands and stepped out of the bathroom.

Don lay on the bed, on top of the bedspread, asleep in his clothes.

"Donald?" He didn't stir. "Donald? Here I am."

He still didn't stir, so she touched his shoulder. The glass on the night table was empty. Half of the new bottle of champagne was gone.

"Don?"

Mumbly, he said, "Don' bother—"

June sat down in the only chair in the room, a chair with wooden arms and an upholstered plaid seat and back, and watched Don sleep. After forty-five minutes or so, she tried to wake him again, but he didn't even mumble. She stood and gazed out the window; it was long since dark, and there was no moon.

After a few tears had run down her cheeks, June went to the large suitcase and found some cheese crackers her mother had shoved in at the last minute. She spent another half hour munching them slowly, then tried waking Don again. When that didn't work, she got a glass of water, drank it one swallow at a time, then took dungarees and a sweater from her suitcase, changed out of the lovely nightgown, which she draped carefully across the back of the chair—the extra care was intended to contain her anger—and went out for a walk.

An hour and a half later, June came back to the room. She let herself in quietly. Don was not there. Feeling guilty, she went into the bathroom and took a shower. When she got out, she looked at herself in the mirror. It was very mysterious, she thought, that you didn't really know who anybody was, not even yourself. "Serves you right, Don," she whispered. Twenty minutes later he turned up.

His eyes were bloodshot. His hair was stiff and stringy, as if he'd been used upside down as a floor mop. She knew he was hung over, but she didn't want to mention it. Instead she said uneasily. "Where have you been?"

He said, "You weren't here." She didn't respond to that. He said, "I went for a walk."

"Where?"

"Over to the Moon Shot."

"But it closed at ten."

"All I said was I walked over there. I didn't say it was open!"

"Oh."

"And then I walked around a while!"

June and Donald woke up early, even though Donald had a hangover and couldn't open his eyes all the way. They dressed silently, facing away from each other, each not wanting to catch the other's eye. They walked together to the office to return the key.

Finally, Donald said, "Sorry about last night."

Thinking for a few seconds, to try to decide whether she was about to lie or be honest, June finally said, "Me too."

Bertine was alone in the office.

June said, "Well, thanks. It was a—it was a really nice cabin."

"Sure thing," Bertine said, but her eyes were red and puffy and she dragged her feet. It took her several seconds to focus on her job. "Have a happy life," she said. "Come visit again some day."

Donald got behind the wheel of the car. June said soberly, "I guess they've been fighting again."

June 6, 1985

From the back seat, Jennifer, who was seven years old, said, "Why can't we stay at a Holiday Inn? They have a swimming pool."

Donald said, "This is your mother's idea. Not mine. I can think of a lot of better places to be."

June said, "We're having a nostalgia trip."

Don Jr. said, "Well, it's your nostalgia. It's not ours."

They pulled off Interstate 55 onto a deteriorated road that once had been Route 66, running parallel to the interstate. They bumped over potholes so crumbly they must have been unpatched for years. Ahead they saw two concrete islands, four big metal caps over ground pipes, and a shell of the old gas station, two oil bays inside still visible as long narrow depressions with a central hole for the hydraulic lift. There was no sign whatever of the Moon Shot Burgers and Fries. The motel still stood—twelve cabins with beech trees shading them from the summer sun. The cabins were painted white with red trim. The red enamel paint was peeling and the matte white looked chalky and cheap.

June said, "Look, Don, they've changed the name. Now it's the Route 66 Motor Inn."

"This is soooo bogus!" Jennifer said. But she was a nice child, really, and didn't grumble when they stopped the car, even though the place didn't appear to be very prosperous.

Donald said, "A Holiday Inn would be better. Let's go find one."

June said, "No."

Don Jr., usually called Donny, said, "This looks weird."

Donny was thirteen years old. They'd had a fertility problem between Donny and Jennifer, but fortunately nothing permanent. Donny was just starting to make his growth spurt. He hoped by next fall, when he went back to school, he'd discover he'd caught up with the girls in his class, most of whom had put on their growth spurt last year.

He's growing so fast, June thought, studying her gangly child. She could have sworn those pants and the sleeves of the shirt fit when they left Chicago. That was all of six hours ago. Now his wrists stuck out an inch and his ankles an inch and a half. He'd gone up one shoe size a month for the last six months and everybody said feet started to grow first, then the legs. Thank God Donald was a hard-working man.

"Why didn't you go to Florida or something on your honeymoon?" Donny asked.

"Well, partly we had never seen the country. Especially the West. And partly your uncle Mort had a house near Los Angeles that he was going to loan us for two weeks."

"The price was right," Donald said. "Free."

June said, "We had this big old car that your great-grandfather gave us. You'd have laughed at it, Donny."

"Yeah. I wish you'd've kept it."

"Can't keep everything," Donald said.

"You remember your great-grandfather, Donny?"

"Not really. He used to ride me in his wheelbarrow, didn't he?"

Getting out of the car, June said, "We took five days to drive to L.A. We saw the Painted Desert in Arizona, for one thing. And in Amarillo, Texas, we saw a real cattle drive."

Jennifer said, "Big deal."

Donny said, "Why not Las Vegas?"

"We didn't have any money. You kids have been much more fortunate than we were, you know. Thanks to your dad being a good provider." Well, perhaps he was a little possessive, a little rigid, too, but maybe being solid meant you had to be rigid.

"We always hear that."

"Well, we didn't have any money, but we saw a lot of the wild West."

Jennifer said, "That's okay, Mom. You're entitled to a life."

"We took Route 66 all the way from Chicago to L.A. Did you know there was even a TV show once about Route 66?"

Looking at the potholed road, Jennifer said, "Route 66 isn't here anymore."

"Neither is George Washington," June said. "But we still study him."

All four of them walked into the central cabin, the one with the OFFICE sign above the door. Donald pulled out his credit card. He had three and was proud of them.

June took one look at the woman behind the cash register. "Why, you're still here!" The woman was older, tougher, plumper, and more frayed.

"Do I know you?"

"You're Betty—no, Bertha—"

"Bertine."

"We were here nearly fifteen years ago. June 11, 1971."

"Oh, my God. The newlyweds!"

Donald said, "Come on, Juney. Let's get a key and go."

June said, "Bertine, do you really remember somebody who was here that long ago? I mean, I remember you and your husband, but it was my wedding trip. Everything was important. You must have a dozen new people here every day."

"Mmm, well, now that I see you, I sort of remember." She hesitated. "Actually it wasn't like every other day."

"Why?"

"I might as well tell you. Pete was killed that night."

"Oh!" June felt shock, even though Pete wasn't anything to her, of course. Not really. She could hardly even picture Pete in her mind's eye anymore, which seemed wrong. She ought to remember him. Handsome, she thought, but she somehow confused him in her mind with Robert Redford. "Was he in an accident?"

"He was beaten to death with a rock. Behind the old Moon Shot restaurant."

"Oh, my God!"

"He never came home that night. I thought he was—um—was out, you know, somewhere. They found him when the Moon Shot opened for lunch."

"Who did it?"

"I don't know. We never found out. A drifter, I guess. The cops asked about who was here, in the cabins, you know, so I told them all about everybody. But none of you had anything to do with us. We'd never seen any of you before. They talked with the people who worked for us, but nothing came of it. Just nobody a-tall had a motive. I guess it was just one of those things. He was only twenty-eight."

Since each "cabin" had only one room and one big bed, they took two cabins next to each other, number three and number four. Donald and Donny took number four and June and Jennifer took three.

"Jeez, this is truly bogus!" Jennifer said when they un-locked their door and she saw the tiny room. June thought it didn't seem as clean as she remembered it.

From one door away, Donny said to Jennifer, "Hey! I think it's excellent. How many times do you get to visit the scene of a murder?"

"Get inside, Donny," Donald said.

"But Dad, let's go look at where it happened! She said over by where the restaurant was. Maybe we can find a clue."

"We are *not*," Donald said, veins beginning to stand out on his face, "going to ruin our vacation. And we are not going to say *one more word about murder!*"

June 27, 1999

The sign on Interstate 55 said HISTORIC ROUTE 66! EXIT! HERE!

Just past it, there was a second sign: STAY AT HISTORIC ROUTE 66 MOTEL! ORIGINAL! NOT REBUILT!

And a third sign: SATELLITE BURGERS! JUKE BOXES! MALT SHOP! ONE BLOCK ON RIGHT!

As they came to the exit, a series of six signs in a long row swept past them saying,

! ROUTE 66 AUTO MUSEUM!

SIT IN A REAL 1956 BUICK CENTURY——TWO TONE!

DRIVE AN EDSEL!

Smaller letters under the Edsel offer read: OUR CURATOR MUST ACCOMPANY YOU.

CHEVY BEL AIR——NOT ONE, NOT TWO, THE COMPLETE LINE!

FORD FAIRLANE!

The last sign was shaped like a long hand with a pointing finger and added, ARTIFACTS! NEWSPAPERS! NEIL ARMSTRONG

WALKS ON MOON! ORIGINAL FRONT PAGES AND BLOW-UPS! 500
HUBCAPS 500!

It was all so different, with its effort at trying to be the
same, June thought. And here we are, back here again, and
again the reason is a wedding.

Donny, who was twenty-seven, had dropped out of college after a year, gone to work for a concrete company,
then decided building wooden forms and troweling ready-
mix was not a lifetime career for him. He had just graduated from the University of Illinois at Champaign in
computer engineering. In his last year he'd met Deborah
Henry, who'd been in several classes with him. On June
thirtieth they were getting married in St. Louis, where
Deborah's family lived.

One more chance, June thought, to drive part of their old,
sentimental route.

Jennifer, who was twenty and a junior at Yale, had said,
"I'll fly to St. Louis. I did your nostalgia trip once and once
was enough."

It wasn't all malt shops and gas-guzzling cars and juke-
boxes, June thought. It wasn't romance. It was a lack of op-
tions. Her children really believed she was nostalgic.
Children were so simple-minded when it came to parents.
She was not nostalgic. If she was looking for anything, it
was understanding. A search. Who was I then and why?

What a funny, naive little thing I was when we first came
here, she thought, uneasily. Brought up with virtually no
knowledge of sex and those unreasonable expectations. All
twitterpated at the idea of my wedding night. It was such a
big deal. Not like these kids.

She remembered Don's anger a couple of years ago when
they found condoms in Jennifer's drawer. Fathers can be so
unrealistic. And when June tried to tell him condoms were a
good thing, and that she had already talked with both chil-

dren about them, he yelled, "My mother didn't even know the *word* 'condom' and if she had, she would never have uttered it in my presence."

"I'm sure, dear," June had said mildly.

They pulled into the Motel 66 driveway.

"Dad, can I take the car over to that museum shop? They might have moon landing stuff. Memorabilia."

"Absolutely not. If you want the car, I'll go with you."

Donny, who'd been through this before, said indulgently, "Yeah, Dad. I know. What's yours is yours." To June he said, "Mom, it's only two blocks. I'll walk fast over there and see what they've got. Five minutes."

"Just three minutes," Donald said. "We need to find a place to eat."

Historic Motel 66 was surrounded by recently mowed bright green grass. Huge beech trees shaded the cabins, except for a gap down toward the end, where a cabin was missing and half a tree remained next to the space, a split trunk leaning eastward. Lightning, June thought.

The bright white and blue paint looked new. The colors struck a chord in June's memory, but she couldn't quite be sure.

She and Donald entered the office. The old cash register was back. The walls were covered with black and white blow-ups of Motel 66, each meticulously dated, and a professionally produced sign above them read, THE HISTORY OF MOTEL 66!

Behind the counter stood a trim white-haired woman in a black power suit over a sapphire blue silk shirt.

June said, "Oh! Isn't Bertha, uh, Ber—um, isn't she here anymore?"

"I'm Bertine."

"Bertine! I wouldn't have known you!"

Bertine smiled. "I figured if I was gonna spruce up the place I'd spruce up myself too. I kind of remember you, honey, but not quite."

"We're what you called the newlyweds. From 1971. June 11, 1971."

"Oh." Bertine's eyes clouded for a few seconds. "I have to say, I've brought the place along a bit since then. Pete would still recognize it, though."

"It looks great!"

"Well, I'm doing okay. This isn't a way to get rich. But I make decent money. Now. It was hard going for a while."

Donald pulled out his credit cards. "Let me get the keys," he said. "We've gotta go eat."

Bertine said, "See, I have the old cash register, but I hardly know how to take cash anymore. My accountant says never take cash and surely never let any of the help take cash." She laughed. "There's a fragment of Route 66 from Oklahoma City to Vinita, Oklahoma, if you're touring. And a piece of historic 66 in Albuquerque."

June said, "We're not going to L.A. this time. Just St. Louis."

She thought about Uncle Mort, who had loaned them his house. Uncle Mort had run off with a girl he met at his health club, where he was working out because his doctor told him to. The girl was a cardio-fitness trainer, but June's mother would still have called her a flibbertigibbet, if June's mother were still alive.

June walked over to the photo blow-ups. One showed the construction of the cabins and was dated March 27, 1969. One showed a line of late-sixties cars on the curved driveway near the motel office.

Bertine walked over to the photos behind her. June had stopped in front of a big photo of Bertine and Pete, holding hands under a MOTEL 66 sign at the door of the brand new office.

Donald said, "Come on, Juney. I'm hungry."

"Poor Pete," Bertine said, but June's back was rigid and she didn't turn around.

Donny came bursting in, shouting, "I got a reproduction 1969 *New York Times* moon landing page. Debbie's gonna think it's real fun." When he entered, Bertine caught sight of him and she froze, staring.

Donny came to a stop next to the photo of Pete, age probably twenty-seven.

For a second, Bertine looked back and forth between the photo and Donny.

Bertine tried to ask June something, but the words caught in her throat. It was something like "no motive." June made a small whimpering sound. Then she turned in fear to Donald.

When she saw the expression on his face, she started to scream.

THE CANASTA CLUB

ELEANOR TAYLOR BLAND

Eleanor Taylor Bland, whose Chicago area police officer Marti MacAlister first appeared in *Dead Time*, has been profiled on the CBS program *Sunday Morning*.

It began snowing as Detectives Marti MacAlister and Matthew "Vik" Jessenovik drove past Springfield, Illinois. Three and a half hours later they had traveled another seventy-two miles. Visibility was close to zero and Route 55 all but impassable by the time they reached their exit. Josephina Hanson, the woman they were going to see, had been told that her eighty-seven-year-old sister Agatha was dead; what she didn't know was that the cause of death was something other than old age and natural causes. Marti pulled into a Phillips 66 and tried to get something on the radio besides static while Vik filled the tank and got directions to the address they were looking for. Over the phone, a Miss Evangeline Roberts had explained that although it could be considered an old folks' home, since elderly ladies lived there, it certainly was not a nursing home.

"We are just getting along in years," she told Marti. "We

are not senile or in any way incapacitated, unless you consider being hard of hearing or visually impaired or using a cane."

Vik had not been eager to come here, but because it looked like a homicide they had no choice. The toxicology reports that came late yesterday afternoon had identified poison, and Agatha Hanson had been dead for almost a month. The case was already cold.

The car door opened. Vik said something but it was muffled by the scarf that covered everything below his eyes. He knocked snow from his boots and brushed it off of his wool cap before he got in.

"We lucked up, MacAlister. And we lucked out. The place we're looking for is only a mile and half up that road." He pointed. "It shouldn't take us more than two hours to get there. The bad news is there's no way in hell we're going to make it back to Lincoln Prairie today. There's close to a foot of snow on the ground and another five to seven inches predicted. And guess what—the storm stayed south of Chicago. If we had waited a couple of days we wouldn't be stuck here."

"Did you remember to phone home?"

"My place, yours, and I left a message for the lieutenant. Everyone knows we made it here, so just stay on the road."

Marti hunched forward with her forehead inches from the windshield. The snow was coming down so fast that even with the wipers on high she had difficulty seeing anything. "I hope I can spot another car's headlights while I still have enough time to stop or get out of the way."

"Just worry about staying on the road," Vik advised. "Nobody but a fool would drive around in this."

"It only took half an hour," she said when she pulled into the driveway alongside a rambling two-story house with a wraparound porch. The force of the wind slammed the car door shut and pushed her against the front fender as soon as she got out. She fought against it, with Vik right behind her, grabbed the railing and hauled herself up the front steps.

"Oh, do come in," a stoop-shouldered woman said, opening the door before they could ring the bell. "I've been watching for you. I didn't think you would make it." The wind blew the door so hard it banged against the wall. The carpet was covered with snow before they made it inside. Vik slammed the door shut.

Vik and Marti introduced themselves and showed the woman their shields.

"I'm Evangeline Roberts; we spoke on the phone." Her breath smelled of peppermint. "I can't remember the last time we've had police officers here, not unless you count the time Claudette Colbert managed to get herself stuck in a drainage pipe. She's one of our cats."

The woman sounded more excited than concerned. She didn't reach Marti's shoulder. As Marti looked down at her blue-gray hair, teased and stiff with hair spray, she could see the scalp.

"Let me take your coats. I'd better take them to the kitchen and hang them up. They are covered with snow. And I'll have to have Elmer mop up in here before someone breaks their neck, or worse, a hip."

Vik took Marti's coat and kept his own. "Let me, ma'am."

As they followed her, she moved quickly and with far more agility than Marti expected. The kitchen wasn't as cozy as the porch had implied. The appliances were commercial and stainless steel. There were enough gadgets to stock a small store. There was just a hint of basil in the air and loaves of bread were rising on a countertop. Marti's stomach rumbled. They hadn't stopped to eat since lunch and it was well past dinner time.

"Have you eaten?" Miss Roberts asked.

"No, ma'am," Vik said.

"Well, the dining room is right over here and I'll fix you a little something right away. Josephina is playing canasta and there is no interrupting them once they cut the cards."

An elevator had been installed by the dining area. Everything was chintz and maple and meals were served at round tables seating four, with seasonal centerpieces of evergreen and holly.

"No need to rush, you won't be going back out tonight. We can put you up right here. This town is so small we don't have anything but that rinky-dink little motel, right off the highway. Route Sixty-six it used to be. They even had a TV show named for it with a song and all. Route Sixty-six it still is, as far as I'm concerned, even if they did make it much too wide and rename it Route Fifty-five."

Marti asked for a telephone.

"The lines are down, dear, but not to worry. We've got an emergency generator if the lights go." She brought them steaming bowls of beef stew, homemade biscuits, and real butter, followed by hot coffee and apple pie.

"I told Josephina you were here. They are right in the middle of their canasta game and were more than a little annoyed by the interruption."

After they had eaten the last bit of pie crust, Miss Roberts led them to the rear of the house. From the hallway, Marti could see an older man mopping up near the front door. Elmer, she assumed. As she watched, he straightened up, put his hand to the small of his back, then continued mopping in a slow circular pattern. Marti wondered what his relationship was to the others. If he didn't live in, and wasn't the next door neighbor, he would be spending the night here too, just as she and Vik would.

"You'll have to wait," Miss Roberts advised. "They play most evenings from right after dinner until bedtime. Once they shuffle and cut the deck, they get madder than buzzards without a carcass if you bother them. Here we are."

Windows ran the length of the porch, which had been closed in and winterized. The windows were bare except for vertical blinds, which were open. A white curtain of icy snow made tapping sounds against the glass. Marti thought of the heating bills first, then the pleasure of looking out and watching the seasons change. A log burning in a fireplace added a homey touch, but Marti doubted that the fire gave off much heat.

Everyone was in pairs. Two ladies sat at the far end of the room, watching a television with the volume turned up. Two ladies were knitting. Two who looked enough alike to be related napped in rocking chairs with their feet on hassocks and fat cats curled up in their laps.

Four women sat at a table. The one with hands crippled with arthritis had arranged her cards in some kind of cardholder. Marti studied each in turn and wondered which was Josephina Hanson. She had seen the dead woman at the morgue, as well as in photographs. None of the card players resembled her. She didn't see anyone to pair with Miss Hanson.

"Jeez," Vik whispered, shielding his mouth with his hand. "Do you think there's anyone in here under ninety? I haven't seen this many old people since my great Uncle Otto died. They had to put him in a nursing home when he was ninety-seven because he kept falling out of his wheelchair."

"I don't think any of these ladies is that old," Marti whispered back. She looked at the two in the rocking chairs and changed her mind. "Maybe those two." She nodded toward them. A walker with wheels and shelves was parked by one of the rockers.

Vik rubbed his arms, then scratched them.

"Old age isn't contagious," Marti said, under her breath. "Cut that out."

"This place is giving me the creeps. There has to be some place else we can stay."

Marti nodded in the direction of the windows. "Got any ideas as to how we'll get there?"

Vik muttered something in Polish.

There was plenty of seating available, but nothing that looked comfortable. The chairs and sofas had straight backs and hard seats that were high from the floor. Most had pillows or an extra cushion. Marti chose a chair close enough to the card table to eavesdrop. The women played like gamblers even though there was no money on the table: all business, no small talk, certainly not any gossip. What conversation there was was mostly about melds. Canasta didn't sound anything like poker or even bid whist. Bored, Marti watched as one of the old ladies by the television stood up and steadied herself with a cane. She thought of her grandmother and how difficult getting up and down had been for her and understood the reason for the chairs and sofas.

Everything had been adapted to meet the needs of the occupants: extra space between tables and chairs; a counter that ran the length of the windows, with books and magazines and needlework and yarn all within easy reach. There were no scatter rugs, no high or low shelves or storage areas. Sweaters hung on hooks and there was a stack of afghans. This was not anything like any nursing home she had ever been in. It was an old house; remodeling it must have been expensive.

A clock chimed the half hour. Marti glanced at her watch. It was after ten. Vik leaned over and said, "I told you old people don't go to bed early. See, they don't do enough to get tired."

The conversation at the table became louder. Chairs were

pushed back. One woman detached herself from the group and walked over to them. Her movements were slow but she was not infirm.

"Miss Hanson?"

"Yes." She was short and plump with a round face and granny glasses. Her deceased sister had been much taller and three years older. There was no facial resemblance whatsoever. "Agatha has been dead for a month now, but if you had to come out in weather like this . . . What is it?"

"Is there some place where we can talk?" Marti asked.

"Yes, right here." She pulled up a chair. "In just a few minutes."

"Here we are, ladies." Miss Roberts bustled in carrying a tray with glasses and a bottle of brandy. All of the women but two shared a nightcap. Marti and Vik declined but accepted mulled cider.

"So," Josephina Hanson said when they were alone, "what is it?"

Marti decided to be direct. "Someone poisoned your sister."

"Oh dear. But who? And how, I mean what?"

"When is the last time you saw her?"

"Oh, it's been ten years now. Not since Howie died. He was our brother."

"Had you spoken with her on the phone recently?"

"Not since June nineteenth, her birthday. We always call on birthdays and Christmas."

Marti supposed that at their age, and with this much distance between them, calls that infrequent might not be considered unusual. Neither woman had married. They had shared equally in their parents' estate. Agatha had lived alone in a small apartment. Frugal until the end, she had directed that there be no service, that her body be cremated and her ashes scattered on a bluff overlooking Lake Michigan. Josephina had inherited more from her sister than from her parents. It seemed as if they should have been closer.

"Do you have any idea of who her friends were?" The neighbors hadn't known of any.

"There was Opal, and Mary Sue, but both of them have been dead ten or twelve years now."

"Was there anyone else?"

"The mailman. She said he was a very pleasant young man and always reliable."

He was close to retirement and had worked that route for years. He found her body the day after she died. She remembered him in her will.

"Was there anyone else? A repairman? Someone trying to sell her something?"

"Agatha was not one to be taken in by strangers."

Agatha had not made any unusual withdrawals or any other bequests either. If someone had tried to swindle or otherwise pry money from her, apparently they had not been successful. If only she hadn't kept so much to herself.

As soon as Josephina Hanson excused herself to go to bed, Vik said, "That's another problem. How much can someone that old remember? And did you see how she leaned forward to listen to you and then talked too loud? Uncle Otto did that, too. He never wore a hearing aid though. One day he just couldn't hear anything at all."

"Vik, she did hear me."

"Right, but will she remember anything you said this time tomorrow? And it's been months since she talked with her sister. How do you expect her to remember any of that? We're talking about old people, Marti, real old people."

Marti leaned toward him and whispered, "What if she hired someone to kill off Agatha for her money?"

"Don't be ridiculous. At her age, how much money could she need? Living here is probably cheaper than her sister's living expenses were."

"I don't think so," Marti said. "This looks like an expensive arrangement. Greed, Vik. Think about it."

"I just did. There's got to be some other reason. You know how old people are. She trusted someone and kept money in the house. They stole from her and killed her when she found out. Or maybe she let them think they were going to get something when she died and they helped her on her way."

"How about the mailman?" Marti suggested.

"For ten thousand dollars?" He considered that. "We'll have to check him out. Did the sister's reaction surprise you?"

"Not if they've only spoken to each other three times a year for the past ten years. I'm wondering why. Something must have happened between them."

Although she would not admit it to Vik, the biggest problem she had questioning the elderly was not knowing how much of what they recalled was reliable. Then there was that ingrained habit of being respectful to her elders. She had also observed that death seldom surprised or frightened them, especially if they were old enough to have lost family members and friends.

"I can't read Josephina at all. There's something very matter-of-fact in her attitude. I don't know if it's acceptance, or indifference, or if she knows more about her sister's death than she's telling us." Tomorrow she would have to rule out two of those possibilities, even if she was disrespectful, even if Josephina did get upset.

Vik went to the window. "It's still snowing. It's drifted up to the windowsill. I bet we can't even see the car. If you tell anyone that we spent the night in an old folks' home, MacAlister, with eleven little old ladies and two cats . . ."

"Me?" If word of this got around the precinct they would both be the butt of everyone's jokes. "As far as I'm concerned, this place has vacant rooms and that makes it a motel."

"Just don't forget that. If anyone ever finds out I spent the night with a bunch of senile old women . . ."

"They are old, Jessenovik, but I don't see any indications of senility. There is a difference."

"Oh yeah? Try telling that to an eighty-year-old man."

Miss Roberts showed Vik to a sofa in a small den. Marti got a guest room on the first floor that was a few feet bigger than a closet. "I'm afraid we've never had anyone sleep over, dear," Miss Roberts explained. "We do have the stray niece and nephew here and there. It isn't something we want to encourage." The nightgown the woman gave her was several sizes too small. Marti stretched out on the bed fully clothed and covered herself with the extra quilt. She didn't like being in a strange bed and the mattress on this one was lumpy. The bedding smelled of sachet and the springs creaked. She doubted that anyone who slept here would want to do it again.

Marti didn't think she would fall asleep. A loud scream followed by hysterical crying awakened her. She rushed into the hall just as Vik came out of the den. He let her go ahead of him.

"Elmer, my God, Elmer!" Miss Roberts sobbed. Fully dressed, she was standing in a doorway.

Marti got close enough to see Elmer lying in a small heap on the floor. The bedroom wasn't any bigger than the one she was in. There was no sign of a struggle.

"Miss Roberts . . ."

The woman turned. "He can't be dead," she said. "He just can't be dead, not Elmer. He's only seventy-three." Her shoulders shook as she sobbed. "He just can't be dead. Nobody in our family has ever died younger than eighty."

Marti stayed with Miss Roberts while Vik knelt beside Elmer and checked for some sign of life. She wished she had asked more questions last night and knew who Elmer was.

Vik looked up and shook his head. "Miss Roberts, we need to call for an ambulance and notify the police."

"The phone lines are still out."

"Then we have to leave him here until we can get help."

"But he . . . he's just lying there . . . he . . . shouldn't we . . ."

"No."

Vik came out of the room and closed the door. "Since everyone in the house seems to be up . . ."

Marti turned to see all of the women, still in their nightclothes, standing close enough to hear what was being said but too far away to see into the room.

"Why don't we all come this way," Marti urged.

"Yes, yes," Miss Roberts agreed. "Breakfast is just about ready. I was so busy making sure those orange yeast rolls didn't burn on the bottom that I didn't even notice how late it was. Elmer always was a late sleeper, never gets up until half past six."

"Perhaps if everyone had breakfast," Marti urged.

"Yes, of course, but poor Elmer. It must have been his heart."

"Did he have heart trouble?"

"No. There was nothing wrong with his health. His eyesight wasn't what it used to be, but I never could convince him to get glasses."

"Is he a relative, ma'am?" Marti asked.

"He's my brother. My baby brother." The tears started flowing again.

"Did he live here with you?"

"Ye-e-e-s." Her shoulders heaved as she nodded.

"At least he didn't suffer," Marti said. That tended to have a calming effect for some reason. Marti wasn't sure why; like Vik said, dead was dead.

"He was always such a good boy, and handy too. He could fix just about anything. I don't know what I'm going to do without him."

"He would want you to go on."

"I know."

"We need to secure this room, ma'am," Vik said. "Just temporarily. Is there a key?"

Miss Roberts took a ring of keys from her apron pocket. "This one."

Vik slipped the key off, locked the door and pocketed the key. "Are there any other keys to this room?"

"Just Elmer's." She dabbed at her eyes and Marti expected more tears. Instead, Miss Roberts squared her shoulders and went into the dining room. "Now my dears, if you'll just give me a few minutes, breakfast will be served forthwith."

The ladies seemed subdued but otherwise okay. If it weren't for the two empty places at the table where the ladies with the cats were sitting, everything probably would have been okay. Within minutes everyone was looking there, and soon tears began trickling down their creased and wrinkled faces.

Marti shook her head when Vik motioned toward the front of the house. She was out of everyone's line of vision and curious to hear what they might say.

"How will we ever manage?" one said.

"How will Evangeline manage?" asked another. "He's been her right hand since Marjorie died. If he hadn't agreed to move in . . ."

"She'll find someone," one of the cat owners said.

"But dear," said the woman sitting beside her, "who can we trust?"

That said, everyone was silent.

When the door to the kitchen opened and Miss Roberts wheeled in a two-tiered tray loaded with food, the ladies hardly noticed. Marti wanted to reach for a crisp piece of bacon, that and one of those yeast rolls.

While the ladies had breakfast, Vik checked outside.

"No change," he said. "If there were any footprints leading to the house the wind has taken care of them."

Miss Roberts brought in orange rolls and a carafe of coffee. "I tried to call Chief Harrolson. Why on earth can't they get the lines fixed? It's never taken this long. Elmer said we needed to get some kind of radio. I don't know why I didn't listen to him."

After she left, Vik reached for one of the rolls, changed his mind and rubbed his hands together. "There's over a foot and a half of snow out there and from the looks of it there hasn't been a plow within miles of here. There's no point in digging the car out and neither of us thought to bring snow shoes or skis. And, all of this stayed south of Chicago. This isn't our case, Marti. This isn't our jurisdiction."

"We're peace officers, Vik." She didn't like this any better than he did and for the same reasons. "We are the only peace officers around."

"I'd be willing to consider natural causes if it wasn't for Josephina's sister," Vik said.

"We'd better treat this one like a homicide, Jessenovik. Just in case."

"You know what that means."

"That the killer is right here in the house."

"And not a day under seventy-five unless there's someone younger hiding in the attic or the basement."

"I think that's pretty unlikely, but let's get permission to take a look."

Vik agreed.

Marti found Miss Roberts in the kitchen. "Is it okay if we take a look around?"

She seemed puzzled, but the oven timer distracted her and she agreed.

"You notice anything about this setup?" Vik asked after they checked the attic and the second floor.

Marti had, but she didn't say anything.

"We've got one room with twin beds, one room with a single bed and the other four bedrooms have a double bed, one with a commode beside it."

"Umm humm."

"And, everyone seems to be in pairs."

"Umm humm."

"The two with the cats look so much alike that they have to be related, and with her sister dead, Evangeline is alone. That accounts for the twin beds and the single bed."

"Umm humm."

"But these are old ladies, Marti. Really old ladies."

"Umm humm."

"I'll be damned."

Vik paced for a moment, stopped, then said, "You know what? I'm going to pretend I didn't notice any of that. And you are not going to repeat it to anyone."

Marti didn't answer. "Lovely old house," she said as they went downstairs.

There wasn't anyone hiding in the cellar either.

They looked in on Elmer again. "Jeez," Vik said. "He's still dead."

"We'd better hope it was natural causes," Marti said, "and not something he ate."

"Ordinarily, MacAlister, when more than one death comes this close to the same person I rule out coincidence, but in this case natural causes makes sense. If the coroner hadn't run those toxicology tests, we wouldn't have known what killed the sister. It's going to take that with Elmer too."

Marti walked around the perimeter of the room. "I think Miss Roberts's permission to look around included looking around in here. Her exact words were 'Do whatever you feel is necessary to make sure we're all safe.' "

"I'm sure of it," Vik agreed. "That certainly includes anything we can do that might prevent someone killing them." He pulled open a drawer.

Twenty minutes later they concluded that Elmer wore his socks until there were holes in the toes and the heels; he owned three rifles, including one that looked like it had seen action in the civil war; and he had probably never thrown away a piece of paper in his life.

"They're organized, though," Vik said. "Some are in alpha order, some numeric and others by type. He must have spent hours in here in sorting them out. Beats the hell out of listening to women talk. He even has other people's pieces of paper. He must have filched them out of their waste baskets. A paper fetish. That's a new one."

"Going through it will give the local force something to do while they're waiting for the toxicology reports."

"Poor man, I bet he was driven to this, living with so many old women."

"Scary, isn't it?" Marti said.

"What?"

"One of these sweet little old ladies could be a real killer."

"Maybe it's time we got to know them a little better,

MacAlister. We've got to do something while we're waiting for an open telephone line or a plow."

"What I'd really like is some food that I was sure was safe to eat."

They waited until all the ladies went upstairs to get dressed, then went to the kitchen.

"Miss Roberts," Marti said, pretending surprise. "You cleaned up everything already. We thought you'd be much too upset to bother, and we haven't eaten anything yet."

"Oh, let me fix you something." She seemed to be getting over the shock of finding her brother dead. Maybe she was just keeping busy.

"Oh no," Marti said. "I'll do it myself, and clean up afterwards. Why don't you just sit and talk with us while I cook." She kept it simple, lots of eggs, plenty of bacon and a stack of toast. "We'll reimburse you, ma'am."

"Why I wouldn't hear of it. If you weren't here, with poor Elmer . . . and all . . ."

Miss Roberts hovered. Marti wasn't sure if it was because she never allowed anyone to cook in her kitchen, or if she was watching for an opportunity to slip a little something into the food. Did Miss Roberts have a reason to want her brother dead? If so, did she want Josephina's sister dead too?

"This is a lovely place you have here," Marti said. "What made you think of it? Has everyone always lived in this town?"

"It was a wonderful idea, wasn't it? We didn't want to end up alone. I'm the only one who was born here. Josephina and I met years ago at the Art Institute in Chicago. A couple of us have known each other since we took an extension course at the University in Bloomington. Then there were the cat shows. I used to raise and show Persians; when the last of them died, I didn't replace her."

"And now you're all here."

"This was my parents' home and my grandparents' before them. We've been together over fifteen years now."

Vik made a face, as if he'd just bitten into something sour. "How do you manage financially?"

"None of us is poor. We could live on our own, at least for a while longer, but eventually we would end up in nursing homes and this is so much nicer. We have a woman who comes in and does most of the cooking, another who cleans. And, when the time comes, there's money put aside for nursing care. We can all just stay here until . . ." She put her hands to her face and cried. "Elmer was my baby brother. He was the only blood relative I had."

Marti put her arms about the old woman's shoulders and walked with her to the porch.

"Money," Vik said when she returned. "If Josephina hadn't seen her sister in years . . . we need to find out about her finances, too."

"And Elmer," Marti said.

"I don't know. He isn't our case anyway. If there is a case."

"These women aren't going to tell us anything, Vik, not unless they tell us accidentally. They are not going to do anything to jeopardize this arrangement." She thought about that. "If the deaths are related, even if they are not, that has to be the motive, something that would jeopardize their being here together."

"Right, MacAlister, and that could be damned near anything. They could all die without us ever finding out."

"Okay, okay. Let's start with what we know. Agatha died from an overdose of this stuff." She took out her notebook and read off the name of the poison. "It's tasteless, and lethal in a very small dose. The best place to find it is in antique shops. People collect the cans that it came in, sometimes there's residue inside."

"So, which one of these ladies do you think was a chemist or a pharmacist?" From the tone of his voice, Marti knew Vik was being sarcastic.

"They were born in the twentieth century. There is that possibility."

"Or it could be a relative or a friend. Then there is always the question of how the poison got from here to Lincoln Prairie. Maybe it was the one with the cane and she walked there, or took the bus. We're leaving Elmer's death up to the locals and focusing on what we came here for. Suspects, motives, and opportunity."

"We're batting zero on all three, Jessenovik, and with Elmer's death, I don't think these ladies are going to be inclined to talk with us about anything."

"Too bad we didn't have a reason to question them last night."

Marti tapped her pen against her notebook. "Antiques. Miss Roberts didn't mention anything about that."

"They've all got a bunch of old stuff in their rooms."

Marti didn't know enough about antiques to know what was valuable and what was not, but maybe that wasn't important. "The second bedroom on the right," she said.

"The one with the junky stuff?"

"Odd stuff, Vik. Things you might pick up on vacation. Nostalgia stuff. The old Log Cabin Syrup can made like a log cabin. That cracked Ovaltine cup. The kewpie doll, the Lionel train caboose, the Route 66 memorabilia."

"A cigarette roller," Vik said. "My father had one."

Everything had been arranged so decoratively about the room that she hadn't thought of it as junk at all. She would have to find out whose room it was without alerting the occupant. "There were a number of old containers. Let's see."

She flipped through her notes and read off a description of the can the poison could have been packaged in.

"Oh sure, MacAlister. Didn't you notice? There was one of those right on the nightstand. Look, killing old Elmer is one thing, but Agatha lived a couple hundred miles away. Assuming that one of these ladies did do it, how did she get there?"

"I'll have to think about that," Marti admitted.

Lunch was served promptly at noon. Another check confirmed that the telephone was still out of order and not only had the street not been plowed, but it was snowing again, with another four to six inches predicted. Marti eavesdropped on the dayroom conversation, which consisted of canasta, a biography of Abigail Adams, and cat habits and behavior.

Vik looked at the tureens of soup and thick wedges of freshly baked bread and shook his head.

"You're getting paranoid, Jessenovik," Marti scolded, not that she intended to eat any of it either. Agatha's last meal had consisted of zucchini bread and preserves laced with poison.

"He has a trick stomach," she explained. "Do you mind if we just fix ourselves something?"

Miss Roberts was busy serving and just nodded.

The ladies did speak a bit loudly. With the dining room and kitchen doors open, Marti could hear most of what was said.

"Did you get the mail yet, dear?"

"What?"

"I ordered a new dish and place mat for Muffie over a week ago."

"Well, they won't come today."

"Why on earth not?"

"The blizzard, old girl. We've got snow out there."

"But why should that . . ."

"Did you see that jigsaw puzzle catalog that come in the other day? I'm ordering if anyone wants to send their order in with mine."

A lively discussion ensued on what was available in the current crop of catalogs as well as which companies misrepresented their products and who took the longest as well as the least time to ship. By the time Vik had approved lunch meat, cheese, and store-bought bread, the ladies had reached the catalog-order-from-hell stage of the conversation.

"I'm not making coffee," Marti said. "It's either what's in the pot or you can drink tap water."

Vik scowled, then relented and held out his cup.

"You'll have to decide for yourself about cream and sugar."

"Black," he said.

The discussion on catalog orders continued.

"Now you know what you have to look forward to, Jessenovik."

"I'm going fishing when I retire."

"I'm sure there's a catalog available with fishing lures if you can't make it to the hardware store in your wheel chair." She wished for the homemade bread as she bit into her sandwich. The cheese was a delicious hard cheddar.

"Delivery companies must love this place," Vik said. "With no deliveries in two days they must have a half a truckload of stuff to bring out here."

"Deliveries," Marti said. "They can pick up stuff too."

"So?"

"What if the poisoned preserves were shipped to Agatha?"

"I like that, MacAlister. I like that."

"Elmer," they both said at once.

Sandwiches and coffee in hand, they went to his room and began searching through all of his mail receipts.

"Here," Marti said, holding one up. "It's addressed to Agatha Hanson and it's dated the day before she died. It was shipped one-day service."

"The sister sent it."

"No, Jessica Perkins did."

"Which one is that?"

"I don't know, but this is as good a time as any to find out."

Jessica Perkins turned out to be a member of the canasta club, the one with severe arthritis. The scent of camphor wafted into the room as she came in. She was not Josephina's partner.

"Miss Perkins," Marti began. "What did you send to Agatha Hanson last month?"

"Why would I send her anything? I didn't even know her."

So much for being direct and catching her off guard.

"Could you explain why your name is on this receipt?"

Miss Perkins looked at it, then gazed calmly at Marti and said, "I have no idea."

Marti doubted that she could have filled out the mailing information. Elmer must have done that.

"Ma'am," Vik said. "Does it seem at all strange to you that Elmer Roberts had this in his possession and now he too is dead?"

"Why no, officer." She actually fluttered her eyelashes. "Perhaps Elmer mailed the package himself, and used my name."

As soon as Miss Perkins walked out of the room, Vik said. "Crafty old bird."

"What did I tell you about assuming senility, Jessenovik?"

Josephina Hanson was next. Marti had little hope of getting anything out of her either.

"Miss Hanson, we found this receipt among Elmer Roberts's belongings."

The woman's expression didn't change as she looked at it, but her hand trembled, unless she had tremors.

"Why are you asking me about this?"

"Did you send a package to your sister?"

"No."

"Do you know why anyone else would send her a package, express delivery, the day before she died of poisoning?"

"What kind of poison?" There was a catch in her voice.

"A poison that isn't sold over the counter anymore but is sold in containers that can be found in antique shops because they are considered collectibles."

"I see."

"Were you close to your sister, Miss Hanson?"

"We were adopted. We didn't have the same real parents. We weren't really sisters. Just legally."

Marti thought of the apartment Agatha had lived in, furnished with only the essentials. She wondered how long the woman's body would have gone undiscovered if the mailman hadn't been concerned enough to look in on her.

"Your sister didn't have any friends, Miss Hanson. She didn't have what you have. She was very much alone. Someone sent her a loaf of homemade bread and a jar of poisoned preserves. She thought it was a gift. She ate it and she died."

Tears ran down Josephina's cheeks. She dabbed at her eyes. "She didn't want any friends. She wanted to be alone. She was always like that."

"She was grateful enough for the gift to eat it."

"She was probably too cheap to buy it."

"Cheap enough to leave you quite a bit of money, Miss Hanson."

"I did not need Agatha's money."

"Didn't you, Josephina?" It was a guess, but Marti saw the woman's hand tighten around a wad of tissue.

"Is that why you sent the package to your sister?"

"I didn't," she whispered. "I couldn't hurt anyone."

Marti couldn't decide whether or not she was telling the truth.

"Who else knew you needed money?"

She shook her head.

"Someone knew. Who was it?"

There was no response. Josephina and Agatha didn't like each other. They weren't related by blood. Apparently Josephina felt little attachment or loyalty to her. But Agatha thought she was receiving a gift.

"Did you exchange birthday presents?"

"No."

"Christmas gifts?"

"No."

"Then Agatha must have been very pleased to receive a package. Even if someone else sent it, she would have believed it was your idea, your way of giving her something. Was that something that would have made her happy?"

"I don't know."

"Did you ever forget to call her?"

"Once or twice."

"What happened?"

"Nothing. I don't know."

"Would the gift have pleased her?"

"Maybe."

"Would it have pleased your parents?"

Josephina hesitated, wiped at tears again. "Very much."

"How would they feel if they knew you were responsible for her death?"

"But I didn't . . . I only told Jessica my money would run out in a few years. A few years, for God's sake, I could be dead in a few years. How did I know . . . I don't know . . . I don't know. I don't."

"You're upset, ma'am," Vik said. "Maybe you need to lie down."

"Yes," she agreed. He helped her from the room.

When they spoke with Jessica Perkins again, there was a defiant tilt to her chin.

"You knew that Josephina was having financial difficulties," Marti said.

"Nobody else here knows how to play canasta."

"Ma'am?"

"How would we play canasta without Josephina? We've played canasta for over twenty years. Just the four of us. How could we replace her?"

"Could you please tell me what happened, ma'am?"

"I couldn't write. Not the label, not anything. Elmer did it for me." She held up her hands. "I can barely eat with them."

"Why did you kill him, ma'am."

"Because he knew, damn it, because he knew. And he would have told you as soon as he found out why you were here."

"Canasta," Vik said, as Marti drove home. "Two people dead because of a card game. I suppose I've heard worse, but you'd think someone that old would know better. She's probably old enough to get away with it, too. They can just keep continuing the case until she checks out."

Marti turned on the windshield wipers. They were approaching the Chicago city limits and it was beginning to snow. This time the storm was expected to hit the city and points north.

WILLING TO WORK

- - - - - - - - - - - - - - - -

Les Roberts

Les Roberts came to mystery writing after twenty-four years in Hollywood, where he wrote and/or produced more than 2500 half-hours of network and syndicated television. In 1987 he won the St. Martin's Press Best Private Eye Novel Contest for *An Infinite Number of Monkeys*. He followed that book with the first in his Milan Jacovich series, set in Cleveland, where he lives and reviews mysteries for the *Plain Dealer*.

Meacham Donalson snaked the big white Caddy along Gravois Avenue, Alternate U.S. Route 66, in the heavy lunch-hour traffic, taking the air conditioner's blast directly on his face. It almost numbed his fingers on the wheel, but the high temperatures of this St. Louis summer made turning it off and opening the windows unthinkable. It was one of those muggy days when the moisture-laden air coming off the Mississippi was almost thick enough to drink.

Meacham glanced through the tinted window at the pedestrians on the sidewalk and sighed. He'd miss St. Louis, despite the heat, miss the majestic rumbling river even though the city had turned its back on it and moved its core several blocks west. He'd miss the Cardinals the most, he thought, even though it wasn't the same any more now that his boyhood heroes, Musial and Marty Marion and "Country" Slaughter and Red Schoendienst had faded. St. Louis was a pretty good town to live in, despite the heat and humidity, and even if it weren't, after thirty-six years you get used to a place, to its shops and restaurants, to its pulse and rhythms.

St. Louis had come back from economic troubles; they were saying the whole country's economy was coming back after the recession of the late 1950s, the pundits on the OpEd page of the *Post-Dispatch* and John Cameron Swayze on NBC. Tell that to all the people in the cities who were still out of work and foraging in garbage receptacles to feed their families.

It was that damn Bobby Troup song Nat King Cole made so popular that had brought them in—kids from downstate Illinois proudly wearing their good conduct medals and combat infantryman badges, farm boys from little towns in Missouri and Oklahoma, all wanting to "go through St. Louis" after the war to get urbanized and get healthy in the wallet. It had worked that way for a while in the post-war prosperity boom, and then reality had set in.

Meacham saw them on the streets now, lined up for a cot and a square meal at one of the many shelters that had sprung up around the city in church basements or abandoned storefronts, or huddled over trash-can fires in the wintertime, living on the riverbank and willing to do just about anything for a buck.

But one man's troubles were another's good fortune.

Meacham Donalson would do anything for a buck, too, but Fate had smiled on him when she'd assigned his birth to a well-off couple, his father in the investment banking business with a nice house in Clayton. Meacham had drifted into that world, too, but it was every bit as distasteful to him as what the unemployed were willing to do—day work on construction gangs or hiring themselves out to homeowners who had tree stumps to pull or rocks to haul, or the small businessmen who needed temporary help and saw the cadre of the out-of-work as inexpensive and off-the-books muscle. Investment banking just paid better, that's all.

But not well enough for Meacham. A hundred K a year wasn't worth the aggravation, the blinding stress headaches and the mainlining of aspirin, the three martinis at the end of the day just to untie the psychological knots.

But that world was all behind Meacham now, or it would be after today. Right in the pocket of his suit jacket he had the airline ticket to Mexico, to a little place on the Baja Coast that no one had ever heard of called Puerto Vallarta. He had the phony passport with his new name, for which he'd paid a whopping two thousand dollars to a counterfeiter in Chicago. He'd made the deposit on the big white villa overlooking the coastline. And he'd sworn he'd never again put on a tie and wing-tip shoes and toady to a well-heeled account, never again feel the crunch in his gut when a stock price dipped or a mutual fund went belly-up.

No, his worries were almost over. Two million dollars plus would go a hell of a long way in an obscure, sleepy fishing village like Puerto Vallarta.

He'd left work early, claiming he wasn't feeling well, that he'd been having dizzy spells for two days and thought he was coming down with the Asian flu. The people in the office had been very solicitous, had even offered advice from the current best-seller, *Folk Medicine*, on how to take care of himself; when it comes to someone else's health, everyone thinks he's a doctor.

But he'd told them he was already taking medication. And when he walked out of the brokerage firm with his briefcase in his hand, he'd been amazed to realize there wasn't a single person he was going to miss. Not his boss, certainly, not the other account executives, not the women in the typing pool, not even the office boys with whom he'd discuss the fortunes of the Cardinals each morning by the coffee machine.

He was getting away clean.

He cruised downtown for about an hour, comforted by the rumble of the Caddy's big V-8 engine, sweating beneath the sunglasses with their heavy black plastic rims. He glanced offhandedly at the pedestrians, because he was looking for one particular guy, someone he'd seen on the streets several times before, the one who'd sparked his great idea in the first place.

Finally, in the depressed area known as Dogtown, he spotted him.

He was about Meacham's age and height, a tall man in an army surplus jacket and worn Levis, and a red Cardinals' cap which looked like it had been through a decade of baseball seasons. As Meacham had seen him so many other days of this long, sweltering summer, he was standing at the curb with a bulging duffel at his feet and a hopeful expression on his face. In front of his chest he held a large sheet of gray cardboard, on which had been scrawled, NEED MONEY; WILLING TO WORK.

Meacham slowed the Caddy to a stop, leaned across the seat and rolled down the passenger-side window. There was a fluttering in his stomach he'd never experienced before, and he coughed to clear an unexpected frog from his throat. "Hi there," he said.

The man stooped down so he could see into the car. He hadn't shaved in several days, and the collar of his shirt was frayed ragged, but he seemed clean.

"I've got some work I need done," Meacham said pleasantly. "Stuff I need moved from the spare room to the basement. Books and things—heavy. I'd do it myself, but I've got a bad back." The man hesitated. "Take you two hours, maybe a little more."

"Sounds okay," the ragged man said, his eyebrows twin arches of hope. "Uhhh . . . ?"

"Twenty dollars, plus lunch," Meacham told him. "If you don't mind the drive out to Frontenac."

Stunned, the man blinked rapidly when he heard the amount; in 1960 twenty dollars was a fortune. "Sure. I guess so."

"Get in, then."

The man opened the car door, putting his hand-lettered sign in the back seat. He slid in beside Meacham, hugging the small duffel to his chest as if it were a child. "I really appreciate this," he said. His speech was more refined than Meacham had expected; perhaps this was an educated man down on his luck. "Appreciate the chance to work."

"Hey, I help you out, you help me out. That's the way the world operates." Meacham leaned across him to roll up the window again and was aware of the man's odor. He smelled almost dusty; it wasn't acrid or unpleasant, but it was an odor nonetheless. Meacham left the window open a crack at the top.

"My name's Chuck," the man said.

"Mine's . . . Mike." Meacham used the name that was on his false passport; he'd spent the last ten days getting used to it. He took a pack of Old Golds from his pocket and offered one to Chuck, took one for himself, and punched in the Caddy's electric lighter.

It took him a few minutes to get back to Route 66. By the time they were rolling along nicely in the westbound traffic flow, Chuck had told him that he'd been laid off from the Budweiser plant more than a year ago, that his unemployment benefits had run out and he'd gone through his meager savings, that he'd been on the streets for about four months now, trying to find a job and a place to live and picking up small change by offering himself for whatever kind of odd jobs he could get there on the street corner in Dogtown.

"That's too bad," Meacham said, trying to make it sound solicitous and caring. "Wife? Kids?"

Chuck shook his head. "No, thank God. It's bad enough to be on my uppers like this without having to worry about feeding a family, too."

As the car picked up speed, the smoke from their cigarettes was sucked out through the top of the open window by the slipstream. Meacham dropped the visor down to block the glare of the high summer sun. The guy didn't sound like a moron. He didn't talk like a Ph.D. either, but he seemed as if he had a brain or two in his head. Meacham had a momentary twinge of remorse, and almost changed his mind about what he was going to do. But he shook the feeling off like a dog shaking water from its coat. He steeled himself. It was too important to his future.

When they finally got to Frontenac, Chuck gazed out the car window at the pristine houses, the well-manicured lawns bright green despite the summer-long drought, the tree-shaded streets. "Nice," he said softly, but there was no trace of envy in it. Longing, perhaps, but no envy. He'd been on the street four months, now; he was already beyond that.

The Caddy turned into a blacktop driveway sloping up a small rise to a six-year-old ranch-style house painted an off-white with tan trim. The door of the detached garage rose smoothly like a stage curtain as Meacham activated his automatic opener and steered the Caddy in next to a battered black 1952 Buick Roadmaster with a big gouge in the paint on the right-hand door.

"Here we are," he said, and cut the motor.

They crossed the small yard to the back door of the house, went in past a washer and dryer in the utility room and into a spacious kitchen with a breakfast nook tucked into a sunny bay of windows. Except for a mug in the sink with the dregs of breakfast coffee in the bottom, the kitchen was spotless. Through an archway Chuck could see a formal dining room, and beyond that a tasteful living room all done in antiques with expensive period furniture. There were two brass, kerosene-burning hurricane lamps on the mantel for decoration, another on a drum table next to the sofa.

"My wife's been gone for a week, now," Meacham explained. "Visiting her sister in New York. You know, shopping and shows." He stopped for a moment, aware that referring to a luxury vacation in front of a man who begged on the street had been insensitive. But then he shrugged off the guilt—what did it really matter?

"I wish I could've gone with her, but I couldn't take the time off from work. Still, I like to keep the place as neat as she does. I don't like clutter in my life." He put down his briefcase, took off his suit jacket and draped it over one of the chairs in the breakfast nook, and loosened his tie. The central air conditioner was on LOW and it was still warm in the kitchen.

"You're probably hungry, right?" Meacham said. "You want something to eat before you start? A sandwich?"

Chuck put his duffel down in one corner of the kitchen. "Uh . . . sure. If it isn't too much trouble."

"No trouble, no trouble at all. That was part of the deal. Take a seat, relax a minute."

Chuck sat down in the breakfast nook and watched while Meacham got out some Wonder Bread, mayonnaise, a jar of pickles, and some sliced chicken wrapped in delicatessen paper and began building a sandwich. He put it all on a plate, took a paper napkin from the holder, a knife and fork from the drawer, and set everything on the table in front of Chuck.

"How 'bout a beer to go with it?"

Chuck nodded, a little stunned. He hadn't expected all this, lunch and chit-chat, and it was making him a trifle nervous. He'd been plucked off the sidewalk for work before—it was how he'd survived the last four months—but in every other case his temporary employer had treated him pretty much like a non-person, speaking to him only enough to explain what the job required. No one had ever offered him lunch and a beer before. He stared out the window at the well-kept pachysandra lawn and the beds of iris and crocus marking off the borders of the backyard as his host busied himself at the refrigerator. He heard the hiss as the cap of a beer bottle was popped, and turned his attention back to Meacham.

"What do you do, flop at one of the shelters downtown?" Meacham asked over his shoulder.

"Whenever I can." Chuck applied mayonnaise to one slice of bread, replaced it, and carefully cut the sandwich in half. "There aren't ever enough beds, and you can only stay there three days in a row. Sometimes I sleep down on the riverbank, when the weather's nice, or down under the Eades Bridge."

"That's rough. But you've got to keep hoping. I'll bet your troubles are going to be over pretty soon." Meacham brought a pilsner glass with a Budweiser already poured and set it next to Chuck's plate. "There you go," he said. He sat down opposite Chuck, leaning forward on his elbows, his white cuffs gleaming. "Go on, drink up. You can have another one if you want."

Chuck lifted the glass in a kind of grateful toast and took a long swallow. It was stinging cold, bitter but good, the first beer he'd tasted in more than a month. He didn't want to appear too interested in the drink so he set it down and bit into the sandwich, shaking off the uneasy suspicion that Meacham was watching him a bit too closely.

"How many boxes do you have?" he asked after he'd chewed the first mouthful of chicken.

"Boxes?"

"You said you had boxes you wanted moved to the cellar."

"Oh. Yes. About thirty, I think. I didn't really count them. But they're heavy suckers—books, papers, things like that. And my back has a way of going out every time I left anything heavier than my briefcase."

"You should exercise," Chuck said.

"Who has the time? They've got me crazy at the office. I don't have time to do any of the things I want to do. But that's going to change." Meacham nodded grimly. "Pretty damn quick now, that's going to change." He seemed to be talking to himself more than his visitor.

Perspiring heavily under his jacket, Chuck drank some more beer to cool himself off. It was so good and cold, it made him a trifle giddy. Perhaps he just wasn't used to drinking anymore, he thought, or maybe it was because he hadn't had anything to eat for the past twenty-four hours. The alcohol burned pleasantly in his stomach.

"You mind if I smoke?" Meacham asked. "While you're eating, I mean?"

"Hell, buddy, it's your house."

"Mike. Call me Mike, okay?" Meacham waited expectantly. All at once it seemed terribly important that Chuck call him Mike, his new name.

"Mike," Chuck said slowly.

Meacham smiled—it was the first time he'd heard it aloud. He took out an Old Gold and lit it with his Zippo. "Want one?"

"When I finish eating."

"Well, feel free." Meacham pushed the pack across the table at him. Chuck just bobbed his head in gratitude and finished the beer.

"Here, let me get you another one." Meacham almost snatched the glass from his hand and took it back to the refrigerator.

"This is really nice of you," Chuck said.

"I'm just glad I can help. I help you out, you help me out, that's the way it works. I won't insult you by saying you've got it easy, because I know you don't." Meacham had his back to Chuck, pouring the beer at the refrigerator. "It must be pure hell, not having a place to live. But for people with jobs—sometimes the rat race gets you down, you know?" He turned and came back to the breakfast nook, handing the full glass to his guest. "Cheers," he said, and took a slug of beer straight from the frosty bottle as Chuck tilted the glass to his lips. "Things. You break your back trying to keep your head above water just so you can have things. Wanting things becomes so important to you, you can hardly think of anything else." He sat back down again. "How's the sandwich?"

"Great," Chuck said, putting the glass down. His tongue was starting to feel a little thick, his lips rubbery, and he was becoming uncomfortably warm. "Mind if I take my jacket off?"

"Be comfortable."

He hung the jacket over the back of his chair. The blue work shirt was faded and its cuffs were beginning to ravel, and he rolled them up to just below his elbows so Meacham wouldn't see. Half-moons of sweat circled his armpits and his shirt was wet at the small of his back.

"Yeah," Meacham was saying, "they hit you with a million bills every month. House payment, car payment, this payment, that payment. Insurance." He shook his head sadly. "That one's a bear, life insurance."

Chuck nodded. He was sleepy all of a sudden. He just wanted to close his eyes, and he had to struggle to keep them open.

"But it's worth it. My insurance premiums would choke a horse, but if I died, my wife would get a cool million. Tax free. Doesn't seem fair, does it?"

Chuck was going to shake his head, but it seemed too heavy for the effort. Meacham's voice sounded as if it were coming from a long, dark tunnel.

"And if I died accidentally—that's double indemnity and she'd get two million. Think about that for a while."

Chuck tried to think about it, but he couldn't. He wasn't able to think about much of anything anymore, just about going to sleep.

"But," Meacham added, "if the insurance company only *thought* I died—why then I could have my cake and eat it, too. Know what I mean, Chuck?"

Chuck didn't say anything; he couldn't. The drug that had been slipped into the beer had practically paralyzed him. He began rocking from side to side, like Ray Charles, fighting desperately for equilibrium. Finally a black liquid wave flowed over his eyes and brain, and he lost consciousness and slipped off the chair onto the floor of the breakfast nook.

Meacham Donalson stayed very still for a moment, not even daring to breathe. Finally he exhaled softly, carefully. "Chuck?" he almost whispered.

There was, of course, no answer; he hadn't expected one. The two men were motionless, like statues, one because he couldn't move and the other because he didn't dare to.

Finally Meacham stood, pushing his chair back into place. He knelt and took Chuck's limp wrist in his hand to feel for a pulse. It was there, faint but racing.

He slipped his arms under Chuck's, clasping him around the chest. Carefully he dragged him through the dining room and living room, down the hallway and into the master bedroom, Chuck's heels leaving twin trails in the thick-pile carpet. Meacham felt a twinge in his lower back from pulling such a heavy weight while stooped over, and thought it would be the supreme irony if this did give him back problems, something he'd never suffered from in his life.

Panting from the exertion, he left Chuck on the floor of the bedroom for a moment. Maybe Chuck was right, maybe he *should* exercise. He sat on the edge of the queen-sized bed, girding himself for the next step, which he wasn't relishing. He watched the man's chest rise and fall in a lazy rhythm.

His energy finally returned to him, and he set to work. He stripped off all Chuck's clothing, grunting as he slipped the trousers from the inert body, handling the gray underwear and badly-mended socks with some distaste, stuffing it all into a plastic grocery sack from the A & P.

He looked down at the nude form, the pale, unhealthy-looking skin beneath the somewhat sunburned face and neck. About what Meacham had expected, given the man's insufficient diet and his prolonged exposure to the elements. Chuck had evidently spent the previous night in a shelter, because he had recently showered; his hands, feet and body were clean.

Meacham then took off his own clothes, every stitch, laying them casually on the bed. He went to his closet, taking down a garment bag full of clothing—a blue shirt, khaki slacks, a lightweight gray sports jacket, blue socks, and a belt—all brand new. No one had ever seen him wearing them before. He put on fresh underwear and donned everything from the bag except the jacket, and slipped his feet into a pair of Florsheim loafers he'd purchased the week before.

Checking himself in the mirror, he smiled with satisfaction. He always looked more youthful when he was wearing casual clothes, he thought, and vowed that once he got to Puerto Vallarta he'd never put on a suit and tie again.

He dressed the unconscious Chuck in the clothes he'd just taken off, all except for the tie, which he tossed carelessly on the floor next to the bed, and the shoes. Meacham was known for his fastidiousness; leaving his suit jacket on the chair in the kitchen and his tie on the floor would reinforce the fact that he had been ill at work and suffered dizziness. It was only logical that he'd go home and lie down immediately.

He left his wallet in the hip pocket of his trousers so they'd find it on Chuck. There was nothing in there he'd ever need again—his wife Bettyann would still have her credit cards when she joined him in a few months.

He took the grocery sack containing Chuck's clothes back into the kitchen, stuffing them into the man's duffel and then taking it out to the battered Roadmaster in the garage next to his Cadillac. He'd seen the car on the street in one of St. Louis' black neighborhoods with a FOR SALE sign in its window, and had bought it for cash, four hundred dollars, from an elderly man who seemed amazed he didn't haggle about the price. The car was a piece of crap, needing a new transmission and God knew what else, but that didn't much matter. It ran, and it didn't have to take him very far. He'd driven it into the garage a few days earlier, at three o'clock in the morning, and nobody knew it was there.

He went back into the kitchen and put away the lunch fixings, washed Chuck's dishes and beer glass, and placed them back where they belonged. He tossed the two empty beer bottles into the garbage, being careful to rinse the fingerprints off them first. He also wiped down the surface of the table in the breakfast nook. Not that anyone would bother lifting fingerprints, but one couldn't be too careful.

With the vacuum cleaner he went over the carpet thoroughly, obliterating the heel marks from when he'd dragged Chuck through the house. Satisfied, he stored it in its usual place in the utility room, winding the cord around the handle the way Bettyann always did.

He returned to the bedroom where Chuck still snoozed on the floor, and hoisted him onto the bed, on top of the spread with his head on the pillow. He opened the bedroom window and nodded in satisfaction when he felt the warm breeze outside circulating throughout the room. Then he went into the bathroom and opened that window, too, creating a nice cross-draft. He took a small bottle of pills from the medicine cabinet, the ones he'd had Dr. Stein prescribe for him over the phone the day before when he'd called up and complained of flu-like symptoms. There were sixteen pills in there, to be taken four times a day until used up. Shaking all but three of them into his palm, he went back into the bedroom and put the bottle on the nightstand with the cap off. Then he wrapped the rest of them in a tissue and put them in his shirt pocket.

He put on his new jacket and thought for a long while, one finger playing idly with his lower lip. Chuck hadn't gone anywhere in the house except the kitchen, and Meacham had cleaned that up pretty well. The bedroom looked about right, too. He'd covered all the bases, he thought.

His guest was snoring softly on the bed, but Meacham rolled him over on his side and the sounds stopped. He arranged Chuck's right hand outflung. Then, sucking in a deep breath, he tipped the antique hurricane lamp from the nightstand over onto the bed, making sure that most of the kerosene inside it spilled over Chuck's head and hand. When they'd bought the house three years earlier, he hadn't wanted to furnish it with antiques, modern being more to his taste, but Bettyann had insisted. Now he was glad.

He stepped backwards, fists on his hips, trying to get the full effect. Yes, it would look very much as if the man on the bed had collapsed there feeling ill, lit a cigarette, fallen asleep, and rolled fitfully over onto his side and knocked the lamp over by accident. He nodded, pleased. He was certain no one would question it.

Still standing well away from the bed, he lit a cigarette, watching the Zippo's flame waver in the breeze between the bedroom window and the bathroom. Then he put the pack and lighter on the nightstand.

He took a few puffs, and then gingerly inserted the lighted Old Gold between the second and third fingers of Chuck's hand. He figured he had about ninety seconds until it burned down and ignited the kerosene.

Moving quickly through the house to the back door, he paused for a mere scintilla of time for one last look. It was a nice house, but working hard enough to pay for it had been killing him. He shrugged away any regrets; it would be a lot better this way.

He went outside to the garage, opened the door with the control mounted on the side wall, slipped behind the wheel of the old Roadmaster, and backed out. He wasn't worried about anyone seeing him, because the couple in the house on one side of his both worked; the widow on the other side also had a day job.

By the time he reached the corner, he could see black smoke snaking out the bedroom window at the side of the house.

He drove east, stopping for a moment in a supermarket parking lot where he deposited Chuck's duffel and the extra pills into a trash receptacle. Then he headed downtown, put his car in a parking garage adjoining one of the big hotels, and crossed the street to climb into a waiting cab. One nice thing about downtown, he thought, is that you could always get a taxi.

"Airport," he told the driver.

Once at the terminal, he went directly to the storage locker where he'd stashed a suitcase three days earlier. New suitcase, new clothes—just enough to get him through the first week in the little seaside town on Mexico's Baja Peninsula until he could buy some more with the twenty-one thousand dollars in cash, also in the suitcase, he'd amassed slowly by selling some stock shares over the past months.

He'd even filled out the luggage tag on the suitcase: "Michael Mitchum," it read, the same name as on his forged passport. Close enough to his own name that he wouldn't forget it, different enough that no one would make the connection.

Not that anyone would try. Meacham Donalson was by now burnt to an unrecognizable crisp in an unfortunate house fire. Poor fellow. His wife was in New York when it happened. She'll be devastated.

Just devastated enough to collect the two million dollars on his double indemnity policy, he thought, smiling, to collect more insurance money on the house, and to join him in Mexico in two months, maybe three, as they'd planned.

However long it took, it would be worth the wait to spend the rest of their lives in the sun with all the money they'd ever need. He briefly considered calling her at her sister's home in Larchmont, just outside New York City, to tell her that things were progressing on schedule, but thought better of it.

He removed four hundred dollars in cash from the suitcase and then checked it through to San Diego where he'd change planes for the short flight to Puerto Vallarta. The truth was, he would have preferred driving all the way, taking his time and seeing the sights along Route 66 like any other tourist, then turning south at Gallup and proceeding on to San Diego. But he knew the old Buick would never have survived the trip, and besides, there was something to be said to getting on with his new life and his new identity as quickly as possible.

With two hours before his flight was scheduled to leave, he went into the cocktail lounge at the terminal and ordered a Budweiser. It would be his last St. Louis beer, he thought; from now on he'd be drinking the Mexican stuff, Dos Equis or something. It would take some getting used to.

He glanced up at the TV set which was playing some witless game show, but he wasn't concentrating, thinking instead about how good it was going to be in Mexico—free from pressure and worry and responsibility, living in relative luxury with Bettyann for the rest of their lives.

It wasn't until halfway through his second Bud that he remembered something, and his face grew ashen as clammy sweat broke out all over his body. He began to shake, spilling some of his beer on the bar top.

The bartender came over to mop it up with a towel and noticed his customer seemed ill. "Hey, buddy, are you okay?" he said.

But Meacham Donalson couldn't answer, because there was a lump in his throat that felt like a basketball, and his stomach was knotted up inside by the harsh twist of fear.

By the time the Fire Department got the blaze contained, half the house was gone. The entire street was cordoned off, much to the dismay of the homeward-bound residents of that particular housing tract who often used it as a thoroughfare to get to their own homes two and three blocks over. The acrid smell of smoke hung in the air for a quarter mile in either direction, and closer to the house was another sweetish smell that few of the neighbors could identify but that the firemen and Detective Sergeant Harry Guska recognized as the scent of burnt flesh.

Guska stood on the front lawn, occasionally bringing a handkerchief soaked with Old Spice aftershave up to his nose and mouth, talking with Fire Department Captain Henry Schreiber.

"There's not much left of the poor bastard," Schreiber was saying, his perspiring face smudged with soot. "Not much left of that side of the house, either. The open windows fed that fire pretty good."

"I wonder why the windows were open on such a hot day," Guska said, shaking his head to fight down the nausea that washed over him like a strong and persistent surf. As soon as the flames had been put out, he'd gone in to look at the body. He wished he hadn't. "You'd think he'd want air conditioning."

"Damn shame," the fireman said. "I met him a time or two—at Chamber of Commerce breakfasts. Not a bad guy. Pretty wife, too." He wiped sweat from his face, turning the specks of soot into long smudges. "Looks like he was smoking in bed, fell asleep and knocked the kerosene lamp over."

"Pretty dumb having a kerosene lamp in the bedroom anyway, isn't it?"

"It was part of the decor," Schreiber said.

A dark Ford pulled up at the curb and the county coroner got out carrying his omnipresent black bag.

"I think he was on something," the fire captain continued.

"What do you mean?"

Schreiber shrugged. "There was what looked like a bottle of pills in the bedroom. Pretty burnt up, though."

Guska scribbled in his notebook. "I'll have my guys check it out."

A uniformed police officer came around the house and walked across the grass toward him. He had a handkerchief to his nose, too, but Guska couldn't tell what it had been doused with.

"Got a minute, sergeant?" He made the word sound like "sarn't."

Guska nodded to Schreiber and followed the young cop up the driveway along the charred side of the house.

"I checked out the garage," the uniform was saying. "The guy's car was in there, all right. A big Caddy."

"So?"

The young cop's nose wrinkled. "Take a look for yourself."

They went into the garage. Since it was a good forty feet from the house it had sustained no damage, although its white paint was darkened by smoke.

The uniformed cop opened the right rear door and stood aside so Guska could see in. On the back seat was a large sheet of grayish cardboard on which the words WILLING TO WORK had been hand-painted.

"What do you think of that, sergeant?"

Guska stood very still, looking at the sign. Then he leaned into the car and lifted it out, holding it carefully by the edges so he'd leave no fingerprints.

"I don't know," he said, frowning hard. "But I'm sure as hell going to find out."

ENDLESS ROAD

John Lutz

John Lutz is the author of more than thirty novels and
over two hundred short stories. He's won both the
MWA Edgar and the PWA Shamus awards, and he
received the PWA Lifetime Achievement Award.
Among his suspense novels is *SWF Seeks Same*, which
was made into the hit movie *Single White Female*. His
recent novel, *Final Seconds*, written in collaboration
with David August, has also been optioned for film.

It was the dry season. A hot, brisk wind whipped out of the
west, snapping taut the white cloth canopy above the verandah. Morgan Hoyt sat next to his aide, Langner, at a round
wicker table in the deep shade of the canopy. The verandah
was part of what had once been the main house of a large
French rice plantation. The clapboard and stone mansion
was in serious disrepair. Beyond the house's immediate
grounds, the vast plain of now-fallow rice paddies remained,
but it was tended by people other than the French.

Morgan sipped from his glass of quinine water and looked
out over the sun-bright fields toward a stone building that
had once been a guest house. It wasn't as badly damaged as

the mansion and had been refurbished and even air-conditioned. It was where the negotiations were being held. Morgan had been using his arts of persuasion since early morning and was glad for this afternoon break before resuming the talks.

"We're down to the short strokes," Langner said. He was a tall young man with a hatchet face and a permanent forward lean, all angles inside and out. "Have you formulated the outlines of a recommendation?"

Morgan smiled slightly. Langner liked to speak bureaucratese, as did many of the people involved in the process. "Not yet," he said.

"You're smiling," Langner pointed out.

"That Dengh's a charming bastard," Morgan said of the other side's chief negotiator. "We have to give him that. But I'm not sure if I trust him even within the context of what we're doing."

"I think he's trustworthy," Langner said, "in that he's bound by his word until his masters change their minds. And I believed him when he told us any kind of traffic on a long road from the North would be impossible to stop."

"I'm not so ready to accept his assessments," Morgan said. "But I do like the man. He reminds me of someone."

From across the fields a woman and two young children were walking toward the mansion, the half-caste wife and offspring of the Frenchman who had fled. They remained and were allowed to live in the ruined mansion.

Morgan sat back in his wicker chair, narrowing his eyes against the bright sun, and watched the three distant figures wavering in the vaporous heat. It hadn't rained in almost a month, and blown dust made the woman raise both hands to shield her eyes. Perhaps it was her casual, elegant gesture, perhaps the dust, that made Morgan's mind travel back more than thirty years . . .

• • •

"Your mother's bringing me back some Coca-Cola," his father said as they watched Morgan's mother walk toward where they sat in the overheated car. She was a tall, graceful woman, burdened by a large straw purse that she used for every purpose. The wind kicked up and blew across the sun-baked road, setting her loose skirt flowing about her legs and carrying a haze of dust that caused her to raise both hands to her eyes.

They'd stopped so she could use the restroom at the Standard Oil gas station, then Morgan's father had driven the car several yards beyond the building to a pump that supplied water for radiators. He'd hand-pumped water into a big bucket, used a funnel to add some carefully to the steaming radiator, then got back in the car with twelve-year-old Morgan and his sister, Julia, and waited.

"Here's two cold bottles," his mother said to both children as she slid into the front seat next to Morgan's father, whose name was Art. She drew two bottles from her straw bag, opened them with the notch on the can opener she carried, and handed them back.

"Nothing for me?" Morgan's father asked.

"Only this," she said, and kissed his cheek.

"Not bad," he said, smiling, "considering the country's in a depression and everything's scarce."

The starter ground, the motor turned over, and the car continued its journey along U.S. 66 toward Morgan's father's promised job with the government in Oklahoma City. He'd been selling ladies' shoes in St. Louis, but the company went out of business just like the other places where he'd worked. It was an old friend who'd offered him this latest job, which would require passing some tests before it was a sure thing.

"There's a restaurant," Morgan's mother said, after another few hours of driving.

"Five o'clock," Art said. "Guess we oughta stop this side of Joplin, get us some supper and let the car cool down."

They had water and cold sandwiches in a booth near a window. It was hot in the restaurant and there were a lot of flies. Morgan remembered there were several dead ones on a brown-stained white windowsill. Julia, who was seven, was out of sorts and deliberately jabbing her older brother in the elbow as she ate. An old woman in a flower-print dress smiled at them when they'd finished eating and were leaving, but Morgan could tell she was glad to see them go and she wouldn't have to listen to Julia anymore.

He was looking forward to the car moving and wind rushing in through the open window. But his father stopped grinding the starter and said, "Damn! She won't kick over, and I'm afraid I'm gonna run down the battery."

He got out, slammed the door hard, and strode back into the restaurant. Morgan's mother sat stiffly, staring straight ahead and saying nothing.

When his father returned he said he'd called a mechanic who told him he'd drive out to the restaurant and look at the car, but it would take him a long while to get there and the Chevy was an old car so he wouldn't make any promises. Then Morgan's father stooped down like an old man and looked in at his wife and children, and Morgan would always remember the stricken, hopeless expression on his face. And his words: "It seems like God's mad as hell at us."

"We passed a motor court just before we stopped here," Morgan's mother said. "I'm sure there was a vacancy sign hanging out. So we're in luck."

And they were. The Do Dropp Inn was a motor court made up of a dozen detached cottages arranged in a wide circle around a small sand-and-earth playground with a swing set and sliding board. The cottages had sharply peaked roofs, ivy growing up their front walls, and inside each was neatly furnished with a double bed, chintz curtains and thick window shades that kept the interior five degrees cooler than outside. There was a bed that rolled out from under the big bed, and Mom called down to the office from a phone right outside to get a cot brought to the cottage. Julia and Morgan both wanted the cot, so their father flipped a coin. Morgan got the cot. Things were looking up.

They settled in while their father left to walk back to the restaurant to meet the mechanic who promised nothing. He would drive the car to the Do Dropp Inn when and if whatever was wrong with it was repaired. A tenuous plan to match the times.

The cottage on the left was empty. Morgan knew the one on the right was occupied because of the big Packard that was parked there. It was old, faded brown and starting to rust, but it was the largest car he'd ever seen, twice as long as his family's Chevy sedan.

He was outside, flipping his pocketknife to the ground so the blade stuck more often than not, when the neighboring cottage's door opened and two women emerged. One was tall and very thin, the other shorter and overweight with a huge wart or mole growing on one of her cheeks near the corner of her eye. Morgan politely answered them when they told him good afternoon, and they both smiled at him as the shorter and heavier of the two women opened the cavernous trunk of the huge car. They got a fancy valise and a leather suitcase from the trunk, closed the lid and started to return to their cottage. Then the tall one, who had short brown hair and was pretty even if she was kind of stoop-shouldered, smiled and said hello to Morgan's mother, who'd stepped out of the cottage to check on him.

The three women talked for a while, and Morgan heard

his mother explain about the car problem. Then Julia came out, letting the screen door slam behind her, and the tall woman, whose name Morgan later learned was Adelle, patted her on the head as if she were a dog. The grown-ups seemed to run out of things to talk about, so they were discussing the heat when tires crunched on gravel and everyone turned to see if Morgan's dad was returning with the Chevy.

But the car that had turned from the highway into the motor court's lot was a new black Ford coupe with a rumble seat. A dark-haired man wearing a sweat-soaked white shirt with a loosely knotted tie climbed out of the car, grinned and said hello to everyone. Then he remarked on how hot it was as he pulled a small suitcase from the dusty coupe's passenger-side seat. He lifted a larger suitcase from the rumble seat and carried his luggage to the door of the cottage on the other side of Morgan's family's. After he went inside, Morgan saw him open the cottage's windows but leave the shades down.

"He's certainly a nice-looking young man," Morgan heard Adelle say. At first Morgan thought she was talking about him, then he realized she'd meant the new guest.

There was more crunching of tires on gravel. This time it was a tow truck that had braked to a halt just inside the driveway. Morgan's father got out, with the suitcase he'd left in the car, said something to the truck's driver, then trudged toward the cottage.

"The driver's going back to the restaurant to tow the Chevy," he said, looking distraught. "Says it needs a new distributor and the water pump's leaking. It'll be late tomorrow before he can get parts and get it fixed so we can drive on."

"You poor man," Adelle said, her sweet, lean face twisted with compassion.

"We have some watermelons we bought at a roadside

stand," the short woman said. "Let us give you one to compensate for your bad luck."

Morgan's father looked embarrassed. "We don't need . . . I mean, I'm on my way to Oklahoma City, got a government job waiting for me."

"Of course," Adelle said. She smiled and made a backhand motion, dusting away any notion of charity. "Some of the melons will rot anyway in this heat if we don't eat them," she called over her shoulder, already on her way to the Packard to open the trunk again.

Behind the women's cottage was a small wooden picnic table. Morgan's mother used a knife borrowed from Adelle to cut the melon, then Adelle and her short friend, whose name was Ida, joined the family. Ida brought a salt shaker she'd found somewhere. Everyone ate watermelon, holding slices like ears of corn and taking lusty bites. Morgan spit the seeds to the side, but noticed that Adelle daintily removed each one from between pursed lips and tossed it away. Morgan decided he liked Adelle, and was even beginning to like Ida despite the mole with hair growing out of it on her cheek.

After the watermelon picnic there was still daylight left, so Morgan and Julia wandered over to the playground and used the swing and sliding board for a while. But Julia started to harangue Morgan the way she often did, and the playground equipment was for smaller kids anyway. So Morgan returned to play with his pocketknife again in a bare dirt area near the cottage.

He was resting the blade's point lightly on his index finger, then using his other hand to flip the knife so it rotated once and stuck in the hard earth.

"Mumbletypeg," a man's voice said. "I used to play that when I was a kid."

Morgan looked up to see the dark-haired man who'd

checked into the cottage next door. He had a friendly smile, with a slightly crooked front tooth that made him look devilish and the kind who'd enjoy a good joke. He kneeled down next to Morgan, took the knife from his hand, and flipped it off his forefinger so it landed point down and stuck three times in a row.

Standing up again, he said, "I ain't lost my touch." He grinned down at Morgan. "You and your family traveling through to California?"

"Nope. Just to Oklahoma. My dad's got him a job waiting there."

The man's grin got wider. "Jobs are hard to come by these days. I just left one and I'm heading up to Chicago for another." He wiped sweat from his forehead with the back of his hand and looked around. "Say, you ever done any fishing?"

"Sure."

"I got the stuff for it in the car and I seen a little lake down behind the motel. Clear it with your folks and you can come with me and we'll see what we can catch."

That sounded great to Morgan. He thanked the man and ran in to ask his father for permission. But he was taking a nap. It was his mother who came out of the cottage to size up the man from next door.

He gave her his grin. "I look upstanding enough?"

Morgan's mother returned his smile. "I suppose. And I see you and Morgan are already friends."

"He and I ain't been formally introduced, but I get a certain sense about some fellas, and I consider us friends. I'm Tom Blake. Headed up to Chicago for a job."

"My husband's traveling toward a job, only going in the opposite direction."

"That's what Morgan said. Lots of folks traveling the highway these days, heading for work or looking for it. A little fishing'd break up the long trip and make it more tolerable."

Morgan's mother shot a glance at him. "I noticed the lake out our cottage's back window. Could barely see it through the trees. But there's a dirt path. I suppose it's okay if you two walk down and fish there."

They both thanked Morgan's mother, then Morgan went with Tom to the car. Tom opened the rumble seat, reached in and came up with a disassembled rod and reel and a bamboo pole broken down in four sections. He then reached down and handed Morgan a small steel tackle box. "We're off," he said breezily, and began striding toward the lake. Morgan fell in beside him.

The tackle box was locked and Tom had forgotten the key, so he used Morgan's knife to pry it open. It was full of lead weights, fishing line, cork floats, and all kinds of fancy lures. There was also a can of worms, but it looked as if the heat had gotten to them.

Morgan and Tom fished until it got dark, catching three small sunfish along with a measly crawdad they threw back in.

When they returned to the cottages, Morgan's mother and father were standing outside talking to Adelle and Ida. The warm night was just past dusk, moonlit and filled with the ratcheting screams of crickets.

Tom introduced himself to the two women and Morgan's father, then offered the sunfish to anyone who was interested. When there were no takers, he smiled and said he'd clean and eat them himself. Before turning to go to his cottage, he ruffled Morgan's hair roughly and said, "This here's a good one, this boy. Gonna be one heck of a man." It was an offhand compliment from a man he'd only just met yet sensed was special, but Morgan would never forget that casual assessment of his character, the rough show of approval and affection. It had come just when he'd needed it most, sensing a weakening in his father that he'd never suspected he'd see.

"You like Mr. Blake?" his father asked, when Tom had disappeared in the dark and they heard his cottage screen door slam shut.

"He's the neatest fella I ever met," Morgan said. He was proud to know Tom Blake and figured he must have an important job in Chicago, probably more important than Morgan's dad's government job in Oklahoma.

Later that night Morgan awoke to the sound of his parents' voices.

"We got no choice but to wait for the car to be fixed," his father was saying. "But if we stay another night here, we'll barely have enough to eat and buy gas when we continue on our way."

"Like you said, there's no choice," Morgan's mother said. "Maybe you should have accepted Tom Blake's offer of the fish."

"The hell with Tom Blake and his new Ford and his job waiting in Chicago!" his father snapped, surprising Morgan with his anger.

Morgan was further surprised to hear his mother apologize for something. They made no further sound, and he drifted off again to sleep.

The next morning the mechanic phoned from Joplin and confirmed it would be another day before the Chevy was repaired. They were stuck at the Do Dropp Inn.

When Tom Blake heard the news about the car he told them how sorry he was, then said he'd hang around for a few hours and keep them company. Adelle and Ida, however, loaded their suitcases into the big Packard.

Then Tom surprised everyone by showing them some canned stew and a dozen eggs in a sack, and offered to make everyone breakfast if they built a little camp fire behind one of the cottages.

Adelle and Ida stared at each other, then Adelle nodded. "We have a small kitchenette in our cottage," she said. "We'll be glad to prepare breakfast and check out later."

Morgan's mother pitched in, and the three women soon had breakfast cooked up, which everyone ate at the picnic table in the shade of a tree between the cottages.

Afterward Tom offered Morgan's dad a Camel cigarette, and they smoked and talked while the women cleaned up after breakfast. The motor court owner, a gray-haired man named Ralph Dropp, and his wife, Alma, joined them, and everyone discussed the sorry state of the economy and the increasing car traffic on Route 66. The Do Dropp Inn was about the only business in or around Joplin that was turning much of a profit these days, Dropp said.

Tom Blake had drifted away from the conversation. Morgan, squatting on the bare earth off to the side and playing Mumbletypeg, glanced up and noticed Tom and Adelle talking near where the woods began. But the next time he looked that way they were gone.

"Seein' as you got stuck here against your will due to car trouble," Dropp was saying to Morgan's father, "we're gonna give you a special rate on the cottage. That 66 is a long, hard road, so that's our policy."

"It's a mighty nice policy," Morgan's mother said, before his father could protest. "And we thank you."

Morgan caught movement in the corner of his vision and saw Adelle stalking toward her cottage. Her blouse was half untucked and she looked angry.

A few minutes later there was the sound of a car starting, and the big Packard rumbled from the motor court lot out onto the highway. Everyone sat silently, listening to the accelerating motor and the gears changing.

"Why, they never said goodbye," Morgan's mother said. "How odd."

"They paid up, though," Ralph Dropp told them. "That's all I request of a guest."

Tom Blake was suddenly alongside them. "I think I still got time for a little fishing before I go," he said, looking at Morgan and winking.

Morgan folded his pocketknife and stood up, looking hopefully at his father.

His father laughed, but not with his heart in it. "Why not?" he said. "You two go ahead. I think I'll read the paper and wait for another phone call from the garage in Joplin."

The morning was still cool, and the fishing should have been good. But all Tom Blake and Morgan caught during the next two hours was a small catfish. Tom said they were the devil to clean so he tossed it back in the lake.

That was when Morgan heard his mother call his name.

He turned to see her standing halfway down from the cottage, her hands on her hips. "I need to talk to you for just a few minutes," she yelled. "You can come right back and fish some more."

Tom grinned down at Morgan and ruffled his hair again in that mock-rough way. It messed it up something awful but Morgan didn't mind at all. In fact, he was glad of it.

"Better do what your mom says," Tom told Morgan. "Man's best friend ain't a dog, it's his mother."

Morgan grinned back and used his fingers to brush his hair out of his eyes. Then he propped up his bamboo fishing pole with some stones and ran toward the cottage.

"I'll catch that big one for you if he takes your bait," Tom called after him.

When he reached his mother, Morgan was surprised to see the tight expression on her pale face. Yet she didn't seem angry. He'd never before seen that look on her and it kind of scared him.

As soon as they'd taken half a dozen steps toward the cottage she hugged him to her hip and began hurrying them along.

"What's going on?" Morgan asked. "What's the matter?"

As they turned a bend in the dirt path he saw at least a dozen uniformed policemen standing around, along with lots of men wearing suits and ties despite the heat. Some of the men had shotguns or rifles. Morgan's father was there too, holding Julia's hand. The two of them walked toward Morgan and his mother. Julia looked blankly at Morgan and he could tell she didn't understand what was going on either.

"We're going over by the office," Morgan's father said.

He almost physically herded them to the edge of the gravel parking lot where there were lots of police cars parked, and about a dozen guests were standing with some policemen. Mr. and Mrs. Dropp were there looking worried. Everybody wore an expression similar to the one on Morgan's mother's face. Morgan noticed that one of the police cars was parked sideways across the driveway.

Another car drove up, and a big man with a thin mustache and wearing a dark suit climbed out, talked to two other men, then strode through where everyone was standing. He seemed to be in charge. Morgan still remembered the film of dust on the toes of his shined black shoes, the hard look in his eyes, and the way he barely moved his lips when he spoke: "Let's do him."

The big man and the two he'd been talking to disappeared in the direction of the cottages.

No one spoke. Several minutes passed. Then there were half a dozen shots that actually had sounded like fire crackers.

The uniformed police cautioned everyone to stand still. Three other policemen came up from where the cottages were. Their faces were pale as bone but one of them was smiling. He nodded to the men who'd stayed with the motel guests.

Then more men came from the direction of the cottages. Two of them were lugging a motel blanket that was half-folded around the soaking wet body of Tom Blake. Morgan could see Tom's peaceful face clearly and knew immediately that he was dead. There was blood as well as lake water glistening in his hair and staining the blanket, and some blood darker than that on the blanket dripped onto the ground.

Morgan was stunned, numbed with anger and despair. "Why'd they shoot Mr. Blake?" he heard himself ask. His voice sounded higher than usual, strikingly like Julia's.

"He's no Mr. Blake," one of the uniformed policemen said. "He's Tommy-gun Blain, and he robbed a bank in Galena, Kansas, yesterday and was on his way to join his gang for another job in Chicago."

That was when Morgan glanced toward the highway and saw the big brown Packard parked on the shoulder. He remembered the look on Adelle's face when she'd come out of the woods after being there with Tom Blake.

"He killed a bank guard and four customers in Galena," the policeman said, "including a mother and her young daughter. Then he killed an old fella about to go on a fishin' trip, just so's he could steal his car. And he didn't have to kill nobody. Lucky we got a tip he was here. And you folks are lucky you're still alive."

Morgan felt his mother's grip on his shoulders tighten as she pulled him closer. He still remembered her scent and how warm her perspiring body had felt through her cheap, thin dress, his cheek pressed softly against the side of her breast.

• • •

The woman and children were near the main house now. Several members of the delegation from the north walked past them, including Dengh, who smiled warmly at them. The woman smiled back and made a kind of respectful bow.

"Dengh *is* a likable bastard," Langner said, standing to return to the negotiating table. "It's hard not to trust him."

As Morgan stood up from his chair, he saw Dengh pause and grin broadly, and with mock-roughness bend over and muss the boy's hair. He saw how the boy looked up at Dengh.

"Hard not to trust him," Morgan agreed.

Later, on the converted Air Force plane traveling back to the United States, Langner set his martini down and looked over at Morgan.

"Have you made your decision?" he asked.

"I have," Morgan said. "I'm going to recommend to the Secretary of State that we commit ourselves to a major effort and introduce armed forces in much larger numbers to Vietnam."

"Could be a long, hard road," Langner said, not looking at Morgan but gazing out the window at wisps of gray cloud.

"Could be," Morgan conceded.

But he was confident he'd made the right decision. This time there would be no misplacement of trust and affection. This time there would be no second guessing.

BLIND CORNER

------- ---- ---- ---- ---- ---- ---- ---- ---- ----

David August

David August is the coauthor, with John Lutz, of the thriller *Final Seconds*. He grew up in suburban St. Louis, only a few miles from Route 66, the Coral Courts Motel, and the 66 Drive-In.

Just outside the town of Palenville, where Route 66 shed the name of Main Street and became itself again, it ran into Blake's Hill. This was southern Missouri, the foothills of the Ozarks, and the country was rugged. Blake's Hill was too steep to go over and too big to blast through, so they'd bent 66 around it. The road took a sharp left followed by a fishhook right.

The way the men at the volunteer fire department told it, the curve began to get its bad reputation when Dr. Stiller had his accident there. The Doc spun out and bounced back and forth from hillside to guardrail, wrecking his brand-new 1946 Buick Roadmaster and putting himself in a bed in his own hospital for a month.

But it wasn't till the Drew Blackmer crash that people started calling the turn Dead Man's Curve. Drew went off the road and rolled his '52 Chevy pickup four times.

They had to cut his body out of the cab with an acetylene torch.

The volunteer firemen would tell such stories for hours to the boys who liked to hang around the station after school. There were plenty of accidents to talk about. Dwayne Becker, who drove the hook-and-ladder truck, even said that the song "Crash and Burn" by Todd and the Styletones was based on an accident that had taken place on Dead Man's Curve. A teenager came around the blind corner too fast, in the wrong lane, and ran head-on into another car. The kid walked away without a scratch, blessing his luck. Then he found it'd been his own girlfriend in the other car, and she'd been killed. In the chorus he begged the Lord to let him change places with her. Some of the firemen scoffed and said no such accident had ever happened around here, but Dwayne listened to the song on his transistor all the time, and he could quote the lyrics. The description of the blind corner matched the curve around Blake's Hill to a T.

The boys wanted to believe Dwayne, especially Zachary Woodrell. Zack was a bright and talkative twelve-year-old, and he'd remind the doubters of what it was like during the summer vacation months. Every time you came to the Curve, you'd find yourself at the back of a long line of cars with out-of-state plates, inching along with their brake lights flashing. It had to be the worst turn the tourists met up with on the whole length of 66, Zack said. Even in Los Angeles, where the people who made up the songs lived, they must know about Dead Man's Curve in Palenville, Missouri.

Zack's mom didn't want to listen to that kind of talk. She thought that there were a lot of other things in Palenville a boy should feel proud of, instead of a bad turn in the road. Maybe Zack shouldn't hang around the firehouse so much, she said, hearing stories about injury and death and getting a kick out of them. He wouldn't think Dead Man's Curve accidents were so much fun, if he ever saw one.

One day in March of '58, Zack's mom got her wish.

It had snowed so heavily the night before that school was closed that day. Zack and his friends spent the afternoon fighting a fierce snowball battle, Yankees versus Rebels, and Zack had fun even though they made him be on the Yankee side. At four o'clock, feeling weary and chilled, he was trudging along the flank of Blake's Hill toward home. He wasn't thinking about anything except dinner. His mother had promised him his favorite meal, glazed ham with yams, and Devil's Food cake for dessert.

The screech of tires made him stop in his tracks. He shivered as if somebody'd slipped an iceball down his back. It sounded like the scream of an animal in pain, even though he knew it was really a car skidding. It went on and on.

It was coming from the other side of the hill. From Dead Man's Curve.

The car was still sliding when it came around the turn. It was one that would have caught Zack's eye even if it had been standing still—a Thunderbird, silver with a black convertible top. The hood airscoop and basketwork grille told him that it was the new '58 model, the one Richard Diamond, private eye, drove on TV. It didn't belong to anybody from around here. There weren't many convertibles in Palenville. Zack had never even ridden in one, never felt the wind in his hair.

It looked as if the car was going to skid off the road but at the last moment the driver straightened it out. The screeching of its tires ceased. It accelerated as it came toward Zack. The front end was dented and one of the headlights smashed.

The car shot past him. He swivelled to look after it. The license plate was black with orange lettering. Out-of-state.

Squinting, he was able to read the number in the moment before the T-bird roared away: 713-WXM.

He shut his eyes. There were too many letters and numbers for him to remember. He felt as if he were carrying
something that was too heavy for him. He was staggering
and his grip was slipping.

Opening his eyes Zack looked down at the snow. He bent
and wrote the license number in it with his gloved fingers.

He straightened up, relieved. Now there was time to
think. The guy in the T-bird must have hit another car. Instead of stopping, he'd stepped on the gas. But he wasn't
going to get away. Zack had him.

For a while he just stood there, looking down at the number then up at the road, waiting for a grownup to come
along. But no car came from either direction, and he was too
excited to stand still. He thought he'd run around the turn to
where the wreck was.

He took one last look at the license number. By now he'd
hit on a way to remember it. First number was seven, meaning lucky for me. Then thirteen, meaning unlucky for you,
Mr. Hit-and-Run Driver. That would get him started, and the
WXM would come to him.

He ploughed through the snow to the road. Once on the
blacktop he started to run. Within a few steps he was breathing hard, blowing gusts of steam into the cold air. He got
even more excited as he imagined what he was about to see.
Maybe the car would be crumpled against the guardrail. Or
maybe it would've flipped over to rest on its roof with its
wheels slowly turning in the air. Or maybe it would be on
fire. That would be best of all, because the volunteer firemen
would be called. They'd be there when Zack walked up to
the sheriff and said he'd gotten the license number.

They'd be telling this story at the firehouse for years. And
he, Zachary Woodrell, would be the hero.

Lucky for me, unlucky for you, Mr. Hit-and-Run Driver. 713-WXM.

But when he came around the turn, he could not see smoke or flames. There was no wrecked car. Just the black road curving along the white hillside. He dropped to a walk, looking around in confusion.

A girl was sitting in the snow by the side of the road. Her head was down. He ran up to her, yelling, "Hey—you see the accident?"

The girl did not seem to hear.

"There was an accident, right? There had to be. I saw this car go by real fast. It was a silver T-bird and its license number was—"

The girl raised her head. Her eyes were so full of shock and pain that Zack flinched and turned aside, as if he had looked straight at the sun.

Before he could think of anything to say she covered her face with her hands. Her shoulders shook as she began to cry. Zack knew her name, Marilyn Bremen, although he'd never spoken to her before. She was a little older, in junior high already. Zack's big sister envied her for her long blond hair. She called her Miss Clairol, and said only her hairdresser knew for sure. Zack had always thought Marilyn was beautiful.

She must have been in the accident. She was not bloody or anything, but she needed help. Had she been alone? He looked around.

A man was lying all crumpled up on the other side of the road. He lay perfectly still. The snow around him was red.

Zack clutched his stomach. He felt dizzy. The man was Mr. Bremen, Marilyn's father. Zack recognized the green overcoat he wore all winter, the one with toggles instead of buttons. He wasn't able to look at Mr. Bremen's face.

Mr. Bremen was a piano teacher. He gave lessons to

Zack's big sister, and sometimes he'd stay afterward and play, just for fun, songs from *South Pacific* or *The King and I*. Zack looked away, blinking back tears.

An upended sled was lying on the blacktop. They must've been crossing the road, headed for the sledding hill on Blake's farm, when the car came around the curve. Too fast.

He turned back to Marilyn. Her shoulders were shaking but she didn't make a sound. He tried to think of something to say to her. What would it help him to hear, if it was *his* father lying there? That was what he asked himself, and the question chilled him to the heart. There was no answer. He stood in the middle of the road, looking down at the weeping girl. He didn't know what to do.

A station wagon rounded the corner. He ran toward it, waving his arms.

The car was a Ford Country Squire with paneling on the sides. It plunged to a halt. A gray-headed woman leaned out. It was Mrs. Mercer, who owned the Five- and Ten-Cent store near school. She knew who Zack was, because his mother had told her not to sell him any candy after school as she didn't want his appetite spoiled. Once he'd tried to talk her into selling him the candy anyway, and she still held that against him.

"Zachary," she called out, "don't you know enough to stay out of the road?"

Zack silently pointed at Mr. Bremen.

Mrs. Mercer got out of her car and went over to kneel beside the man. When she straightened up she looked grim. Mr. Bremen was dead. Zack had known that from the first somehow, even though he had never seen a dead body before.

Another car was pulling up behind the station wagon. It was Mr. Josephson's old Rambler. He leaned out the window to squint at them from under the rim of his John Deere cap.

"There's been a bad accident, Tom," Mrs. Mercer called to him. "Go back to the gas station and call the sheriff, will you?"

Mr. Josephson nodded and turned his car around.

Mrs. Mercer had seen Marilyn sitting by the side of the road and was going to her. Zack hurried along beside her. "I was on the other side of the hill," he said. "But I saw the car go by and—"

"What car?"

"The T-bird." Suddenly it all came back to him. "Mrs. Mercer, have you got a pen?"

"What?"

"I saw the car—the one that hit Mr. Bremen. I got the license number."

She stopped and looked at Zack narrowly, just the way she did at her store. She didn't say anything, though, just reached into the pockets of her coat and brought out a pencil and a notepad.

"Go ahead."

Zack opened his mouth to speak. But the number wasn't on the tip of his tongue. Seeing the pencil poised over the paper made him nervous, so he shut his eyes. It was as if the license plate were hanging there in front of him, but it was a little too far away and the number was fuzzy. He tried to pull it closer. Couldn't.

There had been a trick he was sure would help him remember. He had been so pleased with it when he thought it up. But now it was gone too.

Zack looked up at Mrs. Mercer. Miserably he shook his head.

Her lips compressed and the many lines in her face deepened. She put the pencil and pad away. Then she headed for where Marilyn was sitting.

Zack ran after her. "Wait! Wait!"

Mrs. Mercer kept on going. He caught up with her and grasped her hand to make her turn around. "Wait," he said again. "I wrote it down. The license number."

"Well, let's see it."

"No, you don't understand! I wrote it in the snow. Right where I saw the car."

Mrs. Mercer hesitated. She looked at the girl and then at Zack.

"It's just down the road," he pleaded. "We can get there in a couple minutes."

"All right." She nodded toward Marilyn. "But first I have to see to her. You wait in the car."

He ran over to the station wagon and jumped in. The engine was running and the heater was on. He unzipped his parka. Mrs. Mercer was sitting in the snow next to the girl, talking to her quietly. Marilyn did not seem to hear. Mrs. Mercer took off her jacket and put it over the girl's shoulders.

A snowflake—a big, feathery one—fell on the windshield. Zack watched more flakes drift down to land on the hood. The hot metal melted them. But on the windshield they were sticking. In a surprisingly short time he found it difficult to see out.

Zack jumped as the realization hit him. He threw open the door and clambered out. "Mrs. Mercer," he shouted as he ran across the road, "we've got to go *now*."

She had her arm around Marilyn's shoulders and was leaning close to her. "What?"

"You've got to drive me to where I wrote the license number."

"The sheriff will be here in a minute," she said, and turned back to the girl.

"No, no! The snow will cover what I wrote. We have to go right away."

"I think we'd better wait here for the sheriff. Try to stay calm. At least keep your voice down."

With an effort Zack spoke quietly. "If we wait it'll be too late."

Mrs. Mercer closed her eyes and took a deep breath. "I know you want to help. I appreciate that, and so will the sheriff, but—"

"You don't believe me!" Zack wailed. "I'm not lying. I did see the car. I did get the license number. You have to take me back there."

"Zachary, hush! I mustn't leave her alone. Can't you see that?"

Zack looked at the girl's bent head. Marilyn needed Mrs. Mercer, he could see that. But she didn't need Zack. Not to just stand around doing nothing, anyway.

He turned and started to run up Blake's Hill. Going over the hill would be faster than following the road around it. Mrs. Mercer shouted his name but he didn't look back.

As the slope got steeper Zack had to struggle more, because the snow had drifted. With each step his foot sank in deep and he had to pull it out, windmilling his arms for balance. Snow got into the tops of his boots and oozed down, chilling his feet.

The license number was going to be gone by the time he reached it, he thought. Maybe he wouldn't even be able to find the spot. Then there would be nothing he could do but trudge back over the hill.

The going began to get a little easier. He was nearing the top and the snow wasn't as deep. But there was no shelter from the wind that drove the snowflakes under his parka hood and into his face. He bowed his head. There were old footprints and runner-tracks up here, left by kids on the way to the sledding hill. And they weren't filled in yet, not all the way. Zack felt fresh hope. He had written the license number with big, deep slashes of his fingers. Maybe—*maybe* it would still be there.

He ran down the hill. He was still keeping his head bowed in the wind, and he didn't look up until he heard the sound of the engine.

At first he could see only a headlight—a single headlight—looking dim and yellowish in the whiteness. The Thunderbird emerged from the whirling snow. Zack stopped dead and stared, hardly able to believe his eyes. The car was moving slowly along the near side of the road. The window was down and the driver was leaning out. Zack was close enough to see the snowflakes in his black hair.

Zack's heart was pounding from exertion. Now it seemed to stop.

The man got out of the T-bird and stepped into the snow. Zack could see the line of his own footprints along the side of the road, and the place where he'd written the number. The man swept his shoe back and forth, obliterating it.

"No!" Zack said.

The driver looked up. Maybe he heard, or maybe he'd seen Zack before. He began to walk toward him. He was wearing Ray-bans, so Zack couldn't see his eyes. He didn't have a real coat on, just an Eisenhower jacket over a T-shirt, and pegleg chinos. His black hair swept up from his forehead in a rigid wave. The wind didn't affect it at all. He must have used a lot of Brylcreem.

Zack tried to make himself think that this was funny. It was a trick he used in the schoolyard when some big kid was bearing down on him. He fastened on some ridiculous feature of the big kid so he wouldn't be so scared. But the trick didn't work now.

"Yeah, I saw you," the driver said. "Saw you the first time, too. Only it didn't hit me what you were doing till I was five miles down the road."

He shook his head. "Man, the last thing I wanted to do was come back. I tried real hard to convince myself it wasn't the way it looked and you weren't writing my plate number in the snow. But I couldn't be sure, so I turned around. Even when it started to snow again I kept on coming, because I had to be sure. Good thing I did."

The man didn't sound mad, which was a big relief to Zack. Instead he was grinning. Pleased with himself. It was as if they were playing checkers and Zack was going to have to king him. "You don't remember the number, do you? That's why you're still hanging around here, instead of going for the cops. Right?"

Zack said nothing.

"Yeah, that's right. The number's gone and we got nothing to argue about. Beat it."

So the man was going to let him go. He wanted to turn and run away as fast as he could. But he thought of Marilyn Bremen and stayed put. He said, "You got to go back, Mister."

The man's grin broadened. He shook his head.

"You got to. That guy you hit, he's—he's dead."

"I'm not going to jail, kid. I have other plans." He took a pack of Chesterfields out of a special pocket on his sleeve and fumbled for a cigarette with stiff fingers. "I woke up this morning in St. Louis. Looked out the window and saw it'd snowed again, and said the hell with this. I've had enough winter. So I'm driving away from it. By tomorrow I'll be someplace there's no snow on the ground. Day or two after that, I'll be someplace it's warm."

He peered into the whiteness around him. "Where am I, anyway?"

"Palenville," Zack said.

"Palenville." The man was still trying to get a cigarette out of the pack. Suddenly he stopped and looked at Zack. "You mean—that was Dead Man's Curve?"

Zack nodded.

"Well, what do you know?" he said. "I heard about it, but I never—that's some curve. I didn't see the guy till I was right on top of him. No way I could stop."

"You shouldn't have been going so fast."

"Hey, look. It's not like I wanted to hit him. I'm not going to jail for this. It's not my fault. It's Dead Man's Curve."

The man grinned and spread his hands.

Zack thought of Marilyn again, and of Mr. Bremen lying in the bloody snow. It made him feel angry and kind of sick, to think that he'd first gotten into this because he'd wanted to be the hero of a Dead Man's Curve story. He wished right now that he'd never heard one. He wished that they'd never even given the turn that name.

The man was putting his pack of cigarettes back in his pocket. "Time for me to move on, kid. So you just turn around and run up the hill, okay?"

Zack looked at the T-bird, which stood on the road pouring white smoke from its tailpipe. He realized why the man wanted him to leave first. Because if he just went back to his car and got in, Zack might be able to follow and get another look at his license plate as he drove away. Which meant that as long as Zack stood here, the man couldn't leave.

Zack's heart was pounding against his ribs and his knees felt weak underneath him. But he stayed put.

The man wasn't laughing anymore. He bent over toward Zack, taking off his Ray-bans. His eyes were too scary to look at and Zack dropped his gaze.

"Why, you little bastard. You're trying to hold me here, aren't you? It's not gonna work. Now scram—or you'll get hurt."

Zack thought his knees were going to buckle. But that was all right. He could fall down, just so he did not turn and run.

"You think I won't really hit you. That it? You're wrong, kid. I'll hit you just as hard as I have to."

Zack didn't doubt that. He tried to think of something else to say or do, because right now it looked as if he had only two choices. He could run off and let the man get away, or he could get beat up—and let the man get away.

A thin, high wail came to him from over the hill. It was the sheriff's siren. The man heard it too.

"Get the hell out of here," he said. "I'm giving you one last chance."

Chance. The word caught in Zack's ear. He didn't know why. He stood stock still, his mind racing.

"That's it, kid."

Dropping into a crouch he moved in quickly. His wind-reddened hands were on a level with Zack's eyes. The knuckles of the left one whitened as it clenched in a fist.

Chance, Zack thought. The word stirred something in his memory. The man's right hand grasped Zack by the collar and gave him a hard shake so that his hood fell back. Now his face was open to the coming blows. The left fist drew back.

Chance, Zack thought. *Luck.*

It came back to him, the trick he'd thought up to remember the number. Lucky for me. Unlucky for you, Mr. Hit-and-Run Driver.

Seven thirteen.

713-WXM.

Zack spun away from the man. He heard the tearing of

cloth and he was free. He started running up the hill as fast as he could.

He heard the man give a ragged laugh of relief and triumph. "That's it, you little jerk! Run!"

713-WXM, thought Zack. He wasn't worried about losing it again. He would remember it forever. He reached the top of the hill and looked back. The man and the silver T-Bird were gone.

Two days later, Oklahoma State Troopers spotted the T-bird outside Weatherford. The driver, Bobby Alton by name, wouldn't pull over, and they had to chase him for miles until he crashed into a telephone pole. He was dragged from the car bloody but he still put up a fight.

Or that was the way the volunteer firemen back in Palenville told the story, anyway, to their eager audience of schoolboys. With each telling, they made more improvements to it. That old battle-axe Mrs. Mercer, for instance, had locked Zack Woodrell in her car and he had to smash a window to get out. And when Zack faced Bobby Alton on the roadside, the punk broke Zack's nose and knocked him cold. It was only when Zack woke up that he remembered the number.

Zack himself didn't hang out at the firehouse much anymore. It seemed to him that they liked the story better the way they were telling it, and they didn't want him around to correct them. But that was all right. Zack had lost his taste for Dead Man's Curve stories anyway.

REST STOP

– – – – – – – – – – – –

Lillian M. Roberts

Lillian M. Roberts is the author of the Andi Pauling veterinary mystery series, including the recent *Almost Human*. She also wrote the autobiographical *Emergency Vet*. She supplements her writing income by practicing small-animal medicine in Palm Desert, CA.

Alicia Carmichael thought the people in the blue truck had come from farther up the road than Joplin.

She first saw them at a rest stop outside Tulsa. Even though the little girl wasn't more than eight or nine, she doubted they would have stopped so soon if they were from her parts. The license plate was still Missouri, but they might have started all the way up in St. Louis.

Since her last hospital stay, Alicia had to pee all the time; that's why she was stopping after barely a hundred miles. At this rate it would take her forever to get to California. And she didn't want that. She had set her mind and was itching to get to Hollywood. At the same time, it felt good to be antsy about something after so long not caring about anything.

But she was gonna have to pee her way clear down Route

66. She giggled, picturing that. It reminded her of when she was carrying. Sometimes she pretended the doctors were wrong, that she was gonna have another baby. But most of the time she knew better.

She noticed the child just like she noticed every little blond-headed girl since Jenny. That, and they were the only two in the Ladies'.

Alicia left the stall and saw the kid hunched on the floor, jammed against the cold, filthy concrete block in a corner by the sink. She was intently focused on a pad of paper, balanced on one knee. A red Crayola jutted from her fist, and she used it on the paper like a weapon. Her face drew into a frown of concentration and the pink tip of her tongue showed between pursed lips.

Alicia almost yelled at her to get out from under there. *Your pa'll kill us both!* she almost said. So she waited until the child wasn't Jenny anymore, and she remembered.

She washed her hands, using a sliver of soap that might have been older than she was. *I didn't say it, though. That's a good thing. I stopped in time.* The towel roll was grimy so she dried her hands deliberately on her skirt. Then, casual, "Hey, hon. You going to California?"

The girl had not spoken, but when Alicia smiled down at her she saw the blue eyes had widened and followed her every move.

"Whatcha got there? You drawin a picture? Ain't that sweet!"

The girl's eyes flickered to her paper then back to the woman in the yellow dress. She looked scared. Alicia knew about being scared. But the child might just be startled at being spoken to. Alicia wasn't much good at telling these days.

"Can I see?" It hurt to squat or bend over, so she put one knee on the cold floor, lifting her skirt automatically so the dirt wouldn't show. It was an instinctive, motherly gesture and something in the little girl's face opened up the tiniest bit.

A man's voice hollered from outside. "Lizzy? Let's go!"

Alicia flinched. She couldn't help it. She saw the girl flinch too, then spring to her feet. With the smallest hesitation she tore the top page from her pad and thrust it into Alicia's hand as she dashed outside.

Moments later, Alicia heard the truck engine turn over. She stood alone in the concrete room staring at a ragged drawing of a maple tree done all in red.

The sunny morning faded into a hazy monotony of cattle, crop rows, small towns, and barbed wire. She passed a sign that said, OKLAHOMA CITY 66 MILES. As if that was something to look forward to. She wondered they didn't go crazy living out here, it was so flat. Lord knew, she'd been in hurry enough to get out of Joplin, but for all its grinding sameness at least there was *scenery*. This was nothing like the Old West she'd seen at the movies.

The radio in her Rambler pulled in a Dallas station—imagine that, Dallas, Texas!—and she tried to sing along with the new song by that Kentucky girl, Loretta Lynn. But Loretta sounded like she'd had a hard life too and Alicia wound up just listening. The road got real tiring. It was one thing to move to Los Angeles. Another thing altogether getting there.

The picture of the maple tree sat beside her until a gust of hot wind almost carried it out the window. After that Alicia put it in the glove compartment.

She stopped for gas outside of Oklahoma City, which had not been worth the wait. Gas was cheaper here than back home, only fourteen cents a gallon. The man who came to fill her tank wanted to chat, but she was afraid she'd break out bawling if he asked her where she was from. So she headed for the ladies' then bought a Coke out of the machine by the front door. The man had her hood up and was checking her oil. The way he did that reminded her of Hank, and she shivered.

The blue pickup was in the garage, with one tire off. Hank had taught her about cars some, and she could tell the blue pickup, with its round fenders and rusted spots, was older than her Rambler. The little girl from the rest stop—Lizzy—sat on an apple crate out front, drawing on her paper. Maybe this had been their destination all along. Alicia felt sad at the thought. She liked the idea of knowing someone else who was going where she was.

As Alicia took a swig of her Coke Lizzy's father came out of the garage's office with another man. She recognized the voice. He was laughing at something the other man had said that ended with ". . . get you to the coast." He saw Alicia and looked her up and down the way Hank used to. The way that made her skin tingle when she first met him, and made it creepy-crawl later on. Now she guessed she'd best get used to it if she was going to be a movie star.

" 'Bouts you from?" she asked him.

His smile, which had looked pleasant enough at first, took on a nasty edge without changing much. He'd been carrying a wide-brimmed hat, which he now set on his head with the practiced thoughtless motion of something unimportant done a thousand times. He didn't look anything like Hank, yet he did. "St. Charles. Up by St. Louis," he added when she didn't recognize the first place.

"Pretty little girl."

"Yeah. Watch her a minute while I get this tire back on the truck." Hank would have said it *tar*, but otherwise their manner was the same. Alicia got goosebumps, remembering. Then she turned back to Jenny-Lizzy. Her mouth went dry for a second but then Lizzy was just Lizzy and they were

standing out front of a gas station in Oklahoma at the edge
of a weedy field with oil rigs off in the distance.

The girl had stopped drawing and was watching her intently. Alicia smiled for her, a smile she could produce any-
time, anywhere. She thought that smile had died with Jenny
but was kind of excited to find out she could still do it.
Lizzy's big eyes just stared at her, the half-finished sketch in
her lap forgotten.

"You're quite a little artist, ain—*aren't* you? Bet you're
gonna study in Paris one of these days."

Lizzy's attention returned to the page. The tongue came
out and she drew in a few more details. Alicia watched. It
was the same tree, the foliage like flaming cotton balls in red
Crayola, another pile of fluffy red at the tree's base. Flowers? She wanted to buy the child a new set of crayons. Alicia didn't like red. And something about that pile of fluff
made her want to take the scissors out of her purse and cut
it away. But she didn't.

The blue truck backed out of the garage and Lizzy's father shouted for her to get in. Once more the girl tore the
page from her pad and thrust it at Alicia before running to
comply.

She hadn't made a sound, this time or last. Alicia didn't
think she was deaf and dumb, though—she'd responded to
her daddy's voice.

Alicia decided to follow them, as far as they were going.
Or until she had to stop and they didn't.

She hummed along with the radio, or when there wasn't a
station she just hummed to herself. Once she said, "Lord,
this road's a long one." Then she glanced, embarrassed, at
the empty seat beside her, and saw that Jenny wasn't there.
She'd forgotten. But only for a minute.

It stayed flat and gray for hours. Twice Alicia caught herself almost asleep, the car drifting across the yellow line—

once it was a diesel's air horn that jolted her awake and caused her to overcorrect so that she almost wound up in the ditch on the other side.

"Lordy!" she murmured once all four tires were safely back on the road. "Hollywood almost didn't know what they missed!" Then she realized the blue truck was nowhere in sight. Her already speeding heart threatened to burst from her chest as her foot coaxed more effort from the tired Rambler.

"There!" she said finally. With its lights off, it had been hard to see against the grayness of the road. Funny how everything looked the same out here. It was like that in Joplin too sometimes. California would be different, though. It wouldn't rain there, nothing but golden sun on the blue, blue sea . . .

The haze that dulled most of Oklahoma turned to a misty rain in the Texas panhandle. Alicia almost lost the blue truck again trying to roll the passenger-side window up on the Rambler without stopping. Her hip hurt like crazy when she did that. By Amarillo, Alicia was ready to burst and low on gas to boot. If the blue truck didn't pull off soon she'd have to give up. But then, way ahead, it turned in to a Phillips 66. Alicia nodded and flipped on her blinker.

The child seemed to be waiting for her when she left the restroom. A new picture showed the same maple tree, the same fluff underneath, and a stick figure wearing a wide-brimmed hat. The figure held something in its hands but Alicia couldn't make out what it was. Lizzy regarded her without a word or a smile, her grim face searching Alicia's, waiting. Alicia knew better than to ask the child what the man in the picture was holding. She wasn't even sure it was a man.

"How pretty!" she said. But she knew by the girl's face it was the wrong response.

Then the girl's father came out of the men's and stopped short. She'd have known he was her daddy anywhere—he had the same blue eyes, the same long face and square chin. Except his had the same tense lines that Hank's had. His warning flares, she'd thought of them. His eyes narrowed in recognition and he grunted. Alicia batted her eyes shyly and smiled her smile. The man's face softened, as men's faces did when Alicia smiled.

"Seen you before," he said.

"Reckon we're going the same way." She moved the hand holding Lizzy's picture behind her a little so the folds of her yellow skirt hid most of it. She didn't know why she did that but she felt the girl's eyes follow the movement and thought she approved.

"I hear there's work in Californee."

Alicia, who hated to hear the name of her unseen new home pronounced that way, surprised herself by saying, "I'm going to be a movie star!" She'd never told anyone that dream before, and felt her face turn red.

The man actually seemed a little impressed. "That right?" he said. "No kidding?"

She smiled with new pride, and a giggle escaped. "If my car holds up."

"Pretty lady like you oughtn't be out on the road all alone. How far you aim to get today?"

"Don't really know. New Mexico maybe."

The man nodded as if he approved. "Stick close and I'll keep an eye out after you. We'll stop in Albuquerque. Find a motel maybe."

Alicia wasn't sure she could afford a motel, but said okay. She paid the man for her gas but put off getting back in the car for as long as possible. This rain made the pain in her hip blossom like a flower, and standing gave her a little relief.

She watched the girl follow her father back to the truck and get in.

"Where's your mama, child?" she murmured.

The man who had pumped her gas gave her a Look, but that was all. She made herself get in the car and start the engine. She had a Thermos of coffee and a couple of roast beef sandwiches cut in half and wrapped in cellophane. They were in a bag under the seat, and she got it out now. The coffee would make her have to pee even more, but half of one of them sandwiches sure sounded good.

The radio gave out soon after she passed a faded sign that said, WELCOME TO NEW MEXICO! LAND OF ENCHANTMENT! It helped that almost immediately the flat-topped buttes of west Texas spread their wings, kind of, and became mountains. Enchantment, indeed. The rain quit, too—though she supposed that it was still raining for the people who were still in Amarillo. Mostly it cleared up but not all. She could see little thunderheads here and there sometimes when she crested a hill, tiny private storms for the eagles and the coyotes maybe, because no one else seemed to be living here. Sometimes the sun went behind a cloud, sometimes behind a mountain, and every now and then it would leap out and stab her in the eyes. She didn't mind, not really.

This was the Old West. This was more like it.

She hummed the Loretta Lynn tune, singing the few words she could remember. The blue truck was maybe a quarter-mile ahead, now in sight and now invisible. The Rambler didn't much take to the steeper hills, and a couple of times she thought it would just give up before the road leveled off and started heading down again. She learned to build up speed on the downward sides and downshift for the climb, but she knew something needed adjusting under the hood. And the up sides were longer than the down ones. The little valleys did not hide the fact that the sky was getting closer all the time. Hank had taught her some about cars, and when she got to Albuquerque she'd see what she could do.

Or maybe she'd get the man to fix it for her. Men liked to fix things for women; she'd learned that a long time ago. If you didn't give them something to fix, they'd start breaking things.

She shifted in her seat, trying to relieve the pain in her hip. The aspirin she'd swallowed that morning were a distant memory. After they stopped she'd get them out of her suitcase and move them to her purse.

The sun was no more than an orange slice behind a hill by the time she pulled into a gravel parking lot behind the blue truck. The neon sign in front of a faded adobe building said, 66 MOTEL. MODERN. CLEAN. VACANCY. There was a little NO in front of the VACANCY, but it was darkened. Alicia guessed that meant they had room for her.

She followed the blue pickup to a spot near the lobby and got out. At first the hip almost didn't take her weight and she held on to the Rambler until it would. Lizzy sat in the pickup, drawing in the faint glow of the sign and the motel's porch light. By then the man was inside, and Alicia only heard the end of his conversation with the lady behind the desk.

". . . room back away from the road," he was saying. She assumed he was asking for a quiet room where the highway noise would be less noticeable. It would not have occurred to her to specify which room she wished to sleep in but she thought it was a good idea. When it was her turn she'd ask for a room in back, too.

He turned as she approached and grinned in that ugly way she'd seen in Oklahoma City. "I got it covered, hon," he said. He handed her an oversized key with the number 66 on it. "Why don't you get us unpacked and meet me in the cafe."

She stood there on the cracked linoleum, gaping at the key in her hand. Her mind flew in a spiral the way it always did when she tried to think in a hurry, like a car cranking and cranking but wouldn't start. Who was this man? Why had he handed her a motel room key? What had she done that led up to this?

"Go on, hon. I've got to pay the lady and sign the paper." He turned his grin to the counter lady, who didn't seem to find it ugly at all. In fact, she was looking at Alicia as if her face was on crooked. "She's worn out," the man was saying. "Had to follow me in the other car all the way from St. Louie. Just needs a good meal and some rest."

Alicia turned and went out. She went up to the blue pickup and opened the passenger-side door. She was shaking all over.

"Lizzy, come on with me?" The girl met her gaze quizzically but then climbed out and got in the Rambler, bringing her pad of paper and her red Crayola.

The only clue Alicia had was that the room would be around back. She drove around the end of the motel, past pickup trucks and station wagons and one horse trailer, wishing she was one of the normal people inside those rooms.

"Help me find our room," she told Jenny-Lizzy. "Number 66."

The girl had not spoken in Alicia's presence, but while Alicia drove slowly along the darkened line of yellow doors, she pointed. They pulled the Rambler into the space and got out.

Alicia didn't have much to unpack. She carried her small suitcase inside, put it in a corner and sat on the bed. She wasn't shaking anymore but felt all quivery inside, like the top of a glass of water on the hood of a car.

Lizzy wanted to give her another drawing, and she stared at it without seeing. Not at first anyway. Same red tree, same man. This time it was clear what he held in his hands—a shovel. The fluffy stuff at the tree's base, then, was dirt. A pile of dirt. The man was digging a hole under the tree, or filling it in. A bunch of lines that might have been another stick figure protruded from the dirt.

She had another picture in progress. Not getting the reaction she wanted, the girl went back to her work. Minutes passed. Lizzy drew, and Alicia sat on the bed just waiting. Finally, satisfied with what she'd drawn, the girl offered the picture to Alicia. At the same moment the door creaked open. Alicia stared at the picture and it burned itself into her mind.

The man approached her and she realized she'd been foolish to sit on the bed. Ignoring the child, he leered at her and her skin went cold. "We've got all night," he said. "I told the lady we're married. I told her our name is Smith and we're from St. Louis."

She put the crayon drawing behind her, so it was hidden by her body when he pushed her down. Her purse was on the bed beside her. She said, "Lizzy, hon? Go in the bathroom. Take your paper and Crayolas and go in there until I tell you to come out."

The girl went, as if she'd been listening to the woman her whole life.

The man took this all as a good sign. She'd hoped he would. After all, he didn't know what she knew. And he didn't know about Hank. Her hand found the purse.

His hands pulled at her stockings. Her hip flared in agony and she caught her breath. The man must have taken it as passion because he muttered. "Un-huh, you're a sweet little thing, aincha." And tore her skirt.

When she plunged the scissors between his ribs at first he

didn't react. Then he stiffened and his eyes went wide. "You little bitch!" he screamed, reaching back. It was his own hand that twisted the protruding handles, ripping something important inside and washing them both with his blood.

"That's for Jenny," she said. "That's for my little girl you killed before she was ever even born." Except the man wasn't Hank, not quite. She'd thought Hank was dead but now she wondered if she would have to keep killing him over and over and over.

She struggled to push him off her, onto the floor. Lizzy's picture had been drenched somehow. Red blood obscured the red crayon drawing that depicted a stick figure of a man bringing the blade of his red shovel down on the head of a stick figure of a woman in a red dress. And a red little girl off to one side, watching. The stick figure protruding from the dirt in the earlier picture now made sense.

It was a long drive to Los Angeles. She threw away the yellow dress behind a diner in Gallup. The man's wallet she discarded outside of Flagstaff. Her daughter Jenny slept in the back seat all the way to the California border.

SPOOKED

Carolyn G. Hart

Carolyn Hart grew up in Oklahoma City not far from Highway 66 and has warm (very warm) memories of driving through the desert on 66 en route to L.A. in an old car with a window air conditioner. She still lives in Oklahoma City, loves air-conditioning, and has written more than thirty mysteries, many of which have won awards.

The dust from the convoy rose in plumes. Gretchen stood on tiptoe waving, waving.

A soldier leaned over the tailgate of the olive drab troop carrier. The blazing July sun touched his crew cut with gold. He grinned as he tossed her a bubble gum. "Chew it for me, kid."

Gretchen wished she could run alongside, give him some of Grandmother Lotte's biscuits and honey. But his truck was twenty feet away and another one rumbled in front of her. She ran a few steps, called out, "Good luck. Good luck!" The knobby piece of gum was a precious lump in her hand.

She stood on the edge of the highway until the last truck

passed. Grandmother said Highway 66 went all the way to California and the soldiers were on their way to big ships to sail across the ocean to fight the Japs. Gretchen wished she could do something for the war. Her brother Jimmy was a Marine, somewhere in the South Pacific. He'd survived Iwo Jima. Every month they sent him cookies, peanut butter and oatmeal raisin and spice, packed in popcorn. When they had enough precious sugar, they made Aunt Bill's candy but Mom had to find the sugar in Tulsa. Mr. Hudson's general store here in town almost never had sacks of sugar. Every morning she and Grandmother sat in a front pew of the little frame church in the willows and prayed for Jimmy and for all the boys overseas and for Gretchen's mom working so hard at the defense plant in Tulsa. Her mom only came home about one weekend a month. Grandmother tried to save a piece of meat when she could. Grandmother said her mom was thin as a rail and working too hard, but Gretchen knew it was important for her mom to work. They needed everybody to help and Mom was proud that she put radio parts in the big B-24 Liberators.

Gretchen took a deep breath of the hot heavy air, still laced with dust, and walked across the street to the cafe. Ever since the war started, they'd been busy from early morning until they ran out of food, sometimes around five o'clock, never later than seven. Of course, they had special ration books for the cafe, but Grandmother said they couldn't use those points to get sugar for Jimmy. That wouldn't be right.

Gretchen shaded her eyes and looked at the plate glass window. She still felt a kind of thrill when she saw the name painted in bright blue: Victory Cafe. A thrill but also a tightness in her chest, the kind of feeling she once had when she climbed the big sycamore to get the calico kitten and a branch snapped beneath her feet. For an instant that seemed to last forever, she was falling. She whopped against a thick limb and held on tight. She remembered the sense of strangeness as she fell. And disbelief, the thought that this couldn't be happening to her. There was a strangeness in the cafe's new name. It had been Pfizer's Cafe for almost twenty years, but now it didn't do to be proud of being German. Now Grandmother didn't say much in the cafe because her accent was thick. She was careful not to say *ja* and she let Gretchen do most of the talking. Grandmother prayed for Jimmy and for her sister's family in Hamburg.

Gretchen tucked the bubblegum in the pocket of her pedal pushers. Grandmother wouldn't let her wear shorts even though it was so hot the cotton stuck to her legs. She glanced at the big thermometer hanging by the door. Ninety-eight degrees and just past one o'clock. They'd sure hit over a hundred today, just like every day for the past few weeks. They kept the front door propped, hoping for a little breeze through the screen.

The cafe was almost as much her home as the boxy three-bedroom frame house a half mile away down a dirt road. Her earliest memories were playing with paper dolls in a corner of the kitchen as her mother and grandmother worked hard and fast, fixing country breakfasts for truck drivers in a hurry to get to Tulsa and on to Oklahoma City and Amarillo with their big rigs. Every morning grizzled old men from around the county gathered at Pfizer's for their newspapers and gossip as well as rashers of bacon, a short stack and scrambled eggs. But everything changed with the war. Camp Crowder just over the line in Missouri brought in thousands of soldiers. Of course, they were busy training, but khaki uniforms were no stranger to the Victory Cafe even though the menu wasn't what it had been before the war. Now they had meatless Tuesdays and Grandmother fixed huge batches of macaroni and cheese. Sometimes there wasn't any bacon but they had scrambled eggs and grits and fried potatoes. Instead of roast beef, they had hash, the potatoes and meat bubbly in a vinegary sauce. But Grandmother never fixed red cabbage or sauerkraut anymore.

It was up to Gretchen to help her grandmother when her mom moved to Tulsa. She might only be twelve, but she was wiry and strong and she promised herself she'd never complain, not once, not ever, not for the duration. That's what everybody talked about, the duration until someday the war was over. On summer evenings she was too tired to play kick the can and it seemed a long-ago memory when she used to climb up into the maple tree, carrying a stack of movie magazines, and nestle with her back to the trunk and legs dangling.

She gave a swift professional glance around the square room. The counter with red leatherette stools was to the left. The mirror behind the counter sparkled. She'd stood on a stool to polish it after lunch. Now it reflected her; black pigtails, a skinny face with blue eyes that often looked tired and worried, and a pink Ship 'n Shore blouse and green pedal pushers. Her blouse had started the day crisp and starched, but now it was limp and spattered with bacon grease.

Four tables sat in the center. Three wooden booths ran along the back wall and two booths to the right. The jukebox was tucked between the back booths and the swinging door to the kitchen. It was almost always playing. She loved "Stardust" and "Chattanooga Choo Choo" but the most often played song was "Praise the Lord and Pass the Ammunition." A poster on the wall beside the jukebox pictured a sinking ship and a somber Uncle Sam with a finger to his lips and the slogan: LOOSE LIPS SINK SHIPS. Grandmother told her it meant no one should talk about the troop convoys that went through on Highway 66 or where they were going or talk about soldiers' letters that sometimes carried information that got past the censors. Grandmother said that's why they had to be so careful about the food to make sure there was enough for Jimmy and all the other boys. And that's why they couldn't drive to Tulsa to see Mom. There wasn't enough gas. Grandmother said even a cupful of gas might make a difference one day whether some boy—like Jimmy—lived or died.

Two of the front tables needed clearing. But she made a circuit of the occupied places first.

Deputy Sheriff Carter flicked his cigar and ash dribbled onto his paunch which started just under his chin and pouched against the edge of the table. He frowned at black and white squares on the newspaper page. He looked at Mr. Hudson across the table. "You know a word for mountain ridge? Five letters." He chewed on his pencil. "Oh, yeah," he murmured. He marked the letters, closed the paper, leaned back in the booth. "Heard they been grading a road out near the McLemore place."

Mr. Hudson clanked his spoon against the thick white coffee mug. "Got some more java, Gretchen?"

She nodded.

Mr. Hudson pursed his thin mouth. "Bud McLemore's son-in-law's a county commissioner, Euel. What do you expect?"

Gretchen hurried to the hot plates behind the counter, brought the steaming coffee pot, refilled both men's mugs.

The deputy sheriff's face looked like an old ham, crusted and pink. "Never no flies on Bud. Maybe my youngest girl'll get herself a county commissioner. 'Course, she spends most of her time at the USO in Tulsa. But she's makin' good money at the Douglas plant. Forty dollars a week." Then he frowned. "But it's sure givin' her big ideas."

Gretchen moved on to the next booth, refilled the cups for some Army officers who had a map spread out on the table.

The younger officer looked just like Alan Ladd. "I've got it marked in a grid, Sir. Here's the last five places they spotted the Spooklight."

The bigger man fingered his little black moustache. "Lieutenant, I want men out in the field every night. We're damn all going to get to the bottom of this business."

Gretchen took her time moving away. The Spooklight. Everybody in town knew the army had set up a special camp about six miles out of town just to look for the Spooklight, those balls of orange or white that rose from nowhere and flowed up and down hills, hung like fiery globes in the scrawny bois d'arc trees, sometimes ran right up on porches or over barns. Some people said the bouncing globes of light were a reflection from the headlights on Highway 66. Other folks scoffed because the lights had been talked about for a hundred years, long before cars moved on the twisting road.

Gretchen put the coffee on the hotplate, picked up a damp cloth and a tray. She set to work on the table closest to the Army officers.

". . . Sergeant Ferris swore this light was big as a locomotive and it came rolling and bouncing down the road, went right over the truck like seltzer water bouncing in a soda glass. Now, you can't tell me," the black mustache bristled, "that burning gas acts like that."

"No, Sir." The lieutenant sounded just like Cornel Wilde saluting a general in that movie about the fall of Corregidor.

The kitchen door squeaked open. Her grandmother's red face, naturally ruddy skin flushed with heat from the stove, brightened and she smiled. But she didn't say a word. When Gretchen was little, she would have caroled, *"Komm her, mein Schatz."* Now she waved her floury hands.

Gretchen carried the dirty dishes into the kitchen. The last words she heard were like an Abbott and Costello radio show, a nonsensical mixture, ". . . soon as the war's over . . .

set up search parties . . . I'm gonna see if I can patch those tires . . . good training for night . . ."

Four pies sat on the corner table, steam still rising from the latticed crust. The smell of apples and cinnamon and a hint of nutmeg overlay the onions and liver and fried okra cooked for lunch.

"Oh, Grandmother." Gretchen's eyes shone. Apple pie was her most favorite food in all the world. Then, without warning, she felt the hot prick of tears. Jimmy loved apple pie, too.

Grandmother's big blue eyes were suddenly soft. She was heavy and moved slowly, but her arms soon enveloped Gretchen. "No tears. Tomorrow ve send Jimmy a stollen rich with our own pecans. Now, let's take our pies to the counter. But first," she used a sharp knife, cut a generous wedge, scooped it out and placed it on a plate, "I haf saved one piece—*ein*—for you."

The pie plates were still warm. Gretchen held the door for her grandmother. It was almost like a festive procession as they carried the pies to the counter.

The officers watched. Mr. Hudson's nose wrinkled in pleasure. Deputy Carter pointed at the pie plate. "Hey, Lotte, I'll sure take one of those." There was a chorus of calls.

Grandmother dished up the pieces, handing the plates to Gretchen, then stood at the end of the counter, sprigs of silver-streaked blond hair loose from her coronet braids, her blue eyes happy, her plump hands folded on her floury apron. Gretchen refilled all the coffee cups.

Grandmother was behind the cash register when Mr. Hudson paid his check. "Lotte, the deputy may have to put you in jail you make any more pies like that."

Grandmother's face was suddenly still. She looked at him in bewilderment.

Mr. Hudson cackled. "You sure don't have enough sugar to make that many pies. You been dealing in the black market?"

Grandmother's hands shook as she held them up, as if to stop a careening horse. "Oh, *nein, ne*—no, no. Not black market. Never. I use honey, honey my cousin Ernst makes himself."

The officers were waiting with their checks. The younger blond man, the one who looked like Alan Ladd, smiled warmly. *"Sprechen Sie deutsch? Dies ist der beste Apfelkuchen den ich je gegessen habe."*

The deputy tossed down a quarter, a dime and a nickel for macaroni and cheese, cole slaw, pie, and coffee. He glowered at Grandmother. "No Heinie talk needed around here. That right, Lotte?" He glared at the soldier. "How come you speak it so good?"

The blond officer was a much smaller man, but Gretchen loved the way he looked at the deputy like he was a piece of banana peel. "Too bad you don't have a German *grossmutter* like she and I do." He nodded toward Gretchen. "We're lucky, you know," and he gave Grandmother a gentle smile. *"Danke schoen."*

But Grandmother's shoulders were drawn tight. She made the change without another word, not looking at any of the men, and when they turned toward the front door, she scuttled to the kitchen.

Gretchen waited a moment, then darted after her.

Grandmother stood against the back wall, her apron to her face, her shoulders shaking.

"Don't cry, Grandmother." Now it was Gretchen who stood on tiptoe to hug the big woman.

Her grandmother wiped her face and said, her accent even more pronounced than usual, "Ve haf vork to do. Enough now."

As her grandmother stacked the dirty dishes in the sink, Gretchen took a clean recipe card. She searched through the file, then printed in large block letters:

LOTTE'S APPLE HONEY VICTORY PIE
6 tart apples
1 cup honey
2 T. flour
1 tsp. cinnamon
dash nutmeg
dash salt
pastry

She took the card and propped it by the cash register.

Back in the kitchen, Grandmother scrubbed the dishes in hot soapy water then hefted a teakettle to pour boiling water over them as they drained. Gretchen mopped the floor. Every so often, the bell jangled from the front and Gretchen hurried out to take an order.

The pie and all the food were gone before five. Grandmother turned the sign in the front window to CLOSED. Then she walked wearily to the counter and picked up the recipe Gretchen had scrawled.

"Let's leave it there, Grandmother." Gretchen was surprised at how stern she sounded.

Her grandmother almost put it down, then shook her head. "Ve don't vant to make the deputy mad, Gretchen."

Gretchen hated hearing the fear in Grandmother's voice. She wanted to insist that the recipe remain. She wanted to say that they hadn't done anything wrong and they shouldn't have to be afraid. But she didn't say anything else as her grandmother held the card tight to her chest and turned away.

"You go on home, Grandmother. I'll close up." Gretchen held up her hands as her grandmother started to protest. "You know I like to close up." She'd made a game of it months ago because she knew Grandmother was so tired by closing time that she almost couldn't walk the half mile to the house and there was still the garbage to haul down to the incinerator and the menus to stack and silverware to roll up in the clean gingham napkins and potatoes to scrub for to-morrow and the jam and jelly jars to be wiped with a hot rag.

Gretchen made three trips to the incinerator, hauling the trash in a wheelbarrow. She liked the creak of the wheel and the caw of the crows and even though it was so hot she felt like an egg on a sizzling griddle, it was fun to use a big kitchen match and set the garbage on fire. She had to stay until she could stir the ashes, be sure the fire was out. She tipped the wheelbarrow over and stood on it to reach up and catch a limb and climb the big cottonwood. She climbed high enough to look out over the town, at the cafe and at McGrory's gas station and at the flag hanging limp on the pole outside the post office.

If it hadn't been for the ugly way the deputy had acted to-ward Grandmother, Gretchen probably would never have paid any attention to him. But he'd been mean and she glow-ered at him through the shifting leaves of the cottonwood.

He didn't see her, of course. He was walking along the highway. A big truck zoomed over the hill. When the driver spotted the deputy's high crowned black hat and khaki uni-form, he abruptly slowed. But the deputy wasn't paying any attention, he was just strolling along, his hands in his pock-ets, almost underneath Gretchen's tree.

A hot day for a walk. Too hot a day for a walk. Gretchen wiped her sticky face against the collar of her blouse. She craned for a better look. Oh, the deputy was turning into the graveyard nestled on the side of the hill near the church. The graveyard was screened from most of the town by a stand of enormous evergreens so only Gretchen and the crows could see past the mossy stone pillars and the metal arch.

Gretchen frowned and remembered the time when Mrs. Whittle caught Sammy Cooper out in the hall without a pass. She'd never forgotten the chagrin on Sammy's face when Mrs. Whittle said, "Samuel, the next time you plan to cut class, don't walk like you have the Hope diamond in your pocket and there's a policeman on every corner." Gretchen wasn't sure what the Hope diamond was, but every time any of the kids saw Sammy for the next year, they'd whistle and shout, "Got the Hope diamond, Sammy?"

The deputy stopped in a huge swath of shade from an evergreen. He peered around the graveyard. What did he expect to see? Nobody there could look at him.

Gretchen forgot how hot she was. She even forgot to be mad. She leaned forward, and grabbed the closest limb, moved it so she could see better.

The deputy made a full circle of the graveyard which was maybe half as big as a football field, no more than forty or fifty headstones. He passed by the stone angel at Grandpa Pfizer's grave and her dad's stone that had a weeping willow on it. That was the old part of the cemetery. A mossy stone, half fallen on one side, marked the grave of a Confederate soldier. Mrs. Peters took Gretchen's social studies class there last year and showed them how to do a rubbing of a stone even though the inscription was scarcely legible. Gretchen shivered when she saw the wobbly indistinct gray letters: Hiram Kelly, Age 19, wounded July 17, 1863, in the Battle of Honey Springs, died July 29, 1863. Beloved Son of Robert and Effie Kelly, Cherished Brother of Corinne Kelly. Some of the graves still had little American flags, placed there for the Fourth. A half dozen big sprays marked the most recent grave.

Back by the pillars, the deputy made one more careful study of the church and the graveyard, then he pulled a folded sheet of paper from his pocket and knelt by the west pillar. He tugged at a stone about three inches from the ground.

Gretchen couldn't believe her eyes. She leaned so far forward her branch creaked.

The kneeling man's head jerked up.

Gretchen froze quieter than a tick on a dog.

The sun glistened on his face, giving it an unhealthy coppery glow. The eyes that skittered over the headstones and probed the lengthening shadows were dark and dangerous.

A crow cawed. A heavy truck rumbled over the hill, down main street. The faraway wail of Cal Burke's saxophone sounded sad and lonely.

Gradually the tension eased out of the deputy's shoulders. He turned and jammed the paper into the small dark square and poked the stone over the opening, like capping a jar of preserves. He lunged to his feet and strode out of the cemetery, relaxing to a casual saunter once past the church.

Gretchen waited until he climbed into his old black Ford and drove down the dusty road.

She swung down from the tree, thumped onto the wheelbarrow, and jumped to the ground. The bells in the steeple rang six times. She had to hurry. Grandmother would have a light supper ready, pork and beans and a salad with her homemade Thousand Island dressing and a big slice of watermelon.

Gretchen tried not to look like she had the Hope diamond in her pocket. Instead, she whistled as though calling a dog and clapped her hands. A truck roared past on its way north to Joplin. Still whistling, she ran to the stone posts. Once hidden from the road, she worked fast. The oblong slab of stone came right off in her hand. She pulled out the sheet of paper, unfolded it.

She'd had geography last spring with Mrs. Jacobs. She'd made an A. She liked maps, liked the way you could take anything, a mountain, a road, an ocean, and make it come alive on a piece of paper.

She figured this one at a glance, the straight line—though really the road curved and climbed and fell—was Highway 66. The little squiggle slanting off to the northeast from McGrory's station was the dusty road that led to an abandoned zinc mine, the Sister Sue. The X was a little off the road, just short of the mine entrance. There was a round clock face at the top of the sheet. The hands were set at midnight.

She stuffed the folded sheet in its dark space, replaced the stone. X marks the spot. Not a treasure map. That was kid stuff in stories by Robert Louis Stevenson. But nobody hid a note in a stone post unless they were up to something bad, something they didn't want anybody to know about. Tonight. Something secret was going to happen tonight. . . .

Gretchen pulled the sheet up to her chin even though the night oozed heat like the stoves at the cafe. She was dressed, a tee shirt and shorts, and her sneakers were on the floor. She waited until eleven, watching the slow crawl of the hands on her alarm clock and listening to the summer dance of the June bugs against her window screen. She unhooked the screen, sat on the sill, and dropped to the ground. She wished she could ride her bike, but somebody might be out on the road and see her and they'd sure tell Grandmother. Instead, she figured out the shortest route, cutting across the McClelland farm, careful to avoid the pasture where Old Amos glared out at the world with reddish eyes, and slipping in the shadows down Purdy Road.

The full moon hung low in the sky, its milky radiance creating a black and cream world, making it easy to see. She stayed in the shadows. The buzz of the cicadas was so loud she couldn't hear the cars, so she kept a close eye out for headlights coming over the hill or around the curve.

Once near the abandoned mine, she moved from shadow to shadow, smelling the sharp scent of the evergreens, feeling the slippy dried needles underfoot. A tremulous, wavering, plaintive shriek hurt her ears. Slowly, it subsided into a moan. Gretchen's heart raced. A sudden flap and an owl launched into the air.

Gretchen looked uneasily around the clearing. The boarded-over mine shaft was a dark mound straight ahead. There was a cave-in years ago, and they weren't able to get to the miners in time. In the dark, the curved mound looked like a huge gravestone.

The road, rutted and overgrown, curved past the mine entrance and ended in front of a ramshackle storage building, perhaps half as large as a barn. A huge padlock hung from a rusty chain wound around the big splintery board that barred the double doors.

Nothing moved though the night was alive with sound, frogs croaking, cicadas rasping.

Gretchen found a big sycamore on the hillside. She climbed high enough to see over the cleared area. She sat on a fat limb, her back to the trunk, her knees to her chin.

The cicada chorus was so loud she didn't hear the car. It appeared without warning, headlights off, lurching in the deep ruts, crushing an overgrowth of weeds as it stopped off the road to one side of the storage shed. The car door slammed. In the moonlight, the deputy's face was a pale mask. As she watched, that pale mask turned ever so slowly, all the way around the clearing.

Gretchen hunkered into a tight crouch. She felt prickles of cold though it was so hot sweat beaded her face, slipped down her arms and legs.

A cigarette lighter flared. The end of the deputy's cigar was a red spot. He leaned inside the car, dragging out something. Metal clanked as he placed the thing on the front car fender. Suddenly he turned toward the rutted lane.

Gretchen heard the dull rumble, too, loud enough to drown out the cicadas.

Dust swirled in a thick cloud as the wheels of the army truck churned the soft ruts.

The sheriff was already moving. He propped a big flashlight on the car fender. By the time the driver turned and backed the truck with its rear end facing the shed, the sheriff was snipping the chain.

The driver of the truck wore a uniform. He jumped down and ran to help and the two men lifted up the big splintery board, tossed it aside. Each man grabbed a door. They grunted and strained and pulled and finally both doors were wide open. The soldier hurried to the back of the truck, let down the metal back.

Gretchen strained to catch glimpses of the soldier as he moved back and forth past the flashlight. Tall and skinny, he had a bright bald spot on the top of his head, short dark hair on the sides. His face was bony with a beaked nose and a chin that sank into his neck. He had sergeant stripes on his sleeves. He was a lot smaller and skinnier than the deputy but he was twice as fast. They both moved back and forth between the truck and the shed, carrying olive green gasoline tins in each hand.

Once the sergeant barked, "Get a move on. I've got to get that truck back damn quick."

Even in the moonlight, the deputy's face looked dangerously red and he huffed for breath. He stopped occasionally to mop his face with an oversize handkerchief. The sergeant never paused, and he shot a sour look at the bigger man.

Gretchen tried to count the tins. She got confused, but was sure there were at least forty, maybe a few more.

When the last tin was inside the shed, the doors shoved

shut, the chains wrapped around the board, the deputy rested against his car, his breathing as labored as a bulldogger struggling with a calf.

The sergeant planted himself square in front of the gasping deputy and held out his hand.

"Goddam, man"—the deputy's wind whistled in his throat—"you gotta wait 'til I sell the stuff. I worked out a deal with a guy in Tulsa. Top price. A lot more than we could get around here. Besides, black market gas out here might get traced right back to us."

"I want my money." The sergeant's reedy voice sounded edgy and mean.

"Look, fella." The deputy pushed away from the car, glowered down at the smaller man. "You'll get your goddam money when I get mine."

The soldier didn't move an inch. "Okay. That's good. When do you get yours?"

The deputy didn't answer.

"When's the man coming? We'll meet him together." A hard laugh. "We can split the money right then and there."

The deputy wiped his face and neck with his handkerchief. "Sure. You can help us load. Thursday night. Same time."

"I'll be here." The sergeant moved fast to the truck, climbed into the front seat. After he revved the motor, he leaned out of the window. "I'll be here. And you damn sure better be."

Grandmother settled the big blue bowl in her lap, began to snap green beans.

Gretchen was so tired her eyes burned and her feet felt like lead. She swiped the paring knife around the potato. "Grandmother, what does it mean when people talk about selling gas on the black market?"

Grandmother's hand moved so fast, snap, snap, snap. "We don't have much of that around here. Everyone tries hard to do right. The gas has to be used by people like the farmers and Dr. Sherman so he can go to sick people and the Army. The black market is very wrong, Gretchen. Why, what if there wasn't enough gas for the jeeps and tanks where Jimmy is?"

There wasn't much sound then but the snap of beans and the soft squish as the potato peelings fell into the sink.

Gretchen tossed the last potato into the big pan of cold water. "Grandmother," she scooped up the potato peels, "who catches these people in the black market?"

Grandmother carried her bowl to the sink. "I don't know," she said uncertainly. "I guess in the cities the police. And here it would be the deputy. Or maybe the Army."

Gretchen put the dirty dishes on the tray, swiped the cloth across the table.

Deputy Carter grunted, "Bring me some more coffee," but he didn't look up from his copy of the newspaper. He frowned as he printed words in the crossword puzzle.

Across the room, the officer who looked like Alan Ladd was by himself. He smiled at Gretchen. "Tell your grandmother this is the best food I've had since I was home."

Gretchen smiled shyly at him, then she blurted, "Are you still looking for the Spooklight?"

His eyebrows scooted up like snapped window shades. "How'd you know that?"

She polished the table, slid him an uncertain look. "I heard you yesterday," she said softly.

"Oh, sure. Well," he leaned forward conspiratorially, "my colonel thinks it's a great training tool to have the troops search for mystery lights. The first platoon to find them's going to get a free weekend pass."

Gretchen wasn't sure what a training tool was or a free pass, but she focused on what mattered to her. "You mean the soldiers are still looking for the lights? They'll come where the lights are?"

"Fast as they can. Of course," he shrugged, "nobody knows when or where they're going to appear so it's mostly a lot of hiking around in the dark and nothing happens."

Gretchen looked toward the deputy. He was frowning as he scratched out a word, wrote another one. She turned until her back was toward the sheriff. "They say that in July the lights dance around the old Sister Sue mine. That's what I heard the other day." Behind her, she heard the creak as the sheriff slid out of the booth, clumped toward the cash register. "Excuse me," she said quickly and she turned away.

The sheriff paid forty-five cents total, thirty for the Meatless Tuesday vegetable plate, ten for raisin pie, a nickel for coffee.

When the front door closed behind him, Gretchen hurried to the table. As she cleared it, she carefully tucked the discarded newspaper under her arm.

"A cherry fausfade, please." She slid onto the hard metal stool. The soda fountain at Thompson's Drugs didn't offer comfortable stools like those at the Victory Cafe.

"Cherry phosphate," Millard Thompson corrected. He gave her his sweet smile that made his round face look like a cheerful pumpkin topped by tight coils of red hair. Millard was two years older than she and had lived across the alley all her life. He played the tuba in the junior high band, had collected more tin cans than anybody in town, and knew which shrubs the butterflies liked. Once he led her on a long walk, scrambling through the rugged bois d'arc to a little valley covered with thousands of Monarchs. And in the Thompson wash room, he had two shelves full of chemicals and sometimes he let her watch his experiments. He even had a Bunsen burner. And Millard's big brother Mike was in the 45th, now part of General Patton's Seventh Army. They hadn't heard from him since the landings in Sicily and there was a haunted look in Mrs. Thompson's eyes. Mr. Thompson had a big map at the back of the store and he moved red pins along the invasion route. Mike's unit was reported fighting for the Comiso airport.

Gretchen looked around the store, but it was quiet in mid-afternoon. Millard's mother was arranging perfumes and powders on a shelf behind the cash register. His dad was in the back of the store behind the pharmacy counter. "Millard," she kept her voice low, "do you know about the black market?"

He leaned his elbow on the counter. "See if I got enough cherry in. Yeah, sure, Gretchen. Dad says it's as bad as being a spy. He's says people who sell on the black market make blood money. He says they don't deserve to have guys like Mike ready to die for them."

Gretchen loved cherry fausfades, okay, she knew it was phosphate but it had always sounded like fausfade to her, but she just held tight to the tall beaded sundae glass. "Okay, then listen, Millard . . ."

Gretchen struggled to stay awake. She waited a half hour after Grandmother turned off her light, then slipped from her window. Millard was waiting by Big Angus's pasture.

As they hurried along Purdy Road, Millard asked, "You sure it was Deputy Carter? And he said it was for the black market?"

"Yes."

Millard didn't answer but she knew he was struggling with the truth that they couldn't go to the man who was supposed to catch bad guys. When they pulled the shed doors wide and he shone his flashlight over the dozens and dozens of five-gallon gasoline tins, he gave a low whistle. Being Millard, he picked up a tin, unscrewed the cap, smelled.

"Gas, all right." There was a definite change in Millard's voice when he spoke. He sounded more grownup and very serious. "We got to do something, Gretchen."

She knew that. That's why she'd come to him. "I know." She, too, sounded somber. "Listen, Millard, I got an idea . . ."

He listened intently while she spoke, then he looked around the clearing, his round face was intent, measuring. Then he grinned. "Sure. Sure we can. Dad's got a bunch of powdered magnesium out in the storeroom. They used to use it with the old-fashioned photography." He looked at her blank face. "For the flash, Gretchen. Here's what we'll do . . ."

Gretchen could scarcely bear the relief that flooded through her when the young lieutenant stopped in for coffee and pie Wednesday afternoon. When she refilled his cup, she said quickly, "Will you look for the Spooklight tonight?"

The lieutenant sighed. "Every night. Don't know why the darned thing's disappeared just when we started looking for it."

"A friend of mine saw it last night. Near the Sister Sue mine." She gripped her cleaning cloth tightly. "If you'll look there tonight, I'm sure you'll find it."

It was cloudy Wednesday night, the last night before the man from Tulsa would come to get that gas. Gretchen and Millard moved quickly around the clearing, Gretchen clambering up in the trees, Millard handing her the pie tins Gretchen brought from the cafe's kitchen. She scrambled to high branches, fastened the tins with duct tape.

"You think they'll come?" Millard asked as they un-wrapped the chain, lifted the board and tugged the doors to the storage shed wide open. Gretchen carefully tucked the newspaper discarded by the sheriff between two tins.

"Yes." There had been a sudden sharpness in the young officer's eyes. She'd had the feeling he really listened to her. Maybe she felt that way because she wanted it so badly, but there was a calmness in her heart. He would come. He *would* come.

Millard took his place high in the branches of an oak that grew close to the boarded-over mine shaft. Gretchen clutched the oversize flashlight and checked over in her mind which trees had the pie tins and how she could move in the shadows to reach them.

Suddenly Millard began to scramble down the tree. "Gretchen, Gretchen, where are you?"

"Over here, Millard." She moved out into the clearing. "What's wrong?"

He was panting. "It's the army, but they're going down the wrong road. They're on the road to Hell Hollow. They won't come close enough to see us."

Gretchen could hear the noise now from the road on the other side of the hill.

"I'll go through the woods. I've got my stuff." And Millard disappeared in the night.

Gretchen almost followed. But if Millard decoyed them this way, she had to be ready to do her part.

Suddenly a light burst in the sky and it would be easily seen from Hell Hollow road. Nobody who knew beans would have thought it was the Spooklight but, by golly, it was an odd, unexplained flash in the night sky. Then came another flash and another.

Shouts erupted. "Look, look, there it is."

"Quick. This way."

"Over the hill."

If Millard had been there, she would have hugged him. He'd taken lumps of the powdered magnesium, wrapped them in net (Gretchen had found an old dress of her mom's and cut off the net petticoat), and added a string wick they'd dipped in one of the gas tins. He lighted the wick and used his slingshot to toss the soon-to-explode packet high in the air.

Gretchen heard Millard crashing back through the woods. He just had enough time to climb the oak when the soldiers swarmed into the clearing. Gretchen slithered from shadow to shadow, briefly shining the flash high on the tins. The reflected light quivered oddly high in the branches. She made her circuit, then slipped beneath a thick pine and lay on her stomach to watch.

Two more flares shone in the sky and then three in succession blazed right in front of the open shed doors.

The local *Gazette* used headlines as big as the Invasion of Sicily in the Friday morning edition.

**ARMY UNIT FINDS
BLACK MARKET GAS
AT SISTER SUE MINE**

Army authorities revealed today that unexplained light flashing in the sky led a patrol to a cache of stolen gasoline . . .

It was the talk of the town. Five days later, when Deputy Sheriff Euel Carter was arrested, the local breakfast crowd was fascinated to hear from Mr. Hudson who heard it from someone who heard it on the post, "You know how Euel always did them damfool crossword puzzles. Well," Mr. Hudson leaned across the table, "seems he left a newspaper right there in the storage shed and the puzzle was all filled out in his handwriting. Joe Bob Terrell from the *Gazette* recognized his handwriting, said he'd seen it a million times in arrest records. The newspaper had Euel's fingerprints all over it and they found his prints on the gas tins. They traced the tins to Camp Crowder and they checked the prints of everybody in the motor pool and found some from this sergeant and his were on half the tins and on the boards that sealed up that shack by the Sister Sue. They got 'em dead to rights."

Gretchen poured more coffee and smiled. At lunch the nice officer—she'd known he would come that night—had left her a big tip. He'd looked at her, almost asked a question, then shook his head. She could go to Thompson's for a cherry fausfade in a little while and tell Millard everything she'd heard. It was too bad they couldn't tell everyone how clever Millard had been with the magnesium. But that was okay. What really mattered was the gas. Now maybe there'd be enough for Jimmy and Mike.

INCIDENT ON SIXTH STREET

D. R. Meredith

D. R. Meredith is a split personality who spends her days working in the medical records department of a local clinic and her nights committing murder. A former teacher, librarian, and bookseller, Meredith is the prize-winning author of three mystery series, including the latest Megan Clark Sixth Street mystery, numerous short stories, and a book review column for *Roundup Magazine*.

When I read in the newspaper about the discovery at the old dry cleaner's, I figured the law wouldn't bother much with it, so I was a little surprised when the nurse told me a policeman was here to see me. I don't know how you tracked me down and it doesn't matter. I'm lying in this nursing home waiting to die, and since my people are long-lived, I reckon I'll hang on a few more years whether I want to or not. So long as I'm on this side of the grave I welcome company, even company like you who wants to stir up mud in the bottom of the pond. Sometimes it's better to leave the mud alone, but I guess a man in your line of work doesn't see it that way. You want to ask me if I recall an incident on

Sixth Street? Young man, I remember it like it happened yesterday instead of more than sixty years ago. An old woman's memory is like that: You remember what you saw and heard and felt years ago better than you remember what your granddaughter told you last week. I always thought time was kind in that way, letting you remember things that happened when your sight and hearing and smell was fresh and sharp. Nowadays, if I misplace my glasses I can't see beyond the end of my nose, and folks sound like they're swallowing half their syllables when they talk, and as for smell, a person can forget that and just as well, too. Otherwise you might smell your own aging, that musty odor you can't ever quite bathe away.

But I'm getting sidetracked, another trait of an old woman, although men are worse about it in my opinion. My second husband was the world's worst for talking around a subject, but I best get on with my story seeing as how you're tapping your fingers on that chair arm like you're losing patience. I was saying how I remembered what happened just as clear as could be with none of the details gone from my mind. "Imprinting" my granddaughter calls it. (See, I did remember something she said on her last visit). According to her, and she's got some fancy degree from college—got that instead of a husband and family—incidents that evoke strong emotion burn themselves into our memories. That's more or less a quote from her. Sounded a lot like branding cattle to me, but I didn't say that to her. Besides having a face that looks like five miles of hard road, my granddaughter doesn't have much in the way of a sense of humor. Of course, being close to the change of life like she is doesn't help, but she never had one even as a youngster. She was always too earnest for her own good—and everybody else's, for that matter. Have you ever noticed how folks dedicated to good works and holding the best of intentions toward others always seem to rub some folks the wrong way?

You haven't?

Well, I have. Noticed it sixty years ago and I noticed it last week when my granddaughter visited me. Is it the Bible that says the path to Hell is paved with good intentions? I'm not so closely acquainted with the Holy Scripture as most women of my generation, but around here religion is in the air, and a body picks up odds and ends of scripture whether you have much formal Sunday School or not—and I don't. My daddy's place was so far out in the sticks that we never got to town but every six months. That was before everybody had a car, and besides there weren't any roads worthy of the name. But that was before your time, young man. Likely before your daddy's time, too.

But just because I didn't go to Sunday School doesn't mean I don't know right from wrong. My daddy taught us the difference with a razor strap. He was a hard man, my daddy, and a little too fond of that razor strap. Looking back, I wonder if I would have done what I did if I hadn't heard another razor strap whistling through the air and seen the red welt rise up on that poor girl's thin little arm. I don't know, and there's no way to sort out the might-have-beens now. Likely it wouldn't have made any difference.

Young man, I see you shifting on that chair like it was a red ant bed. You just have some patience and listen to what I'm saying. I'm getting to where you wanted me to start, but like most youngsters, you don't give enough credit to what went on before and what came afterwards. Nothing in this life ever happens without a before and after. You keep that in mind and you'll be a better policeman.

To get back to my story, it was 1938, a Saturday in late March. I don't remember the exact date because the days were all alike for me. One wasn't any different from another except Saturdays were busier and the next day was Sunday, and I could rest up from ironing starched shirts and pressing pants and breathing the fumes of cleaning fluids. I used to sit in my front yard on Sunday mornings and just breathe the clean air. Then on Monday morning I'd go back to work. You know, I can still close my eyes and remember how that dry cleaner's smelled? The bleach was worst of all. The stink of strong bleach will bring tears to your eyes, not to mention what the touch of it will do. But you know about that. And the moist heat smell of freshly ironed shirts. Yes, sir, I was one who thought permanent press was a gift straight from God, and so did every woman who ever lifted a heavy iron or used a pressing machine. And it's not true that permanent press is what drove my boss—his name was Harry, Harry Thompson in case you're interested—out of business. When the city rerouted Route 66 from Sixth Street to Amarillo Boulevard, business dried up like the Canadian River in July. And of course you know that Sixth Street is old Route 66, and that the Mother Road is part of the story. Might not have even been a story without 66. You might even say that if time or place or people had been different, there wouldn't be a story or—what did you call it?—incident on Sixth Street. But once everything came together and all the pieces rubbed up against one another, there was no stopping what happened.

I'll start with the time—or maybe I should say times. It was still hard times in 1938, the Great Depression with capital letters, and it had the whole country in a headlock. Except for here in Amarillo it wasn't so bad as elsewhere. We never had any banks go bust for instance, and our bread lines were a whole lot shorter than the ones you saw in pictures of New York and Chicago. That doesn't mean everything was rosy in the Panhandle of Texas—it wasn't—but it could have been a lot worse. We never saw folks thrown wholesale off their land by the banks like happened in Oklahoma and Arkansas and further south in Texas. We never saw dozens of our neighbors tying their mattresses and box springs on top of their cars and piling the kids in the backseat and driving off down Route 66 into the setting sun. Mind you, there were some who left, some who couldn't wait it out until the rains came instead of the wind, so you could grow crops and livestock again, and somebody would buy them when you did. I'm not blaming those who couldn't stick it out. Some folks have more grit than others. A black duster will show what a body is made of fast enough. But you're too young to have lived through one. Lord, but they were awful, the air so full of dirt that the sun couldn't shine through. It would be blacker than the devil's heart at midday, and a person couldn't see his hand before his face. I remember hanging wet sheets over the windows and stuffing rags under the doors to keep out the dirt. And I'd dip a handkerchief in water and tie it over my mouth and nose so I could breathe. In a couple of hours, less if I went outside, that wet hanky would be caked with mud. It was a sight to behold, those clouds of black dust that reached up into the sky to block out the sun. It was a sight I could have done without. I lost my youngest boy after the black duster of 1936. He was always a sickly child, and hanging a wet sheet over his crib didn't save him. He died of what we common folks called dust pneumonia in those days. I don't know what they call it now. Probably nothing, since we don't have black dusters anymore, thank the Lord.

Anyhow, I told you about my boy so you would know I suffered during the Great Depression and the Dust Bowl, along with my neighbors and the rest of the country. And the country wasn't out of the woods in 1938 despite Roosevelt and the CCC Camps. In a certain way it might have been the worst year of all for some folks, the ones who had held on through all that came before and thought they would make it. But when the weather and the banks and the markets don't cooperate, and you've got a family to feed and clothe and house, and there's no money for shoes in the winter, nor seed for crops in the spring, and once you slaughter that last calf for food, then you got your back to the wall. You have to get out or starve.

The dry cleaner's had a big front window, and while I worked, I watched the caravans of Okies and Arkies and Texies in their beat-up old cars loaded with all they owned—and it was a light load—go driving down Route 66 in search of better times. But the saddest ones, the most pitiful of those caravans, were at the tag end of the Great Migration as they called it, when you thought it was over. In 1938 the cars were older, the tires looking like round checkerboards from being patched so many times, and the faces—Lord, but the faces were gaunt. Did you ever see pictures of the Okies, young man, the ones Steinbeck wrote about in *Grapes of Wrath*? Surprised that I read that book, are you, an old woman with not much schooling? You shouldn't be. It was about my times and the people I saw drive down 66. But it's not the book I'm asking you about, it's the people. The gauntest faces I saw during the Depression were in 1938, and it wasn't starvation that melted the flesh off the bones—although most didn't have enough to eat—it was hope. Hope betrayed them, don't you see. They held on until they thought they saw the end in sight, and then they lost. To lose from the beginning is one thing, but to almost win, to see victory so close you can almost touch it, that's giving yourself over to hope. When you lose then, it's a cruel loss that cuts the heart right out of a person.

Those were the times as best I can describe them to a youngster who never lived through them and won't ever live through anything like them, and you better hope you don't.

Now for the road—the Mother Road, the Main Street of America some called it—'cause 66 played its part, maybe the main part of this story.

What's that you said? What difference does a road make? What does it have to do with what you found in the false wall behind that industrial dryer? Young man, it has everything to do with it. Route 66 was more than just a ribbon of concrete running from Chicago to California; it was the Highway of Dreams. It was Route 66 to a second chance, a new beginning. It was the route you took to start over. It was DX service stations and motels built in the shape of Indian tipis; rattlesnake farms and roadside zoos, and curio shops that sold genuine Indian moccasins made in Japan. It was fantastic sights and outlandish shops and diners that sold fried chicken like Mamma made. It was the road to freedom and adventure even if you didn't have more than a dollar in your pocket and ate peanut butter sandwiches all the way to California. But most of all, youngster, Route 66 was hope, even to those last Okies who had already been betrayed once. And they were afraid to trust hope again—you could see it in their eyes—but they didn't have any choice. Hope was all that was left to them. Hope or just give up and die— and those folks were too tough to die.

And now I come to the people. There's me, of course. I worked at the dry cleaner's and lived just north of Sixth Street in a frame house my first husband bought the one and only time he was flush with money. When he died, he left me the house, a worn-out Buick, and three boys. I went to work at the dry cleaner's because hard work was all I was educated to do, and I was lucky to get the job. That's as much about me as I choose to tell and as you need to know. Opal Bannister was the young girl with the skinny arms, and she sat by her husband, a fellow by the name of Leroy, in the front seat of a Ford that was at least ten years old if it was a

day, with bald tires and a slate off an apple crate in place of
the passenger side window. You could still see the lettering.
"Washington Apples" it said. A mattress was doubled over
and strapped on top of the car, and a couple of canvas water
bottles were tied to the radiator cap and hung down in front
of the radiator. That was back when radiators were in the
very front of the car and you didn't have to open up the hood
to get to them. That's where hood ornaments came from,
you know, radiator caps, because everybody had as fancy an
ornament on the cap as they could afford. There were cupids
and eagles and about everything else you could imagine, and
if you were rich, why then your ornament might be bronze
or maybe even silver or gold.

I saw you nearly jump out of your chair when I mentioned
the radiator cap, but don't interrupt me to ask about it. I'll
get around to it soon enough and in my own way. Now,
where was I before I got sidetracked on radiator caps? Oh,
yes, the water bottles. Most folks carried them because of
crossing the desert, and car radiators in those days were liable to boil over when the engine overheated—which they
did regularly. Also, the folks driving the cars needed to drink
a lot of water. Remember, the only air conditioning those
cars had came from leaving the windows open.

There was something else you ought to know about 1938.
It was the year of the dedication ceremony of Route 66 by
the Will Rogers Memorial Highway Association whose
headquarters was right here in Amarillo. Sixty-six was finally paved from Chicago to Los Angeles, and you had all
kinds of motorcades starting from one city or the other.
There were lots of ordinary folks driving the distance before
and after the ceremony, too, folks who weren't Steinbeck's
people or part of the motorcades, but just wanted to share in
the celebration and had the wherewithal to do it. Adele

Davis was one of those folks, and it was just bad luck that she drove into Amarillo right behind the Bannisters.

In those days there was a filling station right across the street from the dry cleaner's, a Phillips 66 I think it was, or maybe it wasn't, and I used to go over there on my lunch hour and buy a cold Coke. I can't describe how good that Coke tasted after working all morning in a steamy laundry. At any rate, I was sitting inside the garage, kidding with the mechanics while I drank my Coke and smoked a cigarette, when this old Ford drove in. Lord, I thought I had seen some wrecks before, but this car was held together with spit and baling wire. The only fancy thing about it was that radiator cap, a woman dressed up in one of those Roman outfits—togas, I think they're called—pointing a sword toward heaven. Yes, it looks like the one you've got in that plastic baggie. I reckon it's the same one or you wouldn't be showing it to me. But to get back to my story, a tall thin man climbed out of that Ford, a young man aged beyond his years, wearing overalls and a checked shirt that had been washed until it was nearly worn out. It was probably the only shirt he owned besides his Sunday one, and I would have bet my Coke that he was saving that one for job hunting when he got to California. He was an Okie. I could tell the minute he opened his mouth. After years of hearing folks on the Great Migration talk, I could tell an Okie from an Arkie or a Texie. If I hadn't been born poor and the wrong sex besides, I might have gone to school and been what my granddaughter calls a "linguist." I tell you that just so you know I'm in the way of being an expert in where folks originate.

"I need some gas," Leroy Bannister said to the attendant, Elmer I recall his name was. "And you got any kerosene for sale? I got my own can."

"I got kerosene for sale. About how much would you be wanting?"

"I need a gallon of gas, and five gallons of kerosene," Leroy answered, taking a can from the trunk of his car.

Elmer filled up the can with kerosene—filling stations kept a supply in those days—and put a gallon of gas in the old Ford. "That will be nineteen cents for the gas and forty-nine cents for the kerosene."

Leroy nodded his thanks and pulled a ragged leather coin purse from the hip pocket of his overalls. With cracked and calloused fingers he carefully counted out two quarters, a dime, and eight pennies. I know because I'd finished my Coke and was walking by the old Ford on my way back to work. I also know there wasn't much money left that I could see in that coin purse.

Elmer took the money, gave the windshield a last wipe, and smiled at the two white-haired children, a boy and a girl, in the back seat. "You have a good trip now," said Elmer, "and thanks for stopping by."

I tarried a minute, pretending to study the gas pump like I'd never seen one before, while I tried to get a good look at the passengers. I couldn't tell you even now why I was so curious about the Bannisters when I'd seen so many Okies just like them driving down 66, except that there was something noble about that particular family. Whether it was Leroy's clean shirt, or the hole in the little girl's sweater that had been so skillfully darned with thread almost but not quite the right color, or just the way Leroy asked for gas. Everything from clothes to car shouted out defeat, but Leroy still stood tall with his shoulders back. If he had been flat broke, he would have offered to trade labor for gas. His kind never asked for charity. My dad was the same way.

Leroy drove a half block down the street and stopped the car. He got out with the five-gallon can of kerosene and walked to the gas tank. Elmer nudged me about that time. "Watch what he does now. He's going to pour that kerosene in his gas tank. I knew he was going to do it when I sold it to him, but as long as he's not on the premises when he does, then I haven't broken the law. I'm not allowed to sell kerosene for cars, but a lot of these Okies use it when they run low on money for gas, and they're mostly always low on money. Old cars like that will run on kerosene so long as you start them up on gasoline and keep the engine warm."

"Isn't that dangerous?" asked a well-dressed woman who stepped out of a brand new Pontiac.

Elmer and I had been so busy watching Leroy Bannister that we had missed seeing Adele Davis drive up. According to what Leroy told me that long dark night that was to come, she was a rich oil man's widow from Oklahoma City who didn't mind telling you how well-off she was. To me that meant she married above herself, because the only folks I know who tell you what everything they own cost are the ones who started out poor as church mice and haven't adjusted to their new circumstances. The old rich never mention cost, probably because they grew up never having to ask the price.

Elmer snapped to attention like he was still in the trenches in France and an officer had just walked by. "I don't think so, Ma'am, not in these low compression engines like that Ford. Can I fill you up?" he asked with a smile while he wet his sponge and began to wash her windshield.

"Of course, that's why I stopped," she replied while watching Leroy pour the kerosene into his gas tank. "But now that I have, I believe I'll step over there and have a word with that young man. Mixing kerosene and gasoline might be dangerous and he has young children in the car. His kind are often ignorant of the danger their actions cause to others. Makes you wonder why God gives children to them and not to the more deserving."

There was something about Adele Davis that went all over me—probably the way she dismissed Leroy Bannister as "his kind." At any rate, I put in my two cents' worth. "Elmer said it wasn't dangerous, and I don't see as how you have any call to be saying different. Besides, I figure that man has enough worries for two men without you adding to his troubles."

"You know him?" she asked, raising her plucked eyebrows. Women used to pluck their eyebrows into a narrow little line, like a pencil streak above their eyes.

"No, but I know his kind," I said, dragging out the last two words just so she would know I caught her meaning.

She looked me up and down like I smelled bad—which I probably did, sweating like sixty working in the cleaners all day. "I don't believe you need to concern yourself about the young man. You hardly look like you can care for your own needs, much less worry about his."

Honest to God, young man, that's exactly what she said in that Okie accent that wasn't any better than Leroy's. She just used fancier words, is all. Well, if I'd been mad before, I was like a rabid dog now. I reached out to grab her by the lapels of her suit—imagine wearing a suit to drive from Oklahoma City in those days—but Elmer stepped between us. "I reckon it's time you went back to work," he said to me, frowning to beat the band.

I stood there a minute, feeling hot and shamed and not about to take Elmer's advice. It wasn't any of my business one way or another, but I couldn't seem to let go of it. "You don't know anything about me—or about him," I said to Adele.

"I don't know you personally, of course, but since my husband passed away I've had the privilege of sitting on many charity boards, and I have a great deal of experience helping people do what's best for themselves and their families. You, for example, should improve your grooming and personal hygiene if you want to better yourself. After I speak to the young man, I'll jot down a few suggestions for you and leave them with this gentleman. You may pick up the list at your convenience and I hope you find it helpful."

She patted her felt hat with the narrow brim that turned up all around her face. I can't remember now what the style was called, but it was fit closely over the crown of the head. It was attractive on her, and I'm sure she dazzled poor Leroy upon first acquaintance. Opal she merely intimidated until right up to the last. The children she frightened, but then the very young have good instincts about predators.

I watched her walk up to Leroy, then went back to work and tried to forget it. But I couldn't. Even though the Bannisters weren't really any of my business, I watched out the front window anyway, even stepping outside several times to look across the street. That's how I knew that Adele Davis and Leroy stood together talking for more than two hours. Or rather Adele talked and pointed to the children, and Leroy nodded his head every once and a while, looking down at his feet and hooking his thumbs in the front pockets of his overalls. Occasionally he would sneak a glance at his children and I knew Adele was giving him what for on the subject of what was best for the youngsters. She never did appreciate that he was doing his best.

Finally, around four o'clock, Opal got out of the car. She was more than thin. She was skinny, her hip bones jutting against the worn cotton dress when the wind blew the fabric tight to her form. Her hair was pinned up in a knot on the back of her head, and was just as white blond as her children's, but a few locks straggled down her neck. I saw Adele pull a comb out of her purse and hand it to Opal, gesturing all the while. I figured she was giving Opal pointers on personal grooming. Opal just bowed her head and took the comb. I could see her white skin turn red from where I stood in front of the cleaners'.

When work was over I sprinted across the street to the filling station. "Elmer, what happened to the Okies and the rich widow?"

He frowned at me. "I don't see that it's any of your business—or mine either."

"Come on, Elmer. Don't you want to know the end of the story? I'll tell you when I find out."

I never did, of course.

Elmer finally told me that Adele had persuaded the Bannisters to go with her to a travel court further down Sixth Street past Georgia. Travel courts are what we used to call motels, and even a cheap one was way out of the Bannisters' reach, and this one wasn't particularly cheap. It was shiny white frame cabins all connected together in the shape of a U. The building's still there, only it's not a travel court anymore. Anyhow, I couldn't imagine what Adele had in mind for Leroy and Opal, but I knew Leroy, or rather I knew men like him. He would never admit to a woman like Adele that he was too poor to pay his own way. That's how men like him get themselves into messes. Like the Bible says, pride goes before a fall.

I went charging down Sixth Street to the travel court like the Devil himself was chasing me—and maybe he caught up—maybe he caught up with all of us. That time of the year in Amarillo daylight lasted until a little after six, so it was good and dark by the time I reached the travel court. And cold and windy. In late March it's generally cold and windy at night. I kept thinking of that ragged sweater the little girl wore, and how it wouldn't keep her warm in a car with one window boarded up. I nearly stopped right then. Let the

Bannisters sleep in warm beds tonight. Surely to God Mrs. Rich Bitch Davis will pay for their room. She has to know they're the next thing to starving.

But I didn't stop. I went on until I found the battered old Ford with its apple crate window glass parked in front of a cabin, and Adele Davis's new Pontiac in front of the one next to it. I don't know what possessed me to hammer on the Bannisters' door. Maybe it was an accumulation of all the years of watching folks like them drive by the cleaner's on the Highway of Dreams, knowing that what they were fleeing to was nearly as bad as what they were fleeing from. I read the papers. I've always been what you call a well-informed person. I knew California didn't want the Okies and the Arkies and the Texies. The state didn't have enough jobs for their own citizens, much less the thousands that crossed its borders every month. I knew the migrants ended up in tent cities, living on handouts and being treated like dirt, working for pennies a day when they could find work. Of course, we know now that they survived and eventually prospered when the war industries geared up, but we didn't know that in 1938. I didn't know it. The Bannisters didn't know it, and for sure Adele Davis didn't know it. You keep that in mind, young man. In 1938 all we had was hope and each other. That was what struck me the most as I watched the Great Migration through the front window of the cleaner's. It was families—families holding together despite defeat and misery, families like the Bannisters. It was parents sacrificing so their children would have a chance for a better life.

That's what Adele Davis counted on, you see.

Leroy opened the door and peered at me, his forehead wrinkled up like he was trying to remember where he'd seen me before—which he probably was. He had his overalls on without a shirt, like he'd been in the middle of shucking off his clothes when I knocked. The two white-haired children—tow heads, we used to call them—were sitting on the bed, cuddled next to their mother like two frightened puppies. Opal had an arm around each child and didn't look much bigger or stronger than her offspring. Mother and children had red puffy eyes, and Opal's mouth looked loose and quivered every now and then, as a woman's does when she's been crying desperate tears. Did you know, young man, that tears come in different flavors? There's sad tears and grieving tears and happy tears and mad tears, but the worst of all are the desperate tears, the ones a woman cries when she's finally given up on pleading her cause. It's the desperate tears that make you sick to your stomach, and give you such an ache around your heart that it's a wonder you don't die of it.

"Yes, ma'am?" asked Leroy, which goes to show you what kind of man he was. He didn't ask who the devil I was, and why was I knocking on his door. Not Leroy Bannister. His mama raised him right, be polite to women, even strange women who knock on the door at night.

Suddenly Adele Davis appeared at his shoulder. She must have been sitting on the room's one chair against the wall next to the door because I didn't see her when I first looked in. "Did you follow me here, young woman? I saw you staring at me all afternoon, and I didn't know if I should be flattered or afraid. Financial hard times bring out the worst in certain people, you know."

"I know. I have a good example right in front of me," I said.

She put her hand on Leroy's bare arm, just rested it until looking at it sent the shivers up my back. "You misunderstood me. I wasn't speaking of Leroy."

Sexual did you say, young man? Was it a sexual touch? You mean like a widow lady hungry for another man? No,

that wasn't the way of it between those two. Not at all. She
thought she was calming him, like you might rest your hand
on a toddler's head to reassure him when a stranger comes
to the house. Come to think of it, that's a fair comparison.
She didn't think much more of Leroy Bannister's smarts
than she would of a toddler's. They could both be calmed
and talked into doing what you wanted them to—which
goes to show that Adele Davis never had kids of her own, or
else she would know that there's no more stubborn mortal in
the world than a toddler.

Now that I told you how I saw it between those two, and
remember I was an outsider, so I didn't have my feelings involved the way the Bannisters did. I thought I saw the hell
that was the final destination of Adele's good intentions a lot
clearer than Leroy Bannister did.

Turns out that I was wrong, but there was no way to know
that at the time.

What good intentions? Young man, you're beginning to
make a habit of interrupting me. I'll be dead before I can get
to the end of my story at this rate. You just hush up until I
finish. Then you can ask me all the questions you want. For
now, cast your mind back to that tiny cabin in the travel
court, with Leroy standing there in the doorway in his overalls and no shirt, and Adele gripping his arm. It was a sight
I won't ever forget, gaunt-faced Leroy in ragged overalls
and blond-by-request Adele in her fine suit and silk stockings. Sleek as a well-fed cat she was, which only made Opal
with her skinny hips and thin arms and lines that experience,
not age, stamped on her face, look worse in comparison. Just
looking at that scene a person might think Leroy Bannister
was fixing to trade a roll in the hay with the Widow Davis
for a decent night's rest for his family and maybe a little
cash in the bargain. Well, looks can be deceiving as the old
saying goes, although Adele Davis would have been better

off if she had just wanted a man in her bed. All four of us
would have been better off.

There we were—the Bannisters, Adele Davis, and me—
frozen in place like we were subjects in an old Kodak photograph. Maybe if Adele hadn't insinuated that I either
admired her or threatened her—both ideas set me off like a
volcano—I might have backed away from that door and
gone home. Not that my leaving would have changed anything in the long run. Sooner or later, either on Sixth Street
or further down Route 66, murder would have been done. I
just wouldn't have disposed of the body.

"I wasn't staring at you because I admire your mind"—
bearing down on those last two words—"or because I was
planning to steal from you. My mama raised an honest
woman and I don't like you thinking otherwise. I was
watching you because I was curious. I couldn't figure out
what you wanted with these folks, and anybody who knows
me can testify that when I'm curious, I'm like a dog with a
bone. I don't give up without a fight. You want something,
and these folks are in such a fix that I don't think they can
turn you down if there's money to be had. I don't like the
smell of this business, Mrs. High and Mighty. For all me and
these folks know, you could be a gangster's moll."

Oh, I was so mad, I was bristling, young man, but I wasn't
as outlandish as I sound now. Bonnie and Clyde, Pretty Boy
Floyd, Machine Gun Kelly, Ma Barker and her boys, gang-
sters like them got all the headlines in those days. Of course,
they were mostly dead by 1938, but they all escaped from
the cops at some point by driving down Route 66.

"It's none of your business, and if you don't leave now, I
intend to call the manager and have you thrown off the
premises," said Adele before Leroy had a chance to do more
than open his mouth. I never did know what he intended to
say.

"Mrs. Davis will be taking our children to raise," said Opal. She had the most soft, musical voice I've ever heard, soothing is what it was, but her words struck me dumb. "They'll have good food to eat and nice clothes to wear—shoes and each one will have a coat when it's cold. Leroy has tried his best to provide, but we don't have a home anymore and no money, and my babies are hungry all the time. Mrs. Davis says it's best that she take them—at least until we get on our feet again."

I finally found my voice and indignation to go along with it. "They won't ever be on their feet enough to suit you, will they?" I asked. I looked at Adele Davis and she didn't even have the decency to blush. That's the kind of woman she was.

"Leroy and Opal agree that the children would be better off with me. I would provide them with the best money could buy, and they would have a chance to better themselves."

"If you're so filled with the milk of human kindness, why don't you provide the *parents* with the best money could buy, and they could better themselves so they could take care of their own children?" She didn't like me questioning her good intentions because her face turned red just over the cheekbones.

"By the time they bettered themselves it would be too late. Their attitudes are too ingrained to change quickly. No, the best solution is to save the children."

"I ain't going to do it," said Leroy, suddenly coming to life and shaking off Adele's hand. "I ain't giving up my children. I'll find some kind of work when we get to California. I'll provide."

Opal came off the bed at his remark. "But we said we wanted the best for the children. I can't stand to see them go hungry again, Leroy. I'd rather give them up than see them starve."

She took each child by the hand and walked toward Adele Davis. Just when she came even with Leroy, he grabbed her arm. "I told you we ain't giving our children away. They ain't puppies, Opal, they're our babies, and nobody can love them like we do. Just have a little faith in me. We'll manage."

"I don't have any faith left, Leroy. Mrs. Davis made me see how foolish I've been. She says this is the best way, and that we owe it to the children."

Tears were rolling down Opal's cheeks like rivers, and the children were hanging back, scared half to death but not crying. Kids raised during the Depression lived through too much to do much crying. They learned the hard way that crying didn't put fried chicken on the table, or shoes without holes on their feet.

"Please don't do this, Opal," said Leroy, tears of his own streaking down his cheeks. "I'll stop you if I have to, and I don't want to hurt you. I've never hurt you, but I will this time if that's what it takes."

The tears just rolled faster out of Opal's eyes as she pulled away from Leroy. That's when he did it—grabbed the razor strap and brought it down on his wife's arm. She gasped and dropped her son's hand to cover her arm where a huge red welt swelled up before any of us could draw breath. Leroy fell to his knees and pressed his face against her legs, but I could still hear him crying, sobbing really, and that's when I knew for a fact that no good could come from Adele's intentions.

I did what I wanted to do when I first argued with Adele—grabbed her by the lapels of her fancy suit and shoved her away from Opal and Leroy and their children. She stumbled out the door and fell off the wooden step in front of the cabin. She landed on her behind, and I got a lot of satisfaction out of seeing the dirty circle on the back of

her skirt when she scrambled up. It wasn't very Christian to
feel that way, but if anybody ever deserved to be pushed in
the dirt it was Adele Davis.

"Can't you leave them alone?" I asked in what sounded to
me more like a hiss than a voice. "They seem to be decent
people and they're going to kill each other over an idea you
put in their heads. Don't you have any idea of the harm
you're doing?"

She dusted off the back of her skirt and glared at me. "I
see the harm that vicious bully did his wife. The very idea—
hitting her like that. The best thing that could happen to
those children is if I took them away from those people."

"Leroy may have hit her—and I bet it was the first time
ever—but you pushed him into it, putting him and his wife
at odds over their children. You're standing in judgment
when this mess is as much of your making as theirs."

She ignored me like I was a piece of trash she had to walk
around, and climbed the step in front of the door. "Bring the
children out here, Opal. I'll put them to bed in my cabin."

Opal twisted her skirt out of Leroy's grasping fingers, and
walked outside, closing the door behind her. It was probably
close to eight o'clock by then and very dark, with the only
light being what leaked out around the edges of the blinds
on all the cabin windows, that and a weak moon half-hidden
behind clouds. I couldn't see Opal's face and could barely
hear that soft voice over the wind and the sound of the oc-
casional car driving down Route 66 in front of the travel
court.

"I've changed my mind, Mrs. Davis. I can't give up my
children. I can't hurt Leroy like that. He'd never forgive me
for doing it or himself for not providing better."

I was close enough to Adele Davis to feel her turn stiff as
a fence post. I guess she never had people poor as church
mice turn her down before, and she couldn't believe what

she heard. She and Opal were practically nose to nose on that little step, and it didn't take a second for Adele to recover. "Don't be ridiculous, Opal. You and that brute you're married to can't take care of yourselves, much less helpless children."

I don't know whether it was Adele's calling Leroy a brute, or her insinuation that neither one of them was up to the job of being parents, or both remarks, but Opal slapped her. You could hear the crack of Opal's palm against Adele's cheek as clear as anything—or maybe it sounded louder than it was because it was such a shock. Frail little Opal didn't look like she could stand up for herself, but it turned out she could give as good as she got.

Adele stumbled backward off that step, same as she did when I shoved her, but this time she swung her arms around like a windmill trying to keep her balance. I guess she didn't want to get her skirt any dirtier than it already was. She would have done better to have paid a cleaning bill, because she staggered backward another couple of steps, until she fell against the Bannisters' old Ford. She was a tall woman and her heart matched up perfectly with the radiator cap. If she had been shorter, she would have lived. As it was, that sword the lady in the toga was holding went right through Adele. She didn't make much sound, just kind of a whoosh when the breath left her. It was a good thing it was so dark, or someone might have seen her lying across the radiator with just the tip of the ornament showing through the front of her chest.

I can see you're about to burst with questions, so I'll hurry through the rest. It's not very pleasant listening anyhow. Leroy and I did most of the business because Opal wasn't good for much except lying in bed with all the quilts we could find piled on top of her. Leroy, being a decent citizen, wanted to call the police, but I talked him out of it without much trouble. He and I were two of a kind—that kind—and we both knew nobody was likely to believe what really happened. Opal was liable to spend some hard time in prison, or rather, Leroy was, because he was planning to take the blame. I figured neither one would last without the other, so I persuaded him my way was best. We lifted Adele off the radiator and laid her in the Ford's back seat. I drove to the dry cleaner's with Leroy following me in Adele's Pontiac. Mr. Thompson, the owner of the dry cleaner's, miscalculated when he poured the building's foundation. It was two feet shorter back to front than it ought to be, but Mr. Thompson had already paid for the bricks and the lumber and the other building materials, and he didn't want to waste any, so he just built the wall where he intended to in the first place, and threw up another wall where the foundation ended inside the building. But I guess you found out all about that, young man, when that lady bought the building from Mr. Thompson's grandson, then tried to remodel it.

It took Leroy and me most of the rest of the night to tear a hole in the false wall, bury Adele and about ten gallons of bleach in that two-foot space where there wasn't a foundation, and repair the wall as best we could. At the last minute I ran out and unscrewed the radiator cap and threw it in the grave. Don't ask me why I did that because I don't know. It just seemed fitting that Adele be buried with the instrument of death.

The hardest part of the evening was moving that industrial dryer out of the way, then moving it back, that and dumping bleach on Adele's shiny new Pontiac. Have you ever noticed that when people see a car with its paint peeling, they automatically think it's an old car even if it isn't? Well, they do. Remember what I said about appearances being deceiving. Tie a couple of canvas water bags on the radiator cap, and a mattress and box spring on the roof, and you've got a beaten down Okie in a beat up car. Worked like a charm.

I drove the old Ford to Wild Horse Lake and Leroy helped me push it in. He jumped on the roof until the car settled into the mud on the bottom of the lake. The water level dropped a few years later and the Ford was towed out, but everybody thought whoever the owner was just disposed of an old wreck. Certainly nobody tried to track down the owner.

I cleaned Adele's belongings out of her cabin. I tried to give the clothes to Opal, but she wouldn't take them, said they would haunt her if she did. I did sneak all the cash, and there was a considerable amount, into the Pontiac's glove compartment where I figured Opal would find it. I just hoped she wouldn't shrink from using it, but I never heard one way or another. A few months later I visited Harold and his wife, Maude, who owned the travel court. I managed to tear out the page in the register with Adele's and the Bannisters' names on it while he had his back turned and Maude was fixing coffee. I don't guess he ever noticed that missing page, or thought enough of it to mention it. That page was the last clue to what you call the incident on Sixth Street. If that woman hadn't decided to remodel Mr. Thompson's old building, I might have died before Adele's body was ever found, and you would never know what happened.

What's that? Did I ever think I ought to let the police know? No, young man, I didn't. Adele's death was an accident, and I figured that justice was served in the long run better than a judge and jury could do. As far as I'm concerned Adele's good intentions paved the way to her own hell instead of creating a hell on earth for the Bannisters. I can't say that I've slept soundly every night of the past sixty years, but I haven't lain awake much either. And those nights when I do think about it, I remind myself that nothing I could have done that night would have brought Adele back, and that I made the best of a tragic situation. Don't sacrifice a living family for a dead busybody, young man.

Oh, something else. I made up the names of Leroy and Opal Bannister, but not Adele Davis. Maybe there is somebody somewhere who is curious about what happened to her. Then again, maybe her folks were just as glad to be rid of her.

You can ask your questions now, young man, but I didn't say I would answer them.

'53 BUICK

Gary Phillips

Gary Phillips has written articles and op-ed pieces on politics and pop culture and is the creator of the Ivan Monk mystery series. He also wrote *The Jook*, a stand-alone crime novel, and is at work on a couple of screenplays, going through a box of maduro cigars somewhere in the hell of L.A.

Barreling out of Amarillo, the sandstorm swooped in just as Dolphy Ornette steered the black and red 1953 Buick Roadmaster directly into its path. Route 66 lay flat and hard and open before him like a whore he knew back home in Boley, Oklahoma. Some Friday nights men would be stepping all over each other in the service porch off her rear bedroom waiting their turn.

He'd bought the car two years ago when he'd cashiered out of Korea with his corporal's wages. He'd fought a war just like his older brother had not more than a decade before. Of course, just as with that war, the downtown white men suddenly got a lot of "we" and "us" in their speeches, and told the colored boys it was their duty to go protect freedom. His brother didn't make it back from the war.

Back in '42 the enemy were krauts and nips. In '51 they were the goddamn gooks. White man always could come up with colorful names for everybody else except himself. Dinge, shine, jig, smoke, coon, even had dago, wop, mick, kike for those whites who talked their English with an accent or ate food that they definitely didn't serve down at the corner diner.

The NAACP also said negroes should fight, prove they were loyal Americans and that they could face 'em down with the best of them. So they soldiered up. Surely that would show the ofays back home, things would have to improve in housing and jobs once our boys got back. The black soldiers who returned with memories of lost lives and innocence and blood had the nerve to demand what was theirs from the big boss man. Naw boy, things is going back the ways they always was. Sure Truman integrated the troops in Korea, but that was war time. This was peace.

A steady hammering of sand rapped against his windshield. Earlier, before the break of dawn, he could tell what was coming as he stood gassing the Buick at the dilapidated station in McLean. The old Confederate who ran the place wasn't inclined to sell him gas, but business wasn't exactly knocking down his weather-beaten door, so a few colored dollars would do him.

The wind off the Panhandle drove the sand at the glass with a fine consistency that reminded him of the sound when his mama fried up cornmeal in a pan. But the car's road-devouring V-8 and the Twin-Turbine Dynaflow torque converter kept the machine steady and on course across the blacktop. He was glad he'd paid extra for the power steering, even though at the time he did think it was a mite sissified. The twelve-volt charging unit was doing its job. The dash lights didn't dim like his DeSoto's used to do.

He drove on and on with the sandstorm ranging around his car like the song of one of those sea mermaids luring you. Like you'd get so hot to be with her you wouldn't notice until it was too late as a giant squid popped the eyes out of your head as it squeezed your ribcage together.

Dolphy Ornette kept driving, periodically glancing at the broken yellow line dotting the center of the two-lane highway. The pelting sand sounded a lullaby of nature's indifference to humanity. He drove on because he needed to put distance between himself and where he'd left, and because he needed to get where he was going. Not that he thought they'd suspect him. No, the big boss man couldn't conceive of a black man being that clever. A couple of them might wonder what had put it in his head to quit. But he'd waited weeks after filching the doohickey to announce he was going back to Boley.

Anyway the generals and the chrome dome boys would be too busy trying to figure out how the dirty reds had stolen the gizmo. A blast of wind, like the swipe of a giant's backhand, caused the front end of his car to swerve viciously to the right. His hands tightened on the wheel, and he managed to keep the Roadmaster under control. Ornette slowed his speed to compensate for the turbulence. It wouldn't do to flip over now.

He should'a rotated the tires before he left, but he had other matters to deal with. Up ahead, an old Ford F-1 truck with rusted fenders weaved to and fro. The trailer attached to it shimmied like one of those plastic hula girls he'd seen in the rear window of hot rods.

Ornette slowed down, watching the taillights of the trailer blink through the sheet of brown blur swirling before him. It sounded as if a thousand snares in a room full of drums were being beat. The red lights before him swayed and jerked.

On he drove through the gale until it was no more, and all that remained was a night with pinholes for stars, and a silver crescent of a moon hanging like it was on a string. He pulled over somewhere the hell in New Mexico. Using the flashlight, he checked the windshield. The glass was pitted and several spiderweb cracks like children's pencil marks worked at the edges. But the metal molding seemed intact. He tapped the butt of the flashlight against the windshield in several places and it held.

He popped the hood to check the hoses and then cleaned away the grit on the radiator with a wisk broom he took from the glove compartment. Looking toward a series of lights, Ornette figured he'd take a chance and see if he could get accommodations. He had a copy of the Negro Motorist Green Book in the glove box. It was the black traveler's guide to hospitable lodging, and to which lodging was to be avoided.

At the moment, Ornette Dolphy was too tired and too ornery to give a damn. As he drove closer he could see a neon sign of a cowgirl straddling a rocket with a saddle around its mid-section. Blinking yellow lightning bolts zig-zagged out of the rear of the rocket. The motel rooms were done up like a series of movie rockets had landed tail first in the dirt. The place was called the Blast-Off Motor Lodge. Beneath the girl on the sign was a smaller sign announcing cocktails. If they rented him a room, they'd probably take his money for scotch, he wistfully concluded. He patted the trunk and walked inside.

Ivan Monk looked up from the sepia-hued postcard of the Blast-Off Motor Lodge to the elderly woman. They were sitting in her cramped kitchen, the door to the oven open and set at 350 degrees. Its stifling heat made the sitting and listening to the woman's story that much more difficult. Outside, the temperature was in the comfortable low seventies.

"Mr. Ornette liked to keep mementoes. Know where you been, and look forward to where you going, he was wont to say." She tapped the postcard with her delicate fingers.

"And you want me to find his Buick?" Monk repeated, to make sure he wasn't getting delirious from the heat.

She nodded. "1953, Roadmaster Riviera hardtop coupe, yes sir. It was like something out of Flash Gordon that car. What with that bright ol' shiny grill like giant's teeth and those portholes, four of 'em, lined along the side." She shook her head in appreciation. The black wig she had on slipped a little and she adjusted it in one deft motion.

"I remember it so vivid, that Tuesday he drove up in his beautiful car to the rooming house. Had us a wonderful three story over on Maple near Twenty-fourth. All that's Mexican now." She tucked in her bottom lip, willing herself not to go on about the old days.

"Those cars were classics," Monk agreed. "But Mrs. Scott, why do you want to find Ornette's Buick, and why now?" The heat was too much. His shirt felt like it was stapled to his skin.

"It was a gorgeous car, you said so yourself." She touched her head and looked over at the kettle on the stove. "Tea, Mr. Monk?"

Is the old girl part polar bear? "No thanks."

She got up in the quilted housecoat she had on and poured herself some tea. Standing at the stove she said, "Mr. Ornette kept that car in fine running condition. He heard anything wrong with the engine and he'd get it down to the mechanic lickity-split." She stirred and sipped. "There were a couple of mechanics he particularly liked going to. One of them had a shop over on Avalon." She inclined her head. "Had some kind of royal name, you know? The Purple Prince, no that's the skinny child who runs around with the butt cut out of his jeans."

"Kings High Auto Repair," Monk supplied.

"Why yes, that was it. But he couldn't still be around, could he?"

"No, my father died some time ago."

She halted the cup at her cracked lips. "My goodness, that was your daddy's business?" She laughed heartily. "The Lord sure moves in his ways, doesn't he? It's providence then that I got to talking to your mother after church last Sunday, and she getting you to come here and see me about my need." She laughed some more.

Monk's father had won the stakes with a kings high full house poker hand to make the down payment on the garage. The rest he'd borrowed from a gambler he'd been in the Army with in Korea.

"Mrs. Scott, I'd still like to know why you want to find this car. Did Dolphy Ornette skip out on his rent years ago and now for some reason you want him to make good?" He had to find a way out of this silly business gracefully so as not to offend her or his mother.

"Child, Dolphy Ornette died in 1968."

"And he kept the Roadmaster all that time?"

"Yes he did. He wasn't living with us by then, but my sister, who knew some of his friends, used to see him around town in it. Oh yes," she said animatedly, "he kept that vehicle in good running condition."

"And what happened to the car after Mr. Ornette died?"

She raised her head toward the ceiling, the steam from the cup drifting past her. Momentarily, Monk had the impression her head existed detached from her body. "When we heard about his getting killed, my sister and—"

"Killed?" Monk exclaimed.

"Yes, didn't I tell you?" She sat down at the table with its worn Pionite topping again.

Details definitely weren't Mrs. Scott's thing. "How'd it happen? Don't tell me it was because somebody wanted his car."

"No, nothing like this carjacking foolishness we got today, no. When Dolphy got back from Denver he had more get up and go. We'd known him before the Korean action. My sister had gone around with him before. But when he came back to town, he seemed more focused I'd guess you'd say. Before he was just interested in fast cars and club women." She made a disapproving sound in her throat.

"But when he came back to Los Angeles in 1955, he was like a man afire. He got himself into community college while he waited tables over at the Ambassador Hotel on Wilshire. He soon had a delivery service operating for colored businesses in town and on up into Pasadena. He did all right," she said proudly.

"His death?"

"Shot in the face one night as he came out of his office on Western."

"The police find the killer?"

"No. Some said it was a jealous business rival. Others said it was white folks who had delivery services and couldn't abide a black man taking business away from them."

"And the car?"

"I was raising a family and working part-time at the phone company, Mr. Monk. I couldn't rightly say."

Was she ever going to explain why it was she wanted this car so much now? If there'd been rumors of money hidden it, like Ornette didn't trust banks? Surely she didn't believe it would still be hidden in it after all this time. The Buick was probably long since recycled metal, and was part of a building in Tokyo by now.

Mrs. Scott, anticipating his next question, rummaged in

the lidless cigar box she'd plucked the Rocket Motor Lodge postcard out of a few minutes ago.

"Here," she finally said, "this is a picture of the car. You can see Dolphy with his foot on the bumper, right over the license plate. My sister Lavinia took that shot right in front of our place on Maple."

"Come on, baby, snap that damn thing," Ornette growled. He pulled on the crown of his Flechet.

"Take your hat off, the shade from it's blocking your face."

"Maybe I don't want my face in the picture."

Lavinia Scott put a hand on a packed hip.

Ornette complied. He put one of his new two-tone Stacey Addams on the Buick's bumper. His foot directly over the black license plate and yellow numbers and letters. The first thing he'd done coming back was to re-register the car in California. It wouldn't do to get pulled over by the law for out-of-state plates.

She wound the film in the Brownie camera, held the thing against her stomach and sighted his reflected image in the circle of glass. She snapped off two shots rapidly.

"Let's go now," he ordered. Ornette plopped his hat back on and got in behind the wheel of the Buick. Lavinia squirreled the little camera away in her purse and joined him on the passenger side.

"You been back a month now and you still haven't told me about your job in Denver."

"I told you I'm planning on going to school 'fore I get my ideas set up." He steered the car onto Maple and headed south toward Jefferson.

"See, that's what I'm talking about, Dolph, you all the time ducking the question." She studied her lips in her compact's mirror, applying a thin coat of lipstick. "You know perfectly well what I'm talking about. What was it like working at the PX? It had to be exciting what with everybody returning from the war."

He grinned, showing his gold side tooth. "Like any other slave a colored man can get, sugar honey. Punch that clock and hit that lick."

She gave him a playful slap on the arm. "You so bad."

"That's why you dig me."

She giggled. Then she leaned over and kissed him on the neck. He took a hand off the big steering wheel and rubbed her leg.

"Don't you go getting too frisky mister, I'm a church-going woman." But she didn't remove the hand.

"Don't I know it. Got your nosey sister askin' me when it is I'm going to get down to church every Saturday evening since I been back."

"She's concerned for your welfare," Lavinia Scott teased, touching his shoulder.

"Soon, if things go right, we ain't gonna have none of those worries. I mean money or our future." He piloted the Roadmaster west along Jefferson toward the Lovejoy Fish House.

"You been hinting around about something since you been back. What is it?"

Ornette beamed at her and chuckled. "Maybe I'll show you. You keep riding with me, sugar honey, you won't have to ask for no more. For nothin'."

She squinted at him, not convinced but intrigued nonetheless. She was about to speak when the car suddenly lurched to a stop. Behind them, a Mercury slammed on its brakes, its front end meeting the rear of the Buick.

"Goddammit, kid," he yelled.

A boy of about nine looked aghast into the windshield of

the Buick. His ball had rolled back to his feet, but he was too frightened to move.

"Oh lord, I think he's going to cry." She unlatched the door.

Ornette had a hand to his face. "Goddammit, Goddammit."

Lavinia went to comfort the child.

Ornette also got out to talk to the Mercury's driver. He was a small, stout man in horn-rimmed glasses and a beret. Influenced, no doubt, by the fashion fad among be-bop jazz men. The man was looking down at where his bumper had gone over the Buick's and was now pressed against the trunk.

"Looks like we can get them apart. How 'bout you get your trunk open and let's use your tire iron for leverage."

"Ain't got no spare," Ornette said hurriedly. He gritted his teeth, staring at the trunk. "I'll get on it and push, you put your car in reverse."

"You might dent it."

Ornette just stared mutely at the trunk.

The man hunched his shoulders and got back in his car.

Ornette got on his trunk and planted his Stacey Addams on the Mercury's bumper. His weight sunk the Buick's rear enough that the bumpers came free with little effort.

"I'm prepared to call it square if you are," the small man said.

"Yeah." Ornette absently stuck out his hand, still glaring at the trunk.

The other man shook the limp hand, and got back into his car.

Lavinia had calmed the child down. Ornette dabbed at his forehead with the sleeve of his camel hair coat. He parked the Buick, taking care to lock the doors.

By the time he'd done that and walked to where Lavinia stood, the kid was on his way with his ball. The child waved at the nice lady.

"Happy?" He sounded nervous.

"Don't like to see anyone disappointed," she said.

He shifted his shoulders beneath his box coat. "That's what makes you so special."

She hooked her arm in his and together they entered the Lovejoy Fish House, right beneath the huge plaster and wood bass suspended over the entrance.

Monk carefully refolded the brittle newspaper clipping from the Eagle newspaper. A piece on the visit of young starlet Dorothy Dandridge to the Lovejoy Fish House in November of 1952 was accompanied by a photo of the establishment. Mrs. Scott had told him about the incident with the child when she'd chanced upon the clipping. She said too that not soon after that, Lavinia and Ornette had broken up. The sister would never say why.

Mrs. Scott had loaned him the box of small knickknacks, postcards, photos and clippings. Many of them seemed to have belonged to Ornette, or were possibly sent to Lavinia by him. But it was all she had, she'd told him in that Hades of a kitchen. And couldn't he for an old woman, a friend of his mother's, spend a few days looking for the Buick, please?

Listlessly, he shifted through the contents of the box that now sat on his desk. There was part of a Continental Trailways bus ticket, more photos, a couple of rings, some buttons, an old-fashioned skeleton key and another postcard. This one depicted a landscape shot in the Painted Desert in Arizona. It was blank on the back.

Monk threw the postcard back into the cigar box and shoved the thing aside. What a pain in the ass.

Delilah Carnes, the fine all-purpose admin. assistant and researcher he shared with the rehab firm of Ross and Hendricks, entered the room. She wore a mid-thigh-length form-fitting black skirt and shocking blue silk blouse.

"Here's what I got from a check of the license plate number you gave me, Fearless Fosdick."

From the National Personnel Records Center in St. Louis, Monk had obtained Dolphy Ornette's service record which included his social security number. The SSN, the magic number to open up the doors to one's life in the not so private modern world.

"Let me guess, somebody filed a certificate of non-operation with the DMV sometime in the mid-eighties and that was all she wrote."

"Indeed," she said, sitting down and crossing well-defined legs on the couch. "Yet a callback I got from New Mexico showed the car was registered again in Gallup in 1988. Nothing after that."

"Registered to who?" Monk didn't hide his displeasure. "So now I'm supposed to go on my own dime to Gallup and prowl around junkyards for this car?"

Delilah laughed. "Your client said she'd pay you with three fresh-baked sweet potato pies. After all, she *is* on a fixed income, Ivan."

"All her money must go for her heating bill," he groused. "Who re-registered the car?"

Delilah checked her printout. "A Delfuensio DeZuniga. I called the number matching the address, but it's been disconnected. I've got half a white page of DeZunigas currently in Gallup."

Monk groaned. "How about any moving violations?"

"Yeah, I ran that too." She leafed through a couple of sheets, then settled on a page. "DeZuniga got a ticket for having a taillight out in 1989. Here in town."

She got up and handed him the sheet, pointing at the location of the infraction. Monk recognized the area as near

Elysian Park where the LAPD's academy was, and where
cholos and their rukas kicked it in the park. Bordering the
park was the Harbor Freeway, the 110, as it became the
Pasadena heading north.

"The 110 used to be part of Route 66," Monk noted aloud.

"And?" Delilah asked.

"Nothing, really. Ornette had driven Route 66 into L.A.
though."

"The address listed for DeZuniga at the time of the infraction is the one in Gallup," she added, walking out of the
office.

"Maybe he was in town visiting relatives," Monk called
out. He was not going to drive or fly to New Mexico on this
vehicular McGuffin of a favor. His phone bill was going to
be on him though, as he knew he was going to have to run
down as many DeZunigas as he could to satisfy Mrs. Scott
that he'd done what he could. His mother, he told himself,
was going to hear about this for years to come. He marched
into the rotunda to retrieve the white and yellow pages, and
got busy.

Later, tired of getting answering machines, nadas, and
busy signals from DeZuniga households in Gallup, he was
glad to take a break. He left his office and drove his midnight blue 1964 Galaxie with its refitted 352-cubic-inch V-8
east on Washington Boulevard leaving downtown Culver
City. The carburetor had been running sluggish, but he
hadn't had time to fool with the fuel mixture screws. At Cat-
taraugus he cut over to the Santa Monica Freeway and
headed east. Driving in the fairly unobstructed early afternoon flow, he was happy to find the car's engine smoothed
at a higher sustained speed.

Eventually Monk was on the 5 and took the exit in the
City of Commerce. Following the directions, he wound up
at the Southern California Buick Association headquarters a

little before two in the afternoon. On time for the appointment he made. The headquarters was also the business address of Willy Serrano, a machine shop operator where they rebuilt car and truck engines.

A boss black and white 1955 Special Riviera hardtop with the sporty mag rims sat in the slot marked "owner." During the early to mid-fifties, the Special Buick was the car to have among true believers.

Monk chatted with Serrano in his parts- and paper-cluttered office in the rear of the machine shop. Through the door the muffled sounds of lathes turning and metal being ground could be heard.

"I looked back in our membership records there, Ivan." Serrano was a large, gregarious man who favored pointed cowboy boots, a Western-style shirt, and a buckle with his initial on it. A white Stetson with three "Xs" on the band rested on top of a file cabinet.

"Sure enough, there was a Jessie DeZuniga in the club in the early nineties. He didn't renew for ninety-four. I recall talking to him once or twice, I think. But I couldn't tell you why he didn't re-join."

A machinist stuck his head in, and said something in Spanish to Serrano. He answered in the same language and the door closed again.

Monk found out Jessie was in his early thirties and got the last known address for him. It was on Callumet in the Echo Park section, near Elysian Park. He thanked the man and drove back into Los Angeles. Nobody was home at the small frame house on Callumet.

He went over to Barrigan's restaurant on Sunset and had a late lunch, topped off with a Cadillac margarita, one made from the good tequila. Then he called his office from a pay phone. Delilah told him their back check on Ornette's social security number had turned up his employment record. She'd leave the report on his desk.

Afterward, he wandered along the shops on North Vermont, the happening avenue for this season. In the window of a clothing store called Red Ass Monkey, the female mannequin's larger-than-usual breasts strained her top. She was in a latex mini and thick-soled studded boots astride a stuffed wild boar. Around six, he went back to the house. A cherry 1971 Camaro with fat rear tires was now in the driveway.

"Sorry, my friend," Jessie DeZuniga said, taking another swig on his beer at the door. The younger man had been home ten minutes from work, and was in his undershirt and blue work khakis. "Somewhere around here I kept the paperwork, but yeah, I sold the Buick about four years ago. It was a sweet car, I'll tell you, homes. But you know I already got one honey," he indicated his rebuilt Camaro, "plus two kids, and the old lady always going on about how I'm putting more money and attention into my dad's car than her."

He took another pull, then tipped the can at Monk's Ford. "But I guess you know something about that."

Monk nodded agreeably. "My old lady is always yapping about that too, but these are classics, right? A man has to have a hobby." Monk was lying, his significant other, Judge Jill Kodama, liked his Galaxie.

"Yeah," DeZuniga commiserated. One of his children, a young girl who must have been a third grader, popped up. "Pops, when you gonna fix dinner?" She averted her eyes from Monk, who smiled at her.

"Wife works nights," DeZuniga explained.

"I'm going to let you handle your business, Jessie. Do you remember the name of the guy who bought it?"

"It was a woman, young, hip hop Chinese chick. Can't

say what her name was now. She answered my ad in the Auto Trader, and made the best offer."

He'd already mentioned that his father had died. Monk asked as he stepped from the porch, "Do you know how your father acquired the Buick after Dolphy Ornette was shot?"

Jessie DeZuniga looked at Monk as if he'd grown a second head. "Don't you know? My father and Mr. Ornette knew each other from this Army base—I think it was in Alamogordo. Dad worked in a bar in town, and Mr. Ornette worked at the base, janitor or orderly, something like that. This wasn't the bar the Army people went to either. This was the one the townspeople went to."

"Ornette must have been the only black man in there."

"He got along." DeZuniga opened the door wider and gestured with the can. "Look at this."

On a tan-colored living-room wall hung several photos in what appeared to be handmade wooden frames. DeZuniga pointed at one. The shot captured men and women, Chicano, white and one black man who Monk presumed was Dolphy Ornette. All were sitting or standing at the bar.

"That's my father." He touched the can to a smiling bartender leaning on the bar, looking in the direction of the camera's lens. Ornette was a couple of stools down, raising his beer to the photographer. It was an afternoon because through the bar's windows Monk could make out the Buick and several other cars parked at an angle in front of the place. Beyond the cars in the distance were white gypsum mounds.

The backwards script painted on the front window was discernible too. Monk stared at it, trying to decipher the Spanish words.

"Flor Silvestre," DeZuniga aided. "The Windflower Cantina. Anyway," DeZuniga continued, "the car was at our crib

in Gallup months before my dad heard he got shot. Mr. Ornette had brought it there. At least that's what my dad had
said. I wasn't even two when all this went on."

His daughter called him again and he told Monk he'd call
if he found the papers. The PI returned to his office and Ornette's job history. The official record backed up what Mrs.
Scott had related to him, that Ornette had worked in a PX
supply depot in Denver. Yet there was that picture and what
the younger DeZuniga had said. And Monk was no geogra-
pher—Denver might have white hills like New Mexico for
all he knew.

At ten thirty that evening, he had an answer for the dis-
crepancy.

"Who was that on the phone?" Jill Kodama asked, handing him a tumbler of Johnny Walker Black and ice. They
were in the study of the house they shared in Silverlake. Her
name on the mortgage. One day, Monk figured, he'd get
used to calling it his home too. "One of your chippies, darling?" She turned on the TV.

"Information broker I use from time to time. His specialty
is out-of-date locations. He confirms that the Flor Silvestre
Cantina was in Alamogordo in the 'fifties, the time period
Ornette told Lavinia Scott he was working in Colorado."

"What do you make of that?" she asked, interested.

Monk crossed his arms. "Maybe he left behind another
girlfriend he didn't want Lavinia to know about. According
to the sister—"

"The one that's going to pay you in pies."

"Uh-huh. She said her sister and Ornette broke up one afternoon after he'd returned from an errand in Pasadena.
Whatever it was it set something off, and Lavinia came
home swearing she'd never have anything to do with that
crazy man again. Her exact words."

Kodama flipped through channels. "She, that is Lavinia, say what was so crazy?"

"No, Mrs. Scott says she'd never talked about it, even when the two would be out and would chance to see Ornette."

"What happened to the sister?" She settled on the History Channel.

"You know I never really asked her that? I assumed she died."

On the screen a mushroom cloud shot through with colonized oranges and reds blossomed on screen as an off-screen narrator droned on about America's love/hate relationship with nuclear power. This image dissolved to one of 'fifties downtown, fantastically backlit by a nuclear blast in the Nevada desert some 300 miles away, as the narrator continued.

"The stealth bomber flies out of White Sands now," Kodama said, eyeing the explosion. "But in the 'fifties and 'sixties, nuclear testing used to go on there."

Monk made an exasperated sound. "And Roswell's in New Mexico, Jill. You think Ornette was a space alien? Was the car his disguised flying saucer and Verna Scott needs to go home?"

"Okay, smart ass, then why does the old girl want the car? Sentimental reasons? Why did Ornette conceal where he worked? Why take Route 66 when the way to drive from Alamogordo to here is a different highway. Unless he was backtracking to throw somebody off his trail. And why is it the Buick hasn't shown up on any of your checking since Jessie DeZuniga sold it?"

"Whoever bought it never bothered to get it registered. The Buick's probably sitting in some garage now, the tires going to rot, the gas in the tank turning to gum. The proud possession of a weekend shade tree mechanic who keeps telling himself any Saturday now he's gonna get back out there and get this bad boy running.

"Anyway, why does he fill in the gaps for me with that bit about his father and Ornette knowing each other and Ornette leaving the car with his dad?"

"Don't be naive, baby," Kodama responded. "You've done that with the cops. Give them enough of the truth you figure they'll find out one way or the other, but also hold back. That way they believe you, and don't look twice in your direction.

"And," she went on, "why didn't the DMV check you told me you did when you got back to the office this evening produce a release certificate from Jessie DeZuniga?"

"It was a spot check going by the license plate. I don't have DeZuniga's social security number."

"He's the last known owner."

"You're much too suspicious for a judge."

"Press him for the paperwork. Maybe then you can avoid all the bugging your mother and Mrs. Scott are going to do if you leave it hanging."

Monk had to concede her logic.

Over the next several days he called DeZuniga several times and it was one excuse after the other as to what might have happened to those papers. But as much as he bugged the younger man, Mrs. Scott bothered him more. Repeatedly asking about any leads. On Friday, Monk broke down.

"I'm concentrating on a guy named DeZuniga, okay?" Monk rubbed his face as he held the receiver to his ear.

"Can you spell that, dear, my hearing's not so good."

He could just picture her standing in her hot kitchen in her quilted housecoat. He spelled the man's first and last name for her and assured her that he'd have something to report by the end of the weekend. He intended to have something by then one way or the other.

Monk had considered staking out DeZuniga in the evenings. But that would mean renting a regular car on his own dime or at the least borrowing his sister's Honda Civic as he'd done sometimes in the past. His '64 Ford was not what one would call a car that blended. Plus a black man sitting night after night in a car in a Latino neighborhood could not expect to not get noticed.

He hoped DeZuniga was being on the level when he said his wife worked nights, as it would ensure he couldn't move around too much until the weekend.

This turned out to be the case.

DeZuniga, the wife and kids drove out to a small frame house in Whittier early Saturday morning. He went inside and left his wife and kids waiting in her Camry. About fifteen minutes later, he was backing out of the driveway behind the wheel of the 1953 red and black Buick Riviera Roadmaster. It looked and sounded new. The family then drove back to Echo Park. Monk followed in his sister's Civic.

"Look man," he began, approaching a surprised DeZuniga in front of his house. "What you do with your car is your business. If you would just let this old lady, my client Mrs. Scott, see the car." Monk stopped a good few feet in front of DeZuniga so as not to be perceived as a threat. "I don't know why, but she's been—"

A Bell Cab pulled up in front of the house. The driver got out and opened the door to let Mrs. Verna Scott out. She paid him and he departed.

Mrs. Scott looked in awe at the Buick.

The children were bothering their mother for something and DeZuniga waved them inside.

"I didn't want to tell you I had it 'cause some others had been around asking about it around a year ago," Jessie DeZuniga said. "They offered me all kinds of money, but something about them." He frowned. "I told them I'd already sold the car. They said they'd been away but had made it back and needed to have the Buick."

DeZuniga looked at the car longingly. "My dad made me promise him to keep the car. Not to sell it, ever. Normally, I keep the Buick in my neighbor's garage down the street. But I moved it out to my cousin's that first night you were here."

"And my constant calling got you jumpy."

"Yeah. That time a year ago when these dudes showed up, the car just happened to be out at my cousin's pad."

"Where you went this morning?"

"Uh-huh. At that time he was redoing the upholstery. I knew they didn't believe I'd sold the car. I spotted them keeping watch on the house. But I out-waited them and finally they went away. Now, I was going to drive it to Moreno Valley, and leave it with my sister-in-law."

Monk was thinking about Ornette's unsolved murder. And that he'd given the car to DeZuniga's father as if he'd anticipated someone would be coming after him. "What did these men look like?"

"X-Files type, you know. Creepy, pasty-faced white boys. Big overcoats, hands in pockets, lips didn't move and shit."

Monk was about to ask more questions but the gun in Mrs. Scott's hand got his and DeZuniga's attention. It wasn't much of a gun, but it could sting.

"Open the trunk, please," she asked forcefully.

Bemused, DeZuniga did so.

"My sister would lay awake nights telling me," Verna Scott didn't finish her sentence. Like a mouse to cheese, she went to the now-open trunk compartment. Monk and DeZuniga got in position to watch her.

"Ain't nothing back there but the spare and a tool box," DeZuniga offered.

The old girl was halfway in the trunk. "Dolphy showed it

to her and it scared her. It was too much for her then. Years later," she grunted with effort, "she always regretted she didn't help him sell it."

"Sell what?" Monk moved forward to get a better look.

"But who would buy it?" she said to herself. He found out the thing was more trouble than it was worth. But by then, he couldn't turn it in either without going to jail forever. "Here it is, here's the latch."

Monk and DeZuniga moved forward to see what she was doing.

Suddenly a brilliant glow shot from the trunk and Mrs. Scott's wiggling form was swallowed by tendrils like beams of light.

"What the hell is that?" DeZuniga shouted, shielding his eyes. Sound seemed to be evaporating.

"Your dad never mentioned this?" Monk tried to move but it was as if some kind of heavy gravity was weighing him down. He and the other man sank to their knees.

"What the hell's going on?" The scintilla throbbed in his ears and he felt as if his heart was going to stop. Monk's world was a white hot essence where he couldn't tell up or down, back or front.

There was an even brighter flash, then birds could be heard chirping again in the morning air. Once the two men got their orientation back, they realized the Buick and Mrs. Scott were gone.

The men in uniform who arrived to question them just stood there peering at them doubtfully. Their story was that they'd been carjacked by an old lady with a pea shooter. Later, the plainclothes went over and over the story with them separately. They unswervingly kept to their version of what had happened. Each had agreed before DeZuniga had called the law not to mention the light thing. They didn't directly talk about it when they were finally let go seven hours later.

"Sorry about the Buick, that was a beautiful car, man." Monk shook DeZuniga's hand.

"Yeah. Think my dad and Mr. Ornette knew this would happen?"

Monk didn't have an answer. Didn't want to even consider one.

Route 66 stretched before them, the stars overhead like tiny pin pricks of light in an ebony-colored cloth. The moon was full and incandescent. Ornette Dolphy, his Flechet perched at an angle, sat at the wheel with Lavinia Scott beside him. In the back seat of the '53 Buick Roadmaster sat Verna Scott and Delfuensio DeZuniga. On the roadway some had called the mother, and others Camino de la muerte, the four drove on and on. Before them lay hope and knowledge and the road. But they didn't drive with haste, they went as if they had all the time in the world to get there.

DEAD MAN'S CURVE

- - - - - - - - - - - - - - - - - - -

Judith Van Gieson

Judith Van Gieson was born in New York City and graduated from Northwestern University with a BA in English and an insatiable desire to write. She moved to New Mexico in 1981 and has been writing about it ever since. She's written eight mysteries featuring Albuquerque attorney-sleuth Neil Hamel.

The prevailing winds are from the west, giving the east side of the Sandia Mountains more precipitation than the city of Albuquerque. It's colder and wetter in the East Mountains. Winter comes early and spring comes late. But when it does, the fields in the foothills are dotted with purple, white, and yellow wildflowers. Only hard, thorny, desert flowers bloom unattended in Albuquerque.

As the city expands people move further and further east. I-40 is the artery that connects East Mountain commuters to their jobs in Albuquerque, but Historic Route 66 still threads over and under the interstate. When 66 reaches Albuquerque it turns into Central Avenue, where you can buy anything from sailboats to sex. It's hard to drive the length of Central at any time of day or night without seeing hookers or a pimp.

But east of Albuquerque Rte. 66 is a two-lane country road wandering through Tijeras Canyon and the towns of Zuzax, Tijeras, and Sedillo, towns that now have gated communities, new banks and libraries, but also have feed stores and old adobe churches. Most commuters prefer I-40 to Rte. 66. It's newer and faster, but Tijeras Canyon on the interstate can be treacherous in bad weather and the semis that haven't seen traffic since Amarillo don't want to slow down for commuters. In the Canyon they start breathing down your neck. If your car is small enough you feel they will swallow you up.

If I lived in the East Mountains I'd take Rte. 66. It's slower—the hills haven't been flattened or the curves straightened—but it's prettier and calmer. The big trucks avoid it and no one pushes you to drive faster. That's what David Hamilton was doing last March—ambling home from his city construction job at dusk with a package of Devil Dogs on the passenger's seat when a westbound car came around Dead Man's Curve in the eastbound lane.

David turned his truck into the other lane in an attempt to avoid a collision, but the driver of the approaching car swung back into the westbound lane at the same moment. David was driving a three-quarter-ton Chevy pickup. The other vehicle was a subcompact and the occupants, who weren't wearing their seat belts, didn't have a prayer. The driver, Enrique Romero; his girlfriend, Vanessa Gabaldón; and her three girls aged six, nine and eleven, were thrown from the car and killed instantly. The tools in the back of David's pickup were scattered all over the road, but his seat belt was fastened and he remained in the cab. He suffered a mild concussion, a sprained back and contusions and was out of the hospital in two days.

Dead Man's Curve got its name because the trucks that used Rte. 66 before I-40 was built would catch the canyon wind and the driver would lose control in the curve. There was no wind the night of David's accident and no precipitation either. The road was dry, the weather was clear. David Hamilton had the sun at his back, but Enrique Romero was driving into the setting sun with a dirty windshield.

New Mexico is known for its high rate of alcohol-induced auto fatalities and the blood alcohol level of both drivers was tested. David's was .03, consistent with the two beers he'd had at a bar on Central before he left town. But Enrique Romero had had numerous beers at a bar in Sedillo before he picked up Vanessa Gabaldón and her three children. His blood alcohol level was 1.5, .5 over the limit that rendered him legally intoxicated, and close to 1.75, the level at which most fatal accidents occur. Beyond that, drivers start weaving all over the road and are easy for the police to spot and pick up. Romero was driving without a license and he already had two DWI convictions. The evidence seemed stacked in David's favor and I told him so when he came to my law office on Lead to ask me to represent him.

Ordinarily I don't handle traffic fatalities, but David had been referred by a client I respected and the depth of his depression touched me. He sat in my office with his hands dangling between his legs, looking about as forlorn as a man could. David was over six feet tall with a large frame, but he seemed to be wasting away inside of it. His blond hair was pulled back into a ponytail. His face was swollen from the accident and his eyes were a pale and vacant blue.

His wife, Amy, was also blond, but smaller and rounder than David. She had a complexion like the finish on an expensive tea cup and baby-fine hair that curled around her face. She wore a flower-printed dress and sandals. Her fingernails were bitten down to a rough edge. "If David is charged with vehicular homicide would you be willing to represent him?" she asked me.

"I need to hear your version of events," I said to David. New Mexico has more than its share of road tragedies, but this was one of the worst in recent memory and it had gotten a lot of news coverage. In every version I'd heard the finger of blame pointed to Enrique Romero.

David began to sweat. He wiped the back of his hand across his forehead. His eyes wandered out my open window. "I was pulling into Dead Man's Curve when I saw the other car coming over the rise and around the curve in my lane." His hands shook and he clasped them together to still the tremor. His wife lay her hand on top of his.

"I swung into the westbound lane to avoid it, but then the other driver corrected," David said. "You know how it is when you're walking toward somebody and he steps to one side to avoid you? But you've stepped to his side to avoid him. Then he steps back and you step back and you're facing each other again but in a different place. It was like that only I was going fifty and he was going a hell of a lot faster. There was no time to swing back into my lane."

"That's what you told the police?"

"Yes."

Amy was sticking to David's side like a burr, but I felt I needed to talk to him alone if I was going to get all the facts. "I'd like to talk to you alone for a few minutes," I told him.

"We're in this together," Amy protested.

"If David gets on the stand, he speaks alone. If he goes to prison he goes alone."

"That's why we need to be together now," Amy replied.

"It's your decision," I said. "But if I can't speak to my client alone I can't take the case."

"Amy . . ." David pleaded.

"Oh, all right." She picked up her purse and walked out of the room.

After she was gone David pulled some M&M's from his

backpack. I watched the trembling in his hands stop as they
dipped in and out of the pack.

"Was there anything that caused your attention to wander?" I began, taking notes on a legal pad.

"No."

"Any animals in the road?"

He shook his head.

"Did you get any sleep the night before the accident?" I
asked.

He shrugged. "As much as I usually get."

"How much is that?"

"About six hours."

About as much as most of us get. Sleep deficit is a major
cause of traffic accidents. Six hours might be enough for
some people, too little for others.

"What was your state of mind that day?"

"Good."

"How were you and Amy getting along?" I looked up trying to gauge the expression in his eyes, but there was none.

"Fine."

"No fights?"

"Not with Amy."

"With anybody else?"

"No."

"How about your coworkers? Your boss?"

"No problems. I had the beers with a couple of guys I
work with."

"Will they testify to that?"

"Sure."

"How's your vision?"

"Twenty-twenty."

He handed me his driver's license which showed no re-
striction for corrective lenses, but the license was three and

a half years old. "Get your eyes checked and bring me a slip from your doctor."

"Okay," he said.

"What did you have to eat that day?"

"A doughnut and coffee for breakfast at Dunkin' Donuts. I didn't have time for lunch."

Although David answered my questions coherently, his attention seemed to fade in and out. My window, open to Lead, was exerting a magnetic pull.

"How do you feel about what happened?" I asked him.

His eyes turned toward me and were full of grief. "Terrible. How would you feel? Five people died and three of them were children. I can't get those children out of my mind. They haunt my dreams. I see them everywhere standing beside the road."

"Did you know the family?"

"No, but I'd seen them. Sedillo is a small town—that's why we live there. Vanessa Gabaldón rented a house in the village. I used to see the children playing in the yard."

David was obviously deep in remorse and any jury would see that. I told him I'd take the case.

Further research assured me I'd made the right decision. The eye doctor confirmed David's vision was twenty-twenty. The brake marks proved the accident had taken place in the westbound lane just as David had said. He might have been going faster than he said. The investigator put his speed at sixty, five miles over the speed limit but that's not considered a crime in New Mexico. Enrique Romero was going considerably faster—seventy according to the investigator.

The case was assigned to Art Tesch, a pit bull of a prosecutor who I'd always thought had more teeth than brains. The decision was made to try my client for vehicular homicide, a crime that could put David in the State Pen for years. The State Pen might feel like home to some people since their friends and family were already there, but it would be a hell hole for David Hamilton. Art Tesch was trying hard to make a name for himself as a prosecutor. He had recently convicted a couple of Hispanic and Indian drivers for vehicular homicide and maybe he thought the time was ripe to put away a white guy. My client sitting at the defendant's table could play well on the evening news.

Whatever Tesch's reasons *The State of New Mexico v. David Hamilton* went to trial in early September. When the time came I prepared my client. By now the accident was several months behind us. David had gone back to work and was car pooling with some coworkers from Cedar Crest. Whatever physical damage he suffered had healed, but his eyes still looked wounded. In view of the investigator's report David had revised his speed upwards, but otherwise he stuck to his story. Romero was in the eastbound lane. David swung into the westbound lane to avoid him. Romero corrected. The vehicles collided.

The only evidence Deputy DA Tesch had was the skid marks in the westbound lane and David's blood alcohol level. We have no vehicle inspection in New Mexico and while there might have been something wrong with the truck, any evidence of that was lost in a pile of twisted metal. David's attention might have wandered from the road, but the prosecution would have no way of proving that unless I put him on the stand.

"I don't think you should testify," I told him. "Do you have any problem with that?"

He shook his head. "I don't want to testify. The hardest part for me will be facing the Gabaldón family in the courtroom. Every time I drive by their house I feel them glaring at me."

"It would be a good idea if you cut your hair and wore a suit to the trial," I said. "A ponytail and T-shirt might not play well with the jury."

He smiled slightly—the first smile I'd seen from David Hamilton. "That's what Amy tells me," he replied.

Enrique Romero was new to the East Mountains and appeared to have no close ties to the community, but Vanessa Gabaldón's friends and family packed the courtroom.

"Vanessa's mother is staring holes in my back," David whispered as we sat down at the defense table to begin the trial.

I didn't turn around until we broke for lunch. It wasn't hard to pick Vanessa's mother out of the crowd. Her face resembled the photographs I'd seen of Vanessa, but with all the youth and hope drained out. Her hair was black as a raven's wing, her nose was aquiline, her eyes burned with rage and grief. A teenage boy sat next to her. He wore a black T-shirt and his hair was shaved close to his head. Tattoos snaked across his bare arms. Throughout the trial we could hear the family's emotions bubbling behind us. Testimony was punctuated by hisses and gasps and sobs.

Art Tesch's case had started out weak and it remained that way. In my opinion it was a waste of taxpayer money to bring it to trial. Tesch put his expert witnesses and the State Police on the stand and hammered away at the fact that my client had been drinking, that he had been speeding, that he had been in the wrong lane when the collision took place. But my witnesses established that my client had not been very far over the speed limit and that he hadn't been legally intoxicated. Tesch couldn't come up with any convincing reason for my client to have been in the westbound lane, although there were a number of reasons for Enrique Romero to have entered the wrong lane: He was legally drunk, he was speeding, and his vision was impaired by the dirty windshield and the setting sun.

Tesch produced a witness who said he'd seen David

driving in an erratic fashion on Rte. 66 on a previous occasion, but the witness couldn't say when or how often David had driven that way. On cross examination I established that the witness was a friend of the Gabaldóns.

I thought I gave a convincing summation, and the jury—which represented Albuquerque's ethnic mix—came back in a few hours with a not guilty verdict.

Unfortunately, as happens all too often in New Mexico courtrooms, that wasn't the end of the story. When the verdict came down the emotions in the courtroom boiled over. Vanessa's mother stood up, pointed a finger at David and shrieked, "What kind of verdict is that? That man killed my precious grandchildren and my beautiful daughter and you're letting him go free?"

The judge banged his gavel and called for order.

Amy rushed up, gave David a hug and said, "Thank God." I hustled them out of the courtroom and into the parking lot behind the courthouse where we encountered friends and well-wishers and lingered too long saying good-bye.

David thanked me and shook my hand. "You did a good job," he said.

"We're so grateful," said Amy. "You've given us back our lives."

Mrs. Gabaldón came around the corner of the courthouse and approached us, leaning on the teenage boy. The contrast between this dark, sad family and the elated Hamiltons was striking.

"No matter what that jury decided God knows what you did," she said to David.

"I am very sorry for what happened," David told her. "If there was any way I could make it up to you I would."

"We're victims, too, you know," Amy blurted out.

"Quiet, Amy," David warned.

Mrs. Gabaldón's face was a road map of pain and suffer-
ing. "You people don't know what being a victim is," she
said. "I only hope some day you will suffer as we have."

The teenage boy spat at David's feet and led her away to
their car. The Hamiltons got into Amy's Saturn and headed
back to the East Mountains with Amy at the wheel. I returned to my office, put the Hamilton file away and began to
work on a new case.

David paid his bill promptly. I didn't expect to hear from
him again, but several weeks later he called to say he was
feeling threatened by the Gabaldón family. A car had been
driving past his house at night with the power stereo blaring.
Someone kept calling and hanging up when he answered the
phone. One night he neglected to put his truck in the garage
and the tires were slashed. "Is there anything I can do?" he
asked.

"Did you call the sheriff?"

"Yeah, but he won't do anything; he's related to the Gabaldóns."

"Get an alarm system," I said. "And a guard dog. Get an
unlisted phone. Keep your vehicles locked in the garage. Do
all the things city folks do."

"We moved out here to get away from all that."

"Move again," I might have suggested but I didn't think
David and Amy were ready yet to give up their East Mountain retreat.

A few weeks later David called back to tell me the guard
dog had been poisoned, the threats continued and that he and
Amy had decided to leave the East Mountains and move to
Rio Rancho.

"We're very sorry we have to do it," he replied. "Rio Rancho is the suburbs. This is the country. We've got a great
spot here. I hate to give it up, but this business with the Ga-

baldóns is terrifying Amy. We're having a farewell party a week from Sunday and we'd like it if you could come."

"I'll be there," I said.

When the day came I took I-40 to the Sedillo exit. Somewhere in the village I took a wrong turn and missed the Hamiltons' dirt road so I stopped at the feed store to ask for directions. A sign outside said they were selling rabbits for ten dollars apiece. One room was full of caged birds, another full of caged rabbits. A couple of bales of hay were stacked in the corner. The air inside had enough dust and dander to gag a maggot. One breath and I thought I would suffocate. I turned to let myself back out again.

"Wait a minute," the boy behind the counter said. "I remember you. You're the lawyer who got David Hamilton off." I remembered him, too, as the teenager with the clipped head who had supported Vanessa Gabaldón's mother. He stepped out from behind the counter with his hand deep in the pocket of his baggy gangster pants. A chain looped from his belt to his pocket. Tattoos snaked up his bare arms.

"I am very sorry about what happened to your sister," I began.

"She wasn't my sister," he replied. "She was my mother. Those three little girls Hamilton killed were my half sisters."

"I didn't know that," I replied. "I can imagine how terrible it is for you, but David was tried by a jury of his peers and he was found not guilty."

"He wouldn't have been found not guilty if he had been tried here," the boy sneered. His eyes narrowed. His hand went deeper in his pocket. "What are you doing in Sedillo anyway?"

I hesitated.

"Hamilton's having a farewell party today. That's why you're here, isn't it?"

"Yes," I admitted. "I got lost and I stopped to ask for directions."

"Go up the road a half a mile, turn right. The second driveway is his."

"Thanks."

"*De nada*," he replied.

He stood in the doorway and watched while I got in my car and drove away. His directions were better than the sketchy map David had sent me. The Hamiltons' log cabin was tucked in the woods. When I got there the lawn was brilliant with sunshine. The aspens had turned this side of the Sandias to gold. But as soon as the sun went behind the mountain I knew the shadows would be cool and deep.

I parked my car beside the road and walked to the house. David, Amy and their friends were gathered in the backyard. He looked better but his eyes still had that quality of fading in and out. He was letting his hair grow again. Amy was soft and neat in a flowered dress. She took my hand. "We're so glad you could come."

"It's a beautiful place you have here," I said. "It must be hard to give it up."

"Very hard," she answered. "What we could buy in Rio Rancho for the same money can't compare with the privacy we have here. But it will be good to feel safe again. I know it was the Gabaldóns who poisoned our dog. I feel like they are in the woods watching us." She shivered. "Well, we'll be out of here in a few days. Can I get you something to eat?"

She lead me over to a table laden with brown rice, tofu salad, fruit plates, veggie plates, rice cakes. I'd been expecting a barbecue and a charcoal-grilled hamburger. "Vegetarian?" I asked.

"We're macrobiotic," she replied.

A large chocolate cake at the end of the table reminded me of a former boyfriend who'd gone macrobiotic and was always sneaking out for chocolate. "Every macrobiotic I've ever known craves sugar," I said.

Amy laughed. "Some people feel that way at first, but they get over it," she said.

David introduced me to the guys he worked with then he moved on to greet another guest. The coworkers and I struggled to make conversation. About all we had in common was our disappointment in the food. They complained that there was no beer and nothing but lemonade to drink. They talked longingly of pizzas they'd had, barbecues they'd enjoyed. The afternoon dragged on. The feeling that someone was watching from the woods grew more intense as the shadows lengthened. One by one the guests began to leave. When I felt I'd paid my dues, I said good-bye, and wished the Hamiltons luck with the move. David walked me around the house and down the road to my car which was resting drunkenly on its rims because all four tires had been slashed.

"Son of a bitch."

"Those bastards," he said.

"I got lost and stopped at the feed store to ask for directions. Vanessa Gabaldón's son was there, and he knew I was coming to your party."

"I'm sure it was him," David said.

The spare in my trunk would get me nowhere. Sedillo had spooked me, and I wanted to get out of there. "I need to get back to town," I said. "Is there anyplace around here I can buy tires?"

"Not on a Sunday."

"Shit," I replied.

"I could drive you home," David said, watching me with careful eyes. "I'll take care of the tires for you tomorrow."

"Do you want to leave your party?"

"It isn't a party," he said. "It's a wake. It's just about over anyway."

Wakes can be cathartic, but this one had just been depressing. The expression in David's eyes shifted to something that resembled hope. This situation we'd found ourselves in had all the elements of a test. Was I willing to drive back to town with David Hamilton at the wheel? He was my client. I was the one who'd gotten him off. What could I say but, "Let's go"?

I hesitated long enough, however, to cause him to smile wryly and say, "Don't worry. I haven't had anything to drink. Amy doesn't allow alcohol in the house."

He went behind the house to tell Amy he was driving me back to town. She couldn't have protested too much because in a few minutes he was back with the keys. He opened the garage door and let me into the cab of the Chevy truck he'd bought with the insurance money from the wrecked vehicle. We both buckled our seat belts. He backed out of the driveway and we bounced down the dirt road trailing a dust devil behind us and leaving my car high and dry. When we reached the village where there was access to the Interstate, he said, "I still prefer to drive Rte. 66. Is that okay with you?"

"Sure," I replied.

He turned south. As we drove through the village, I had the sensation that faces were watching behind the curtains. We passed the feed store, which appeared to be closed. There were no cars in the parking lot. I looked into the side view mirror, but saw no one following us. Rte. 66 turned into a rambling country road as soon as we left town. David picked up his speed. I kept an eye on the speedometer, but he never exceeded the speed limit. The sun had dropped behind the Sandias, extinguishing the Aspen glow and silhouetting the mountains against the waning light. A white cat leapt from the weeds and darted across the road. My foot went automatically to the floor where the brake pedal would have been had I been driving.

"Hey," David said. "Don't worry."

But the truck swung wide when he saw the cat and began a flirtation with the center line, swinging up close, swinging back. A Blazer came around a curve, forcing David to return to his lane. As he did he overcorrected and spun gravel on the shoulder. If there had been a steering wheel on my side, I'd have been gripping it tight. I remembered how spaced-out my former boyfriend got on his macrobiotic diet, the way his attention wandered when he needed a sugar fix. David had been tested for alcohol and drugs but not for diabetes or low blood sugar and both were known to cause lapses in attention. My adrenal glands started working overtime. If I intended to get home I suspected I'd have to be alert enough for both of us.

"Did you have anything to eat at the party?" I asked David.

"There wasn't anything I wanted. Maybe I'll have a hamburger when we get to town."

"You don't stick to the macrobiotic diet?"

"Only when I have to. Amy swears it's healthy, but it just makes me hungry."

"How long have you been a macrobiotic?" I asked him.

"One year too long," he sighed. I understood now what could have caused his attention to wander the night of the accident and put him in the wrong lane. The dead children who haunted his dreams would be also standing beside my highways. I clenched my fists tight as the truck, approaching a blind curve under the influence of David's hungry hands, began again to drift.

A FLASH OF CHRYSANTHEMUM

J. A. Jance

J. A. Jance writes two police procedural series. Detective J. P. Beaumont (fourteen books) hails from Seattle, while Sheriff Joanna Brady (six books) calls southeastern Arizona home. As bi-regional as her characters, J. A. has divided her life between Arizona and Washington state. She has a husband, five children, three grandchildren, and three dogs.

The year goes out in a flash of chrysanthemum:
But we, who cell by cell and
Pang upon pang, are dragged to execution,
Live out the full dishonor of the clay.

I first heard those words in a college auditorium on a January night alive with orange blossoms and promise when C. Day-Lewis, the English Poet Laureate, came to the University of Arizona to read his work. *Baucis and Philemon*, one of the poems he read that night, was delivered to an audience made up primarily of English Major, poetry devotees.

Only nineteen at the time, it was hard for me to imagine what those words meant. Oh, maybe my hips and waist would thicken one day, making my figure match my fifty-year-old mother's, but in reality that possibility seemed remote. In fact, it wasn't until I hit fifty myself when the idea of aging gained an actual foothold in my consciousness.

At fifty-one and finding myself beset with nights of sleep-depriving hot flashes, it was far easier to imagine what might happen. I could see then how that single troublesome molar—the lower left-hand one that for years had shied away from everything cold—might one day do something so drastic as to simply fall out. Or else have to be pulled. Or that my chins—all several of them—would gradually subside into the suddenly excess folds of skin that now flowed down what was once a reasonably slender neck.

It even crossed my mind at times that fading into what I imagined to be the gentle haze of Alzheimer's-induced forgetfulness might be simpler, for me, than dealing with either the ongoing battles between my two feuding daughters or with the once-favored son who hasn't spoken to Ted and me since two years ago last Christmas.

Those ideas came on gradually, creeping up almost imperceptibly over a period of time. But what I never imagined, not in all my wildest dreams—nightmares, if you will—was the appalling reality of what was actually to be. Or what is. No, I didn't see that coming, not in a million years.

We talked about it, Ted and I, when the diagnosis first came in during those stunned but strangely intimate and innocent days when Lou Gehrig was still a baseball player whose life and death had nothing whatsoever to do with me. We started out by reading all the available books and literature on the subject and by trying to imagine what it would be like. No matter how many books we read though, we weren't really prepared. Nobody ever is.

In our naivete, we didn't nearly grasp the grimly inexorable way in which my limbs would be deprived of all usefulness; how they would gradually give up the ghost while still apparently attached to what passes for a living, breathing body. We reassured each other, saying that we understood and that it would be all right. We were in love and we would get through it together somehow. But now, as my ruined body lies virtually helpless on a rail-lined hospital bed or sits trapped as a strapped-in prisoner in this damnable chair, my mind still roams free.

In my imagination I am once again a carefree child, clambering over the dusty, ocotillo-punctuated hills of my Arizona desert youth, leaping off rough burgundy chunks of long dead lava, or wading in the murky depths of some slime-bottomed, polliwog-teeming pond. That's part of the irony of it all. The body perishes but the mind persists, as though the stillness of the one somehow drives the other further and further into frantic hyperactivity.

In the beginning I thought that having time on my hands would be an unheard-of luxury, that I would find solace in doing some long-delayed reading or maybe in listening to books on tape. But that whole idea was an outright lie, a cruel hoax. Time is now my enemy—there is far too much of it—and I no longer have any patience for other people's words. As for my own words, the laborious process of typing them out, one arduous letter at a time, using the computer and my one big toe, takes too long. Far too long.

As I said, Ted and I talked about it all in the beginning. Now I can't talk anymore, and he barely does. At the onset, we both thought we were being very straightforward. And honest. And brave. Ted promised me then that he would gather up a cache of pills—enough to do the job—and that he would put them in a safe place so I would have them "when the time comes." That's how we always put it back then. "When the time comes."

It sounds now as though we more or less expected a timer

to go off somewhere in the vast universe announcing that I was ready for the next step. Like a school bell ringing in an almost empty corridor, or like the stove-top timer that used to announce, with an annoying, noisy buzz, that it was time to take the cookies or the loaves of bread or the pumpkin pies out of the oven. Come to think of it, there's not that much baking going on in our house these days. I don't believe I've heard that buzzer sound once during the last two years. I don't suppose I'll ever hear it again.

But getting back to Ted and me, between the two of us, we never actually spoke about death or dying. Those words were far too blatant. Too blunt. Too coarse. They were always there between us—assumed but unacknowledged—like the stifling but unspeakable odor of a first-date fart. Except Ted and I weren't on a first-date basis anymore, not by a long shot. We have three grown children between us and two grandkids. We've barely seen them—the grandchildren, I mean—and I sometimes wonder if they'll even remember me when they're grown. Probably not. Maybe that's just as well.

The problem is the time for decisive action came and went. The bell rang and we did nothing. Ted probably still has that deadly assortment of pills, squirreled away somewhere out of sight if not out of mind, but they're useless to me now—useless to both of us. I can no longer swallow. If he gave them to me now—if he mashed them up in a selfless act of love and somehow mixed them into the gray gruel that flows through my feeding tube, the authorities would have him up on murder charges so fast it would make his head swim.

At the time we were discussing the pills, back when we both still believed them to be our option of last resort, I guess we both thought they would be a blessing for me, an escape that would allow me to dodge the worst of what was coming. I know now, that isn't true, either. At this moment, the pills would help me and I would welcome them, but Ted's the one who really needs them. Not for him to take himself, of course, but for me. He needs to be set free of me and of everything that goes with me—of all the unrelenting labor and responsibility. And of the awful sores. But most of all, of the smells.

They say you can't smell yourself, but that's not true. I wake up sometimes in the middle of the night with my heart pounding in my chest and feeling as though I'm drowning. When I come to my senses and can finally breathe again, the first thing I notice is the odor. *What is it?* I wonder. *Is something rotten? What can it be?* Eventually I realize that what I'm smelling is me. I can't get away from that appalling stench, and neither can Ted. There's no perfume strong enough to disguise it or to cover it up, and there's no escape from it, either.

Did I mention before that I am writing this with my big toe? Poor, patient, loving Ted never said a word about how much it cost to rig this keyboard so I could use it with my one good foot, but it does take forever, tapping out one paltry letter at a time. In the good old days, I used to be a touch typist. Sometimes, in my dreams, my fingers still fly over the keyboard. The letters appear on the screen seemingly by magic, almost as fast as I can think them.

It's a wonderful dream when it happens. It reminds me of one I used to have when I was a child—a dream about running side by side with a guy named Jim Thorpe. He would smile down at me encouragingly and say, "Come on, kid. You can do it. We'll run fast enough to catch the wind."

Moving fingers. Moving legs. Catching the wind. They're all just dreams now. Figments of my imagination. Pieces of a long-lost if not forgotten past.

But where was I? Oh, I remember, Ted—poor Ted. Sometimes I feel more sorry for him than I do for me. Back in the old days, when sticky murder plots still leaked out through my fingers as easily as a slender thread of spun-glass Karo Syrup flows out of its crystal clear bottle, I could have told him how to do it. I probably could even have given him some pointers about how to get away with it. But Ted's beyond that now. I can no longer swallow, and he's too worn out with taking care of me to think about doing anything else.

I've been busy dying, and so has he. I don't think he even has enough strength left over to consider how life will be for him once all this is over; once I'm gone and he no longer has to spend every waking moment worrying about me—worrying and taking care.

I started writing this weeks ago, whenever Ted was out of the room and unable to see what I was doing. Now's the time to finish it.

It's our wedding anniversary today—our thirty-fifth. Yesterday, just as I asked, he brought me here to the same place we came years ago on our wedding night. We were both beginning teachers then, with matching first-year contracts in Bullhead City. It was semester break, and we had been on our way to the Grand Canyon. We had honeymoon reservations in Bright Angel Lodge, but we never made it there. A sudden late January blizzard closed roads all across northern Arizona and New Mexico. We spent both days of our two-day honeymoon stranded in a godforsaken place called Kingman.

I think we must have rented one of the last rooms left in town. We spent the whole time in an upstairs room in this same motel, although now there's a different name on the sign out front. Tonight we're in a downstairs, wheelchair-accessible room. On our wedding night, we had a glorious dinner in the dining room—prime rib and baked potatoes, followed by baked Alaska. We spent the rest of the evening in the bar dancing to a three-piece country combo.

It wasn't until we went upstairs to bed that we discovered how close our room was to the railroad tracks. Freight trains came rumbling past at least three times overnight and woke us up. Each time that happened we made love. It was wonderful.

Things are different now. The trains still run, but making love is out of the question. The motel is a little rundown. No band in the bar. I couldn't eat the food, of course, but Ted said it wasn't all that good anyway, certainly not as good as he remembered. After dinner, he asked me what I wanted to do. He offered to put me to bed and turn on the TV. He was being so nice about it—so good and patient and loving— that it took a while for me to pick the necessary fight. It's hell starting a fight when you have to squeeze the ugly words out through your body one impatient letter at a time.

GO AWAY, I told him. LEAVE ME ALONE. He read the words I'd written on the screen, but even then he was still willing to get me ready for bed before he went out. I told him, NO. JUST LEAVE. Finally he did.

He must be mad or hurt or maybe both, because he's been gone for at least two hours now. That's longer than he's ever left me alone before. And that's exactly what I've needed— time alone.

The wheelchair runs on commands from the same keyboard I'm typing this on. G is for GO and S for STOP. This is a handicapped room, so the door has a handle rather than a knob. After half an hour of terrible struggle, I've finally managed to pull it open.

The air outside is cold as I sit here drenched in sweat with the door wide open and with the wind whistling in. I know timing is everything. Last night I stayed awake all night and clocked the trains. The next one is due in twenty minutes.

The track is just a little more than a block away. If I go too soon, someone might see me at the crossing and try to pull me out of the way. If I arrive too late, I'll miss it—miss my only chance. My last chance.

I've come as far as I want to down this miserable road. I don't want to travel any farther—not for me and, even more so, not for Ted.

It can't be too much longer now. I wish I could leave the computer here in the room and out of harm's way, but it's attached to the chair and so the machine has no choice. Whither I go, it must go too—sort of like Ruth and her mother-in-law.

It's cold now. Dreadfully cold. And the light blanket Ted draped over my legs when we were inside isn't nearly enough out here in the freezing night air.

Back when we were here before, the whole building shook each time a train came through town. That was what woke us up—the shaking. I'm shaking now. I don't know if it's because I'm cold or if it's because the train is finally coming. If it is the train, it's still so far up the track that I can't see the headlight. But it will have to come soon, looming up over me out of the darkness, turning night to day. And, like Philemon's chrysanthemum, changing my life—or what passes for it anyway—into something else entirely.

Thank you, Ted. Thank you for everything, and especially for the flash. I love . . .

_HELL

Charles Knief

Charles Knief is best known as the author of the Honolulu-based mystery series featuring private eye John Caine. His first novel, *Diamond Head,* won the St. Martin's Press contest for best private eye novel in 1995 and is being made into a motion picture. He and his wife divide their time between Hawaii and Irvine, California.

Billy came over the rise, the windstream blowing around the Mustang's windshield as warm and liquid as spit. Lights glowed in the little valley ahead, a desert crossroads settlement topped by a towering yellow sign, a SHELL sign with its s burned out, giving the town an unexpected moniker.

Static crackled on the radio, the weak country station blocked by the hill. There had been no news of it. The cops he'd seen did not seem to be looking for him. He wouldn't know until he reported in, and he had to report in. Failing to do so would point the finger directly at him. He might as well stop at the next town and turn himself in.

He glanced at the dashboard. Gas was low. His eyes were full of grit; he'd been on the road some nineteen hours.

Maybe Hell had a bed where he could crap out for a while. He didn't have to report until Tuesday. Today was . . . what? Saturday? No, Sunday! The dashboard clock confirmed it. Sunday morning. Two A.M. Two days, more or less, and then back to the leash and off to the war.

Below the gasoline sign another said, ESSEX CAFÉ, OPEN 25 HOURS, 8 DAYS A WEEK. Billy slowed and all but coasted off the highway pavement through sparse gravel to the gas pump. A thin, bony young man, burned nearly black by the sun, his shock of hair bone-white, shuffled through the café's screen door.

"Fill 'er up?"

"Leaded premium."

"Hell of a ride," said the boy, grinning. "Pop the hood, okay? I'll check your fluids."

"Sure."

Inside, the heat seemed trapped, pressurized by the enclosure, making the small café feel even smaller. Two marines, wearing Levi's and white sidewall haircuts, looked up as he entered. They studied and dismissed him. His haircut betrayed him as one of theirs. Off-duty, they wanted to keep company with others unlike their own. Two hippies wearing tie-dye, sunglasses, and long greasy bangs camped at a corner booth. One sat cross-legged on the bench seat, four empty beer bottles on the table in front of him, working hard at being cool. He smoked a hand-rolled cigarette and eyed the stranger from behind the darkened lenses, categorized him as military and no threat and went back to his pose.

If only he knew.

Billy took a place at the counter.

"Welcome, soldier. Coffee?" The waitress, a plump red-headed woman in her forties, moved slowly, as if her feet hurt and she didn't dare stress them any more than she had to. Her name tag read ROSE.

"Please." He rubbed his eyes, feeling the grit.

"Up kinda late, aren't you?"

"Been driving."

"You're a serviceman. You a marine?"

"Army."

"Got a son in the army. He's been to Vietnam and now he's back in Carolina."

"Bragg?"

"That's right." Rose seemed to brighten when she spoke of her son.

"I'm glad he's home."

"Thank you. So am I."

She poured his coffee and smiled at him. "That's on the house. How about some pie?"

"I'll pay." Billy didn't feel like being mothered. He didn't want human contact of any kind.

"Suit yourself," she said, visibly hurt, and went back to her side work.

Vietnam. The defining event of his generation, he had once heard someone say on television. He had no idea what that meant, but he liked the phrase. Vietnam. He'd been there, too. Was on his way back of his own accord, had volunteered for his second tour of duty to hurry up his time in the army. Once he finished this tour he'd be out for good, six months early. He was not afraid of dying. Not now. He was still afraid of being legless, or losing his balls, or becoming blind. But everyone shared those fears. Everybody was terrified of losing a piece of themselves more than they were their lives.

He thought about the gas sign overhead. Hell. Now he'd been to both places. He looked around, studying the room. Not like the war. Still, his hands shook as he brought the cup to his lips. Maybe this was worse, he thought, deciding it was so.

The boy came in and gave him his keys and a receipt for five dollars and forty-seven cents. "That's a big engine," said the boy, smiling shyly. "She sure is beautiful."

"Thanks." Billy gave the kid a quarter.

"Thank you. You can pay for the gas at the register on your way out."

He nodded. And turned back to the counter.

"I parked it right in front, there by the window."

"Thanks." Billy did not turn around.

The boy shrugged and went away.

Companionship was not something Billy craved at the moment. He wondered if he ever would again.

"I want you to kill my husband," she had told him. Just like that. They'd been in bed at the Sooner Motel north of town, covered in nothing but sweat, the sheets and blankets thrown on the floor, the air conditioning turned up high but not cutting the heat and humidity. "You're leaving this morning. He's coming home tonight at ten. You'll be long gone, on the road. Everybody thinks you're already gone."

"What?" He couldn't believe she was asking him to kill the man. The son of a bitch beat her, Billy knew that. He was a mean bastard, even when he wasn't drunk. And while drinking, his abuse was legendary. He whored around whenever he got the chance. And there were rumors that he was the biggest wholesaler of weed in three Oklahoma counties. But killing him?

"They won't catch you. Nobody knows about us. He's got real enemies. Those Mexicans he stiffed for the pot last month, when he stole their load and threatened to jail them if they complained. They swore they'd kill him. People know that. It got around fast. I'll say there were two of them. Mexicans, one big and one small. They killed him. Shot him on the toilet. Then they left."

"You got this all worked out, don't you?"

She kissed his belly, then lower. In spite of his recent exertions he found his erection growing. She took him fully into his mouth, working him like a piston, her fingers playing lightly on the tactile nerve endings of his scrotum. He lay back and enjoyed the experience.

She brought him to the brink, then took her mouth away, clamping her fist around the base of his member.

"You want it?"

"Yes," he managed.

She put her mouth back on him, brought him nearly to eruption, then clamped down on him again and repeated the question. "You want it?"

"Yes."

"You want it bad?"

"Yes!"

"Will you kill him?"

"No."

"For me?"

"No." He almost strangled on the effort of speech, his brain consumed with more urgent needs.

She went back to work on him until she couldn't stop him anymore and he felt as if his lower body detonated. The orgasm went on and on as she continued working him. When the pain came, replacing the ecstasy, he waved her off, but still she kept on. He had to pull her hands from his tender tissues. She struggled and he forced her over onto her back, pinning her with his lower body, his hands on her wrists. They lay on the sweat-soaked mattress, mimicking the position they had earlier applied to what he thought of as more sympathetic pursuits.

"You like that?"

"No." He began to ease off of her, and she reached for his hair and he had to restrain her again.

"You like this, don't you. Admit it. You like dominating me."

"I don't like you pulling my hair."

"You don't have much."

"You going to behave yourself?"

"Are you brave enough to take the chance?"

Billy shook his head. Twelve years older than he, Debra dominated him in all things, but nowhere like the bedroom. They had met two months before and, in the military family society, where no one had secrets from anyone else, where everything you do is everybody else's business, they'd had a hot, quick romance under absolutely secret conditions.

Her husband, a military police sergeant, was known as a brute, as well as corrupt. Officers and enlisted alike steered clear of him, knowing that he had a power that went far beyond his office, and that rank made no difference when he wanted something or wanted someone to suffer. He owned the fort and had the undisputed run of it.

Billy had discovered Debra's car with a flat tire on a country road twenty miles from town. He stopped to help her and, after he had changed the tire and shared a couple of friendly drinks with her in a nearby tavern, he found himself in a hot pillow motel some twenty miles the other direction, flat on his back in the middle of a queen-size, being ridden like a bronco.

She liked him, she said. He liked the sex, the sight of her naked body, all soft curves and white skin, the cast of freckles across her generous chest, the pale curls at the fork of her legs, not quite hiding her sex. She excited him. Everything about her excited him. He knew he was in mortal danger if caught with her, even if a hint of the relationship surfaced, but that only added to the excitement. Sneaking away, coordinating their actions, their rendezvous as calculated as a military maneuver, he liked all that, too. He felt that he'd traveled a long way from the boy who'd attended the Fairfield Methodist Church and had sung in the choir most Sundays. More than the war, he now felt like a real man because a grown woman loved him.

"If I let you up, will you behave?"

She moved under him, rubbing her sex against his flaccid member. It hurt and he tried moving away, but she told him, "No," the breathless way she did when she was working toward her final orgasm, so he lay there and let her grind against him until she satisfied herself. He held her down until she finished, feeling superfluous to the process, and rolled off of her, watching her breasts rise and fall.

"I'm going to miss you," she said, staring at the ceiling.

"Yeah," he said, wondering where he would ever meet a woman like this again, and whether it would be good or bad if he did. Part of him still sang in the choir.

"I mean it, Billy. I have to be rid of him. You can do it. You can free me from this."

He thought he understood what she meant, but he didn't dare ask her anything.

"I got a twenty-two I bought at the fort from a soldier that went to Germany. He bought it from a guy that got killed in Nam. It wasn't registered to anybody. No way it can be traced here. Wear gloves. Wait until he comes home. He always spends half an hour on the toilet as soon as he gets home. He reads the paper, or something, I don't know. Open the door, shoot him sitting there, go out the door, down the alley, and you're gone. You already left, remember? No one will hear the shots. Not with a twenty-two. I come home later, find the body, call the neighbors, call the cops."

"No."

"I've got some money. It'll help you get over whatever you're going through."

"How much?"

"There's enough."

"How much, Debra?"

"Almost ten thousand dollars. All cash. Twenties and fifties, mostly. It's his drug money. He doesn't think I know where it is, but I found it."

Billy thought about it. She may have found much more, but it wasn't any of his business, and it was more than enough—about the same as his life insurance policy.

Ten thousand dollars would do wonders for him.

"Do you have the gun?"

She smiled, leaned over and kissed him, a long, deep kiss. The choir boy in him flinched. "Oh, sorry, sugar. I forgot to brush my *teeth*," she said, still smiling. "The *things* you have to put up with. Won't you be *glad* to be gone?" She had changed into a Southern belle in front of him, lacking only the bonnet, and the rest of the outfit. She crawled over him and ransacked her purse. Finding what she wanted, she bounced back, holding a wrinkled paper bag. The way she held it he could tell it had weight.

"I bought this a year ago, waiting for my Galahad to rescue me. I hid it under the cleaning supplies. He never looks there." She opened the bag and took out a small-framed revolver, a single-action cowboy gun in .22 Long Rifle, scaled down to match the diminutive caliber. She handed it to him.

"Looks clean," he said, inspecting the six-shooter. It wasn't much of a weapon. Hardly more than a toy. "Will it fire?"

"I don't know."

"Would be a bad time to find out it doesn't, standing there, aiming at him over the sports section. There's just no way to explain something like that."

"I got bullets." She reached into the bag and brought out a fist full of tiny brass cartridges.

"You don't know if these work, do you?" He picked then from her hand and examined them. They were ancient. Verdigris covered them. "How old are these?"

"If you don't *want* to do it, just say so! You don't have to be so hateful!" She rolled away from him, presenting him with a perfect view of her bottom. He admired her for a while, knowing this would be the last time he would see that bottom in this particular state of repose and abandon.

"I just wanted to know if the gun will work when it's supposed to," Billy said. "*You* want to explain it to him?"

She rolled back over. "Okay," she said, her voice syrupy sweet. "I'm sorry. I'm just really nervous."

"I'll take the gun out to the country and try it. I can't buy ammo for it because somebody might remember me."

"I'll buy some—"

"That would not be so smart."

"Yes," she considered it. "You're right."

"There are five cartridges here. I'll test one, maybe two. If I can find a gas station that sells Long Rifles I might buy a new box, but only if I don't feel guilty."

"You won't be guilty of anything. You're saving me."

"And I need the ten thousand dollars now."

She stared at him, blinking her eyes. "You mean you don't trust me?" The vicious belle had returned.

"Honey, you and I are planning to murder your husband. Of course I don't trust you."

She laughed. "I thought you'd say something like that!" She bounced out of bed and retrieved her purse, opened it and tossed the loose money to him, all cash, fifties and hundreds, spilling it onto the sheets. "You want to count it? I'll lie down and you can count it on my tummy."

He shook his head. "Not now, Debra. There's only one thing I can concentrate on now."

She kissed his cheek. "I understand. Go do what you have

to do and come to the house at ten fifteen. If the Plymouth is in the driveway and the porch light is on come around back. The door will be open."

She reached down and gave his penis a yank. It startled him.

"Just for luck," she said, giggling.

"Jesus Christ!" said the choir boy.

Billy hiked two miles from the highway before he even thought about taking the revolver from the bag. He wanted to be out of sight and sound of any traffic. After three hills, in a little canyon filled with sagebrush and boulders, he decided that he had found the place he sought.

He dug down into the bag and came up with six rounds, not five, discovering an errant round tucked inside a paper wrinkle. They were tiny cartridges, easily misplaced.

He found a deformed rusty can and set it on a rock and strode four measured paces from the can. At two or three feet he didn't think he would miss the man, but it never hurt to know if the piece could hit its mark if it had to. The extra round helped, too. He could fire twice, if necessary, and not have to worry about running out of ammunition when it counted.

That had been a reoccurring nightmare for him in the war. His gun jammed or gone empty, gooks with fixed bayonets running at him through the barrier, the night sweats hitting him hard. It never happened because he habitually took over four hundred rounds for his rifle whenever he ventured beyond the wire, but the dream came back night after night, the war ruining his dreams as it made desolate his days.

Billy cocked the little revolver, lined up the sights on the lopsided can, gradually increasing the pressure on the trigger until the piece fired. The can leaped into the air.

He walked over and examined the target. The bullet had drilled a neat round hole through the center of the can.

He thought about another practice shot and decided against it. You never could tell. The man was so big he might need the five remaining rounds. Besides, one pistol shot out here could be discounted if other ears heard it. With two, someone might come to investigate. He did not want to be caught with a gun in his hand on the day Debra's husband was shot dead. If that happened, he'd just take the money and run.

But he couldn't do that, either. She would do something. Of that he was certain. She would accuse him of theft or rape or whatever she had a mind to. And they would bring him back to the tender mercies of her husband. If he had the money on him and he was caught it would be difficult to explain. First lieutenants didn't have that kind of cash money. Not law-abiding ones, anyway.

What would he do with the cash? He couldn't take it to Nam. It was too bulky to carry, and he wouldn't be able to guard it all the time. He couldn't mail it home. His mother would open the package, no matter what he wrote instructing her not to. And once she did, she would know that her dire warnings of life in the Army had come true, and she would do something with the money to provide penance. She might donate it to the Fairfield Methodist Church. And take the tax deduction. He shuddered. He would not send it home.

He thought of a bank box but rejected that, too. He didn't trust banks. His father had lost almost a thousand dollars in the Great Depression, and he railed against the pin-stripe-suited bastards for the rest of his life.

The solution came to him suddenly, like an Oklahoma sunrise. He would bury it, go back to town, buy a plastic container, one of those airtight things that preserved bread, and bury it out here in the woods. He'd have to find a high place that was not a part of a watershed so it wouldn't be exposed by run off. If he did not return from Vietnam it would be just one more treasure buried in the wasteland. If he did come back he would dig it up and use it to start his new life. If something went wrong with the hit there would be no way to tie him to the money. No matter what she said.

The doing of it took the rest of the afternoon. He chose an anonymous grocery store on the outskirts of the fort where he was just another faceless soldier standing in line among others of his kind. He paid cash. At another store he bought a cheap garden spade, a small one he could easily dispose of later and could conceal during his walk into the wilderness with the money. A man with a shovel going for a hike in the woods can only have one of two purposes: He was burying something or digging it up.

He chose an innocuous jumble of boulders that could charitably be called a mountain if one had a Romantic streak, not that there were any mountains in Oklahoma. It was surrounded by such tortured and rugged wasteland not even cattle or sheep grazed there. It would not be turned into a shopping mall or a tract of crackerbox houses in the year of his absence. Barring fell circumstance, the cash would wait for him, a faithful companion in a world of betrayal.

A sandy spot beneath a boulder, an abandoned coyote den, was his choice for the money's resting place. Someone had used the tiny shelter as a fireplace sometime in the distant past, blackening the granite above. He moved the stone fire ring and dug down two feet before hitting solid rock. The depth pleased him and he placed the Tupperware into the hole and refilled it, compacting the sand as best he could with his hands and feet. Finally, he replaced the stones as he had found them and burned the bags and receipts in a smokeless fire, leaving the ashes to scatter in the wind.

When he finished, satisfied that nothing on the surface betrayed the contents buried below, he stood and triangulated the surrounding terrain so he could locate the stash. He lined up monuments that would lead him back to his treasure. He didn't move until he was certain he could find his way back to this place.

"You want a fill-up?" The query came abruptly, shaking him from his reverie. When he looked up, the waitress's face was neutral and tired. She didn't mother him, his link with the distant son no longer a bond.

"Sure," he said, pushing the cup toward her.

She filled it and left him alone again.

The money wasn't a problem. Other worries blossomed.

Had he left fingerprints? He'd wiped the gun and cleaned the verdigris from the old ammunition, making certain he left nothing of himself there. He wore his leather driving gloves while handling the revolver, the thin supple leather a gift from his mother two Christmases before. The gloves had been discarded in a Flagstaff trash dumpster after an argument between his conscience and his apprehension, a running battle that spanned four states. He buried his clothing just across the Texas line. Everything. Even his shoes and socks. Nothing of his survived the shedding of his deed.

He was fairly sure no one saw him leave the residence. No one accosted him as he got into his Mustang four blocks away, parked in a busy shopping center lot. A hot shower at a truck stop between Albuquerque and Gallup washed away the Oklahoma grit, the astringent soap stinging his eyes, cleansing him of everything but the horror.

Billy eased into the house through the rear door. Right on time, as if punctuality made him a better person. The choir boy in him had some second thoughts.

"He's here! Be quiet!" Debra hissed at him like a viper, inviting him to take a bite from the apple. Her presence in the darkened kitchen shook him, nearly made him turn and run.

She turned on the light.

Her left eye was bruised and swollen. She had a lump on her forehead. A ragged cut ran down her right cheek, surrounded by a deep bruised cameo of a fist. The brute had beaten her.

"He's really pissed," she explained. "He had a bad day."

Not as bad as it was going to be, he thought.

"Do you have the gun?"

He nodded.

"Does it work?"

He nodded again.

"You tried it out?"

"It fired." He had decided that she did not need to know the details. He felt uncomfortable talking about it.

"Did you buy more bullets?"

"No. Got enough."

"Shoot him. Empty the gun. Look what he did to me!" She raised her voice above a whisper.

He shushed her, but it was too late.

"Debbie! Who're you talking to?" The voice came from behind a closed door in the little hallway.

"Nobody, Pete. I'm just talking to myself."

"Cut it out! You know that drives me ape shit!"

"Okay, Pete."

"Guy can't take a crap in peace."

"I'm sorry, honey."

"I said shut up!"

She looked at Billy and mouthed the word "See?" in an exaggerated mime.

He nodded, taking the revolver from his waistband and heading for the bathroom. She backed away, then disappeared into the living room.

He tried the bathroom knob just as a phlegmy cough exploded on the other side of the door. Startled, he jumped back, collected his wits, cocked the revolver, and twisted the knob. It rattled, but did not turn. It was locked.

"God damn it! What now? Fuck!" He heard movement in the bathroom from behind the door. The toilet flushed.

He stood outside the door, his heart pounding, knowing what a stupid thing it was to be here, wondering why he'd agreed to this in the first place.

The door wrenched open and Billy found himself facing a big florid man in blue and white boxer shorts and undershirt, holding a newspaper in one hand and a bottle of beer in the other. "Who the fuck are you?" growled the man.

He shot the man in the chest.

The man looked down at where he'd been struck by the bullet. He raised his gaze back to Billy and charged.

He shot the man again, backed away, cocked the revolver and shot him a third time.

It was one of his nightmares. He kept firing and the brute kept coming, moving in slow motion, but still advancing, meaty, hairy arms reaching for him. Billy backed away, putting all three shots right into the man's heart, or where it was supposed to be. Seeing no change in the man, he aimed carefully and put the forth round into his left eye, firing from less than a foot from the angry orb.

The man dropped to his knees, still reaching, blood leaking. He stared curiously at his killer from his one good eye for a heartbeat and then toppled over and lay still.

Billy cocked the revolver and pointed it at the man's head, refusing to abandon the target.

"Is he dead?"

He looked carefully. "If not, he will be soon enough."

Debra stood behind him, blocking out the light from the kitchen. "Well, is he or isn't he?"

"As dead as it gets." He kept the gun trained on the big man, unsure if the weapon had done its job.

"Good."

Something about the way she said the word made him turn around.

Sunlight streaming through the window woke him. It took some time to come fully awake and stretch the cobwebs from his body. They had let him sleep at the counter. Rose had been replaced by a young Indian girl with a ready smile and generous hips. He stared back at her smile and watched it fade. She turned away.

I'm a real shit, he thought. She did nothing to me. He tried to feel shame, but nothing he did could add to the load he already carried.

What was today? Still Sunday? Outside the window his Mustang brooded on the gravel, parked beside the white-painted rock curb. The blond-haired boy had vanished, too. Overhead, the blue skies were stainless of clouds as far as the eye could see.

Two days to get to San Francisco. No problem. It was a trip he'd wanted to take ever since he'd seen George Maharis and Marty Milner in their Corvette on the TV. Take Route 66 all the way to LA and then follow Pacific Coast Highway up the coast to the Golden Gate Bridge. He would report in with time to spare. He'd sell the car in Frisco. He had no use for it and was not attached to objects the way some folks were.

He got up and paid for the gas and coffee and left a five-dollar tip for Rose and the Indian girl. It was extravagant, he knew, but he felt some appeasement necessary. If they wouldn't grant it, perhaps the gods might.

He climbed into the driver's seat, wincing at the heat already baking the leather. The engine coughed once and then

turned over in a throaty roar. It gave him pleasure to hear the
big mill power up and down the scale. When it had warmed
to suit him, he spun the big rear tires and shot from the parking lot, gravel slapping the concrete block walls of the café
like buckshot.

The narrow ribbon of asphalt rode the terrain like a roller
coaster. His stomach fell with each descent. He liked that,
reminding him how it was as a child when he stood in the
rear seat of his father's sedan as they drove down the steep
Fairfield hills.

She held a .45 automatic in both hands, aiming it at his head.

BLAM!

The big bullet missed him by a hair, plowing on through
the wall beyond. His left ear went deaf.

He heard her swear and bang on the pistol with her fist as
he shot her. Her eyes widened and she put her hand to her
throat, trying to staunch the bright arterial blood pumping a
pulsing stream. He caught the .45 as she dropped it, deftly
turned her around, cleared the jammed round, placed the big
muzzle against the bloody blue hole already made by the .22
and pulled the trigger. She collapsed.

Still moving automatically, not thinking, ears ringing,
Billy put the .22 into her hand and dropped the .45 onto the
asbestos tile next to the brute's corpse. Not missing a beat,
he went out the back, climbed over the fence and moved
quietly down the alley before the neighbors had time to
come awake and investigate, to differentiate between
dreams and reality and decided to call the police. It wasn't
until he reached the shopping center that he heard the sirens
in the distance.

He had to wait until a cop going Code Three passed before he could pull out of the lot. In two minutes he was on
the interstate, heading toward the Texas panhandle.

•   •   •

A few miles down the road Billy remembered that he was hungry. He did not want to go back so he vowed to stop at the first place he came to that served hot breakfast.

But for her shooting skills and the unaccounted jamming of the pistol, he would have been her perfect alibi. She would have been the hero wife who grabbed a gun and administered quick Oklahoma justice, killing the killer on the spot. And she would have been free from both of them. Probably thought he'd have the money on him.

He shivered in the heat like the shimmering Mojave reflections on the road ahead. It had been a close thing.

A highway sign, partially blocked by a grove of pale spindly trees, proclaimed that Amboy was twenty-six miles ahead. Beyond that was Barstow. Billy thought he might stop there and have breakfast. Maybe call his mother. Let her know he was all right, that the Army had not completely ruined him.

As he came over another one of those rolling hills, flashing red lights and a siren ambushed him from behind. A jolt of ice-cold adrenaline flowed down his back and settled in his groin. His foot automatically tapped the brakes, his leg acting independently of his brain. He studied the rearview mirror. The cop was hot on his bumper, a highway patrolman wearing mirrored sunglasses stared at him, the mouth a hard line.

Was there anything that could tie him to the killings? His mind raced, reviewing everything, a useless endeavor. Everything that could have been done had been done. There was nothing he could do now but play it out.

Billy pulled over.

The highway patrolman parked his cruiser behind him on the shoulder and waited, doing something Billy could not see through the rearview. He didn't want to turn around and look, so Billy sat behind the wheel, his arms across the seat back, hands in sight, letting the California sun wash across his face. It felt hotter when the car was parked. He wished he had his gloves. That steering wheel was going to be a son of a bitch to hang onto if he sat here too long.

The cop got out of the patrol car and strolled his way.

Billy looked up when the cop stood beside his door. "Good morning, sir."

"Can I see your driver's license and registration?"

Billy slowly reached into his glove compartment and pulled out the envelope with the insurance and other papers that made his car legal on base. He sorted through the thick wad of officialdom until he found the current registration and handed that over. In his pocket he found his wallet and took out the Texas driver's license that had expired two months before. He handed that to the patrolman, too, hoping it would not be a problem. The way they'd explained it to him, soldiers on active duty had some kind of exemption until they got home.

"You got a military ID?"

"Yes, sir." Billy dug back into his wallet, took out the pink card with his shaved head and stark young face staring back at him. His mother hated the photo, taken during his first few days in officer's training. It made him look evil, she said. In a flash of insight, he came up with the manila envelope containing his orders and passed that over with the ID card.

The cop glanced at the card but did not bother to open the envelope. "Thought so," he said, handing everything back. "You on your way to Nam, I wouldn't be in such a hurry. Clocked you at seventy-six back there. This is a muscle car, but you can't go that fast without asking for trouble."

"You gonna give me a ticket?"

"You want one?"

"No, sir."

"Just be careful. You're not in Texas, anymore. Not every cop out here's been to a war. Or has a son serving in one right now. Just slow it down a little, okay?"

"Yes, sir."

The cop patted his shoulder. "You're down for a warning, soldier. Take it slow. You're in no hurry to get where you're going. It'll still be there. You want to live, don't you?" The cop strolled back to his cruiser.

Billy looked back for traffic and rolled off the sandy berm onto the asphalt. Keeping the cop in sight, he took the Mustang up to sixty-five and kept it there, resisting the urges.

The cop had posed the question. Did he want to live? That was easy. Damn right! Billy could think of thousands of reasons why.

He would, too. The war could be lethal, but Billy felt protected. He'd been there before, he'd make it through again. He knew how to stay alive and he felt lucky.

His luck continued to run. Billy knew when that happened all you can do is run with it. It would run out soon enough. He prayed that it would keep on running for at least a year.

He would be back. In a year he'd drive this same road, stop in Essex, get some gas, and overtip Rose and that Indian girl again. Then he'd continue. Head east until he found his mountain with the granite rocks that sheltered his treasure.

He'd be back, all right. Nothing anybody could do could stop him.

If it all continued going so well.

First Lieutenant William Mitchell, of Fairfield, Texas, died as a result of enemy action last week. A graduate of Fairfield High School and Missouri State University, Mitchell was on active duty with the United States

Army at the time of his death. He is survived by his
mother, Beatrice, and his sister, Maryelizabeth Parker.
Graveside services will be held at the family plot at
Mount Hope Cemetery. The Reverend Milo Farnsworth,
of the Fairfield Methodist Church, will officiate.
Mitchell is remembered as the quarterback of the 1962
championship Fairfield High football team. He is the
second Fairfield man to die in action in 1969. He was
nearing the end of his second tour of duty in South Vietnam when he suffered his fatal wounds.

Page A-3, *Fairfield Post Gazette*, July 9, 1969

BLUE TIME

Earlene Fowler

EARLENE FOWLER is a native Californian who was raised by a Southern mother and Western father. She has been married twenty-five years to her high school sweetheart and owns twenty pairs of cowboy boots. She is the author of the Benni Harper mystery series.

Christmas Eve, Em thought, is a good time to flee. The season brought to mind the stories she remembered from early in her life, age ten or so. Mama was still alive then and they'd gone to a Christmas Eve service at the Baptist church next door to Dart's Liquors and Sundries where Mama bought her vodka and on occasion, when she was feeling generous, Slim Jims and Abba Zabbas for Em and Jessie. Jessie, being only six, had a hard time with the Abba Zabbas, but was stubborn even then, refusing to give in and eat something softer like a Three Musketeers. The yellow and black checkered wrapping of the taffy candy tempted her beyond reason. Even then Jessie didn't know what was good for her. At the service Mama was sober and she dressed in a red silk dress that set off her shiny black hair, as shiny, Em would recall when she stood over Mama's coffin two years later, as one of those black enamel jewelry boxes that Jessie wanted so bad the first time she saw one in K-Mart. The preacher at the Christmas Eve service had talked a lot about fleeing. He made the innocuous holiday of red-suited Santas and glowy-nosed reindeer seem fraught with danger and intrigue. Em remembered his words, "Arise, and take the young child and his mother, and flee into Egypt, and be thou there until I bring thee word: for Herod will seek the young child to destroy him."

Actually, she hadn't remembered them so exactly. She'd only remembered the words "flee" and "destroy." The verse was quoted, word-for-King-James-word, by Marisol Felicia De La Torre, her coworker at Pang's Commercial Cleaning Service and at last count, her only friend. At thirty-eight Marisol had hips and arms so solid and certain they seemed formed especially to jiggle fussy babies and rescue skinny, desperate white girls. She was one of those strong and sure born-again Catholics, the kind who pray holding their hands high in the air, palms out, like they were small children expecting to be picked up by some wonderful, loving Somebody.

Em had long since realized there was nobody to pick her up. She'd done the picking up for as long as she could remember. Em relayed her doubts to Marisol often though she attended evening Mass with her friend every week, claiming she only went because she liked the mysterious smell of the burning candles and the peace she saw etched on the old Spanish women's faces.

"Oh, *chiquita*," Marisol would say as they cleaned the executive bathrooms of the Santa Ana office building assigned to their swing shift crew. "You are too young to be so cynical of God." She sprayed Lysol on the rim of the urinal, curling her full, red lips in an Elvis Presley sneer. "Bad shots, these *big* shots." She pointed her green can at the porcelain throne and gave it one more squirt before wiping it down. Her yellow rubber gloves glistened with water.

"Where was God when I needed Him?" Em would reply. "Where was He in the ten foster homes, the times I begged Him to make it so Jessie and I would be together?"

Marisol would just shake her head and wipe down the wall behind the urinals. "He found you me, didn't He?"

Em was always hard pressed to answer that one since her meeting with Marisol had been a miracle of sorts. She'd been only three days past eighteen with no place to go since foster care ended when you became old enough to vote. The state still had her fourteen-year-old sister, Jessie, whom she hadn't seen in two years. Em's vague plan was to somehow reunite them, though she didn't have a clue how. That rainy April day four years ago she'd ended up in the back pew of Marisol's church in downtown Santa Ana, the area some call "Little Tijuana," because it was the only place open that didn't expect you to buy something. Marisol had been polishing the altar and after prying Em's story out of her, took her home with her, got her a job at Pang's and let her stay in the converted garage in back of her peeling, slat-board house until Em could afford her own place.

"You and Jessie are together now, no?" Marisol pointed out.

"Yes, but it took me four years of fourteen-hour days. I didn't see Him down on his knees helping me scrub toilets so Jessie would have a place to come to when she turned eighteen."

Whenever they had this conversation Marisol would end it with a roll of her eyes and a murmured Spanish prayer. Em knew her bitterness bothered her friend, but also knew Marisol wouldn't hold it against her. Though she didn't voice it, it was understood that Em felt God had forgotten her and Jessie a long time ago.

Em already missed Marisol's unwavering faith even though it had only been a few hours since she and Jessie left. She wished her friend was here beside her, spouting her Spanish homilies, as they rattled along in Em's rusted-out Toyota on this long, lonely stretch of Interstate 40. Jessie dozed in the seat next to her, her black, swollen eye turned toward Em. Every time she saw it, a white-hot rage burned in Em. A rage at Douglas Johnston Rayburn II, the person responsible. The person they were running from this Christmas Eve day.

The water-stained Rand McNally atlas she'd bought for a dollar at the used book sale at the library showed that if a person took a notion, they could drive the interstate clear from where they caught it in Barstow, California, a town a few hours from Santa Ana, across the country through seven states to North Carolina and the Atlantic Ocean coming out near a town called Wilmington. It was such a straight shot she'd barely have to turn the steering wheel. Right now, that seemed as good a plan as any. She'd stared at the atlas for hours last night, planning their escape, Jessie sleeping unaware in the bed they shared in the one-room apartment above Irma's Cut and Curl—*Se Habla Espanol*. She had every town memorized. It hadn't escaped her notice that the nearest destination to Wilmington, North Carolina, was Cape Fear.

She chose Christmas Eve because there was no way Douglas would come looking for Jessie until the day after Christmas. She was not the type of girl, according to him, you brought home to the family in Newport Beach. Sleep with her in the business suites of side-of-the-freeway motels and slap her around occasionally when the pressures of work got too bad, that was fine and dandy. But take the new office receptionist home to Mother and Father for Christmas Day roast duck and champagne? That was definitely not in the plan of Douglas Rayburn II, newest partner in Lobel, Tungsten, Billycock and Rayburn, attorneys at law. But just like in court, he didn't like to lose in bed so when Jessie, at Em's urging, tried to break it off with him, he blackened her eye and told her he'd hunt her down and see her dead before he'd ever let a white trash slut like her leave *him*.

Yes, fleeing on Christmas Eve carrying your life savings of nine hundred thirteen dollars, a Toyota in need of a new carburetor, all your clothes and a few books, was sometimes a person's only viable option. With the holidays, they'd have a two-day head start. Anyone could disappear in forty-eight hours.

"*Vaya con Dios*, Emmalina," Marisol had said only hours ago, her brown, shiny face anxious and sad. "Cleaning the offices without you will be not so much fun." She pressed two worn twenties in Em's hand, her velvet eyes brimming with tears.

"You can't afford this," Em said, trying to shove it back in her friend's closed fist. Marisol had six children under the age of fifteen and a husband on disability.

She hid her hands behind her back. "Remember, *chiquita*, *Dios es más grande que tus problemas*. God is bigger than your problems."

Em clutched the warm, damp bills, determined not to cry, fearing if she did, she'd never stop. "I'll miss you."

It was five o'clock when they came to the small black-and-white road sign that said, "Historic Route 66." On a whim, tired of the whine of the interstate and the constant dodging of the big rigs rattling their old car with every pass, Em turned onto the small highway. She'd loved maps as a child, and travel stories, always wishing she was the person hitchhiking across America or driving the backroads like

John Steinbeck in a homemade camper with a dog named Charlie. Though she'd never seen the old *Route 66* television series, she read books on "The Mother Road."

She knew there were three little towns on this stretch of 66—Ludlow, Amboy, and Essex. The Ludlow Cafe had long since been abandoned, its white stucco surprisingly bare of graffiti. Driving along the two-lane highway, Em could see Interstate 40 in the distance, the colorful cars and trucks like Matchbox toys. It seemed appropriate to be on this old road, this less traveled highway. Interstate 40 was the real road now. The road normal people took. People who knew where they were going.

Fifteen minutes later, Jessie woke up. "What's going on?" she asked, her blackened eye only half open. "Where are we?"

"Just a small detour," Em said. "I'm tired of the freeway. The truckers are crazy trying to speed home for Christmas."

Jessie readjusted her seatbelt and stared out at the long stretch of two-lane highway. "It looks like the moon out here."

Em nodded. In the falling dusk, the dry, mesquite-covered desert did look like another planet.

"I'm hungry," Jessie declared. "We'll never find a place to eat out here. How long is this road?"

"It'll be a while. There's some beef jerky in my purse."

"I don't want any jerky," Jessie said, her voice petulant. "I want a hamburger and french fries. This is boring. Let's go back to the big road."

"Can't now. We're committed."

Jessie gave a dramatic sigh, but didn't try to argue. She knew that Em was the one person whom she couldn't manipulate with her pouting. Though Em was proud of her little sister's striking beauty, she knew better than anyone it was also the thing that landed Jessie in the most trouble.

"I wish I had a camera," Em murmured, gazing out over the moonscape desert. The tans and browns would be difficult to capture in color, but the stark, black shadows of the jagged mountains, the spindly fingers of the matchstick brush, would make dramatic black and white photographs.

"Oh, you and your old pictures," Jessie said, inspecting her green-painted nails. They looked to Em like she'd dipped them in guacamole.

Em didn't answer. Her love for photography, born from a one-semester class in the last of the twelve high schools she'd attended, was something she refused to discuss in any depth even with the person she loved most in the world. It was her secret dream to someday own a good camera, like the one she was allowed to borrow from school, and all the film in the world. She closed her eyes for a brief second, remembering the feel of the second-hand Nikon in her hands. The teacher, old Mr. Dublin, had said she'd shown promise, had let her borrow the camera more times than students were usually allowed. He was a small, slight man with round plastic glasses and jackets with suede elbow patches worn glossy with age. His voice reminded Em of the low, bubbling water fountain in front of the library. She remembered with a quiet pride how he'd praised her work, his gentle hand on her shoulder, her sharp, sad feeling when he removed it. For a moment, she'd felt safe, a feeling that caught her by surprise.

"There's a place," Jessie said as they came to the small town of Amboy. *Small* was the operative word. Roy's Cafe sat next to a row of neat white cabins. When they pulled in front of the cafe, an old man was turning the sign to closed. He gave them an apologetic shrug and turned his back.

"Well, shit," Jessie said.

"We'll find something else," Em replied patiently.

"Right, like, where?" Jessie was starting to get pissy now, like she always did when she was hungry. Then she'd get a bad headache that would last for hours even if she ate. Sometimes the headaches were so bad she'd rock back and forth holding her head, mewing like a hurt cat. She'd always been like that, even as a child. That was one of the hardest things about being separated as kids. Em worried constantly that wherever Jessie was staying, they wouldn't understand that she had to eat at regular times and that it helped if someone put a washcloth on her head when the headaches were bad.

"I'll drive fast," Em said. "Eat some jerky. It'll help until we find something." This idea of taking off on Route 66 had turned out to be a bad one and Em was angry at herself for not sticking to her original plan.

Up ahead, a long distance away, a light glowed.

"I wonder what that is?" Em said.

"It better be a restaurant," Jessie answered, picking a piece of jerky out of her teeth with a green fingernail. "You got any dental floss?"

"Somewhere," Em said. She concentrated on the lights, willing them to be a cafe. She was surprised when they came upon the square, brick and stucco building. The sign read ESTA'S CAFE.

"Thank goodness," Jessie said, unbuckling her seat belt before Em could get the car turned off. They were the only ones in the parking lot, which gave Em a nervous feeling deep in her stomach. One of the things she'd learned early being bounced from foster home to foster home was safety in numbers. Especially after dark.

"I don't know about this," Em said. "It can't be much further to the Interstate hookup. Maybe we should wait."

"I'm not waiting one more minute," Jessie said, slamming the car door. "My head's already starting to hurt."

The cafe was small and warm with brown vinyl booths and red formica tables. Near the old cash register sat a small artificial Christmas tree. The ornaments were dime store cacti and coyotes. Lettered on a star-shaped tree topper was "Forgiveness was born on Christmas Day." Em and Jessie were the only ones in the room.

Her fear calmed slightly when their waitress brought them menus. She had to be eighty years old and looked as harmless as a poodle. Her wrinkled face reminded Em of the maps she'd studied for so many years. She wondered what stories lay behind those wrinkles. In her mind, she posed the old woman against a large map of the United States. On her head she placed a jaunty English driving cap.

"Chicken fried steak's the special tonight," the old woman said, smiling down at Em and Jessie. "I'm Ruth." Em smiled back, resting for a moment in the woman's kind watery eyes. Jessie ignored her, sucked on her bottom lip and studied the plastic menu with a concentrated frown.

"We was just getting ready to close up," the woman said. "My girl and I are heading out to Laughlin day after Christmas." She pointed to the kitchen where a sixtyish woman with dyed red hair waved from behind the griddle.

"What's Laughlin?" Jessie asked.

"It's a gambling town on the Colorado River," Em explained. "Near Bullhead City, Arizona."

"Rooms there are cheap as dirt this week," the old woman said. "We're going to double our money then spend it at the outlet mall there."

From the kitchen, her daughter let out a cheerful laugh.

Em and Jessie were halfway through their hamburgers when the man walked in. The old woman got up from her stool behind the counter, picked up a menu and said, "Sit anywhere you like."

The man was tall and skinny with a red and black scorpion tattoo on his hand. His denim jacket was black with grime on the sleeves. He sat at the counter, glancing briefly

over at Em and Jessie, his pale eyes lingering longer on
Jessie. Involuntarily, a small smile tugged at her mouth.

"Stop it," Em whispered. "I don't like the looks of that
guy."

"I was just being friendly. It's Christmas Eve, Em.
Lighten up."

"Just coffee," he said in a low voice. Em watched him
warily. One thing she'd picked up in all those foster homes
was a sixth sense about trouble and meanness. This man was
both, she'd stake her savings on it.

She and Jessie had just started their cherry pie when the
man pulled out a large handgun and pointed it at Ruth. He
was smart and had waited until her daughter was standing
next to her, away from the phone.

"All your money," he said. "In a bag."

Jessie's eyes widened and she gave a small gasp. Em
glanced over at the pay phone hanging near the door. At
Jessie's sound, the man turned and saw Em's eyes. He
calmly aimed the gun and shot the phone. It exploded, black
plastic pieces flying across the room. Jessie screamed. Em
grabbed her hand. The old woman, Ruth, instinctively covered her daughter with her thin, freckled arms.

"You," he said, pointing the pistol at Em. "Lock the front
door."

Em's mind flew from one possibility to another, trying to
figure a way for her and Jessie to escape. She looked over at
the two old women, her heart pounding in her chest. She
couldn't leave them. For a moment, the responsibility over-
whelmed her and her heart felt ready to burst. She took a
deep breath and said to the man, "Take the money and we
won't call the police."

He gave a guttural laugh. The glassiness in his eyes was
familiar to her, drugs or alcohol. Or just plain cruelty. That

also gave people's eyes an ugly glow. If you'd ever seen it before, you never forgot.

"Of course you won't," he said. His smile showed perfect white teeth. "I shot the phone." He turned back to the old ladies. "Get me the money."

As Ruth silently put all the cash in a brown paper lunch sack, he told her daughter to sit in the booth behind Em and Jessie.

"I need rope," he said to Ruth when she handed him the bag. She shook her head no, murmuring they didn't have any.

He gestured for her to join her daughter and he ripped the small plastic radio from the wall and cut the cord with a bone-handled buck knife he pulled from a leather sheath. He did the same with a toaster, using the cords to tie the women's hands behind their back.

Then he looked over at Jessie. She stared back at him, her blue eyes wide and unblinking with fear. He smiled and walked over, sliding next to her in the booth.

"What a cute little piece of ass you are," he said, scratching his jaw with the barrel of his gun. He reached over and grabbed her breast.

"Stop it!" Em said, standing up.

He pointed the gun at her, his smile gone. "Sit down."

Frozen, Em stared into the black circle of the gun's long barrel.

"Do as he says, sweetie," the old woman's gentle voice came from behind her. "Sit down."

Em slowly obeyed the woman's voice. He turned back to Jessie and trailed the barrel down her white throat. "It's been a long time, honey."

It was at that moment Em realized that he'd rape Jessie, then kill all of them. This is how it all would all end, after everything, here in a Godforsaken cafe on a forgotten road in the desert.

He grabbed Jessie's blond hair and yanked her head back, biting her hard on the throat. Jessie screamed low in her throat. Em grabbed a fork and lunged at him.

Catching her movements from the corner of his eye, he swung his corded arm out, hitting her in the face with the gun's barrel.

She fell back against the seat, blood gushing from her cheek. She could feel the familiar throb and swell of a blackening eye.

He swiped the table clean of dishes and silverware. Em flinched when a glass burst on the floor. "Try that again and you're dead."

She held her palm against her throbbing, bloody cheek.

"Use some napkins," he said, his voice disgusted.

Deliberately keeping her movements slow, she reached across the table, pulled a wad of napkins from the metal dispenser and held them against the wound. He watched her, his hard, pale eyes measuring her every move.

"I'm hungry," he said to Em. "Get up and fix me something. But stay in my sight and don't be trying anything or blondie's brains here will be all over this window." He held the barrel to Jessie's temple.

Em sat frozen, staring into his marble blue eyes.

"Sweetie," the old woman, Ruth, said. "There's some chili behind the counter that opens with a pop top. Heat some of that in the microwave."

"Good thinking, granny," the man said. "Do what she says."

Em slid out of the bench seat and walked around the counter. She set the wad of bloody napkins down in the sink. To make a large bowl of chili she had to use three of the small pop-top cans. She put it in the microwave and stared at the food times on front looking for chili.

"Hurry up," he said. "And keep your hands where I can see them."

"Four minutes, sweetie," the old woman called. "I know it by heart."

Em continued to study the list, finally finding chili—two minutes.

She turned and looked at Ruth, her face blank.

"Four minutes," Ruth said, her creased face encouraging.

"Yes, ma'am," Em answered and punched in the time.

It was the longest four minutes of Em's life. Behind her back she heard Jessie's scared whimpers as the man amused himself with her sister. The sounds burned a black hole in Em's already pock-marked heart.

When the chili was done, Em carried the steaming bowl over to the man who had already branded her sister with purplish bite marks on her neck. When she reached him, he sat the gun down for a brief second on the formica table, his greedy eyes turning from her sister to the bowl of chili, the expression of hunger almost the same.

Em threw the overheated beans in his face. His scream bit the air, mingling with Jessie's. Without hesitation, she picked up the heavy gun, pointed the barrel's tip at his face and fired.

She fell back from the force of the shot, the gun flying out of her hand. The sound of the shot ringing in her ears mingled with Jessie's animal shrieking.

A calm came over Em as she watched her sister scramble over the table, her feet slipping on the chunks of hot chili and bits of brain and blood. Em stared unfeeling at the mass of mangled human flesh, then turned to the old women in the booth. The daughter's face was shiny with tears, but no sound came from her open mouth. The old woman said calmly, "Untie us, sweetie. Now that's a good girl."

Em untied the women, then went to search for her sister. She found her cowering in a corner of the kitchen, her thin, bloodstained arms hugging knees pulled tight to her chest. Em sank down and surrounded her sister with her arms, humming softy under her breath a tuneless song their mother sang to them as children.

After a few minutes, Em stood up. "We have to go help."

"I want to go home," Jessie said, her voice trembling.

And where exactly would that be, Em wanted to ask, but didn't.

"Stay here. I'll go see what I can do and then come back."

In the cafe, the old woman was setting a cup of tea in front of her daughter. The daughter sat at the counter, her back to the dead man. The smell of burnt chili and fresh blood reminded Em of the Mexican butcher shop she went to with Marisol one time when they visited her family in Ensenada.

"Good girl," Ruth said when Em walked in the room. She didn't know if she was talking to her daughter or Em.

"Should I go get the police?" Em asked. Her first instinct was to grab Jessie, jump in the Toyota and run. Once the police were involved, there would be reports and possibly a newspaper story. Her plan to disappear so Douglas Rayburn couldn't find them would be ruined. She might even go to jail for killing a man. Who would protect Jessie then? Yes, her first instinct was to run. But she couldn't leave this old woman to face the police alone.

Ruth came around the counter and stood inches from Em. "You're running from someone, aren't you, sweetie?"

Em just nodded, wondering how this woman could know that. Was the desperation so obviously carved on her face?

"Then you don't need to get involved with the police. Me

and my girl here will take care of it. You just take your sister and go."

"I can't do that," Em whispered. "I can't . . . I killed . . ."

"Sweetie, that man was dead long before you pulled the trigger," she said, taking Em's cold hand in her warm, old one. Then she dropped it and picked up the gun from the floor, wiping it carefully and thoroughly with her gingham apron. Then she gripped the handle and put her finger on the trigger.

"He tried to rob us. He tied up my girl there and then threatened to kill us. The sheriff's deputy around these parts is an old student of mine. We're a tight little bunch here in the desert. He'll believe me. There will be few questions asked."

What should I do? Em begged silently. Give me some sign. Her mind flickered briefly to the gold-leafed crucifix hanging above the altar in Marisol's church. The agony on Jesus' face had always been too much for her to stare at for any longer than a few seconds.

"Flee, child," the old woman said softly. "Take your sister and go."

They reached the interstate in less than a half hour. They passed Essex, the last town on this stretch of Route 66. A town consisting of an empty, black-windowed school, piles of tires and a desolate Cal Trans yard. Jessie sat frozen in her seat, staring straight ahead at the dark road. Em concentrated on the broken white lines flashing like gunshots past their tires, one after the other. When they'd traveled for a few minutes on the freeway, Em couldn't wait any longer and pulled over. Down on her knees, into some greasy weeds, she vomited until there was nothing left but dry retching.

Back in the car, she wet an old teeshirt with some bottled water and washed her face and hands, then did the same for her sister, who still hadn't spoken. She helped her sister out of her stained blouse and into a thin faded sweatshirt.

"We'll be okay," Em said, pulling off her own teeshirt, soaked with chili and blood. She contemplated throwing the stained shirts on the ground, wanting to just be rid of them. But they might cause questions so she stuffed them under the seat to burn later.

"I know," Jessie finally said, turning her head away and staring out into the black night. The purple bruises on her neck were almost the same color as the star-dotted sky.

They drove without speaking, finally stopping in Needles at an all-night Jack in the Box for something to drink. Em remembered as they sat in the parking lot of the fast food restaurant what the old woman, Ruth, had said about Laughlin, how the rooms were dirt cheap this time of year. She looked at her watch. It was a little past midnight. Christmas Day. They needed somewhere to rest, somewhere that didn't cost an arm and a leg before continuing their journey. She deliberately kept her mind away from what had happened the last few hours. It was better to just think of necessary things—where to stay tonight, what to eat. She glanced over at her sister's white, exhausted face. They needed to find someplace soon. Em looked at the map and saw that Laughlin was only an hour away. She lay her head back against the headrest, intending to close her eyes for only a second.

Hours later, the squawk of a police car radio startled her awake. She jolted up and looked out the window. Next to her Toyota, a Highway Patrol car pulled up. The officer climbed out of his car, stretched and nodded at Em before walking up the front door of the Jack in the Box. A weak yellow sun struggled over the horizon.

"What's going on?" Jessie mumbled, blinking sleepy eyes open.

"Nothing," Em said, starting the car. "We have to go."

She glanced at the rearview mirror every few seconds as she drove through the streets of Needles, a small desert town filled with sand-burnished tract homes and car parts stores, searching for the road to Laughlin. Once she found the highway, she gave a sigh of relief. As the air started to warm from the car's heater and the rising sun, she felt the chunk of ice in her chest begin to thaw.

In Laughlin they had their pick of hotels. There were plenty of rooms, any one of them fifteen or sixteen dollars a night. Em picked Harrah's because she liked the cheerful Southwestern decor. Because it was Christmas, the desk clerk threw in two free dinner buffets. In their room Em and Jessie took turns taking showers. While Jessie dried her hair, Em cut up their blood-stained shirts into tiny pieces and wrapped them in a plastic grocery bag. After they'd taken a nap, she found an outside trash bin at the back of the hotel parking lot.

Jessie silently watched her throw the bag away. A small, involuntary moan caught in her throat when Em let the metal lid slam close.

"Let's go check out the buffet," Em said.

Jessie held her sister's eyes for a moment. "Okay."

Em knew they'd never speak of the incident again.

At four o'clock, they stuffed themselves at the buffet with burritos and turkey and dressing and five kinds of salad and baked potatoes and pumpkin pie. There were only a few other people in the room, all of them safe-looking retirees. One silver-haired woman called a man plopping sour cream on her taco "sweetie" and Em felt her stomach catch. What was Ruth doing right now? What was her Christmas like?

Oh, God, Em thought. The words more of a prayer than she'd ever prayed. I killed a man and let an old woman take the blame.

She dropped her fork. The clatter on her white plate caused Jessie to look up, startled.

"Are you all right?" she asked.

Em nodded, carefully picking up her fork. "Just tired."

After dinner they walked along the sidewalk that bordered the Colorado River flowing next to the line of hotels in this mini-Vegas. Across the river, the lights from Bullhead City started sparking on, one-by-one, looking like rhinestones under the deepening early evening sky.

"Can we afford some magazines?" Jessie asked Em, her voice subdued.

"Sure," Em said, digging in her pocket and giving her sister a ten-dollar bill. "I'm going to stay out here a while longer."

"Okay. I'll be in the gift shop."

Em leaned against the railing and watched the sun dip toward the horizon, turning the air a soft, gentle gray-blue.

"Blue time," she remembered Mr. Dublin telling the class of fidgety high school students, "comes twice a day. Once, before the sun comes up and then again, at dusk. Light is perfect during those two forty-minute intervals. It is a magical time for photographers. It's when anything can happen."

Anything, Em wondered as she watched the rolling desert hills of Bullhead City turn shadowy and beautiful. The smell of burning candles seemed to tinge the air. Behind her, the bright lights of the casino and hotel flickered on, causing an almost chain reaction of neon down the long row of hotels.

Anything can happen at blue time, he'd said.

The smell of burning candles. Candles that were prayers.

She said a prayer for the lady Ruth.

Thank you.

Anything.

Hope.

Maybe even forgiveness.

She let those thoughts float gently, tentatively around her mind. Something to dwell on later. But now she watched the lights from the casino dance across the black water of the Colorado River, red and orange and green, looking for all the world like ripe, beautiful fruit, ready to be picked.

RAPPIN' DOG

Dick Lochte

Dick Lochte has written two novels about Leo Bloodworth
and Serendipity Dahlquist, the prize-winning *Sleeping
Dog* and its sequel, *Laughing Dog*. His New Orleans private detective Terry Manion appears in *Blue Bayou* and
The Neon Smile. A reviewer of fiction for the *Los Angeles
Times*, Lochte is also the coauthor (with attorney Christo-
pher Darden) of the recent novel, *The Trials of Nikki Hill*.

> *Go to school,*
> *And play the fool,*
> *You get no help in the cruel world.*
> *Play it smart, get a fast start,*
> *There's an art*
> *To livin' large in the cool world.*

The words of rapper B. A. "Big Apple" Dawg reverberated
through the unmarked police van. I turned to Mr. Leo
Bloodworth, the renowned private investigator, who was sitting next to me and said, "You're playing the fool when you
go to school? That's the dumbest advice I've ever heard. The
man's a cretin."

"You're preaching to the already converted, Sara," he said, using his own clever diminution of my given name, Serendipity.

The three LAPD detectives in the van, members of an elite team known as the Star Squad, were busy with their surveillance. The leader, a Detective Gundersen, asked, "You getting a good level, Mumms?"

"Just like stereo," Officer Mumms replied. She was a very cool black woman, seated at a table that had been bolted to the floor of the van, studying the various indicators on a tape recorder secured to the table.

"Wire's workin' fine," Detective Gundersen said to our driver. "Give Doggie Boy a honk."

The driver, Detective Lucas, tapped the van's horn twice. He was a rather handsome man with more than a passing resemblance to Mr. John Kennedy, Jr., except that his dark hair wasn't as curly. Detective Gundersen's hair was straight, too, but gray and lay flat on his head like the hair of legendary singer Mr. Frank Sinatra. My grandmother, who is an actress and should know, says Mr. Sinatra's hair wasn't totally his own. Maybe Detective Gundersen's isn't either, but I'd like to think that the Los Angeles Police Department would insist that their officers eschew such nonessential cosmetic touches.

The horn was a code Detective Gundersen had set up with Mr. B. A. Dawg, who was driving a peach-colored Rolls Royce maybe two car-lengths ahead of us on Sunset. It informed him that the transmission was working well and he could stop testing it with his dreadful singsong.

But he didn't stop.

> Show some sense,
> Keep Mr. Pig on the de-fense.
> He comes aroun', puts you down,

Expects to find you shiverin' and shakin'.
Take the pledge, use an edge, cut that mutha oinker up
    into bacon.

"What the heck's he saying, Mumms?" Gundersen asked.

"You don't wanna know, Herm," Officer Mumms called to him. She smiled at me. "How old are you?"

"Fourteen and a half," I replied truthfully.

"And you don't like rap?"

"Vachel Lindsay is about as far as I go," I said.

"Never heard of her," Officer Mumms said. "But I dig the Dawg man. I hope we can catch the guy messing with him."

Mr. Dawg moved on to another of his ditties, one exploring his total lack of respect for womankind. "He's giving a concert at the Shrine tomorrow night," Officer Mumms said.

"I know," I said.

She leaned toward me and, in a voice loud enough for Mr. Bloodworth to hear, asked, "Your boss like rap?"

Mr. Bloodworth isn't my boss, exactly. Though officially categorized as a "high school student," I am sort of his apprentice, spending my afternoons and some school holidays at his detective agency, mainly observing the art of criminology. I also do a little filing and billing, which I was in the middle of the day before, alone in the office, when the call came in from Ms. Lulu Diamond, Mr. Dawg's manager. If Mr. Bloodworth had been there, he probably would have turned down the job. But he wasn't and so he and I were in the van, sharing an adventure with the members of the Star Squad.

"Does Mr. B. like rap? No," I told Officer Mumms, "rap really isn't his thing. His idea of popular music is 'Moon River.'"

He glared at me with those odd yellow-brown hawk's eyes. "Careful, sis," he said. "You're talking about the late, great Johnny Mercer."

Cops, they got the wrong approach,
Like the cockroach,
Crawl around in the dirt,
Gonna meet up with a hero, burn 'em up like Nero, and
*   make 'em face the big hurt.*

"Jeeze," Detective Gundersen said. "If he don't change the tune, I may wind up killing him, myself."

Mr. Bloodworth sighed.

As I said, the big, rawboned sleuth hadn't wanted to get involved with Mr. Dawg at all. But I'd explained to him that because of his recent illness—he'd been felled by a strain of the Outback flu—the month had been a gloomy one, financially speaking. And there was no sign on the horizon of any other ship coming in.

On arriving at Mr. Dawg's suite at the Beverly-Rodeo Hotel, I must admit a certain trepidation on my part, too. The place was filled with an assortment of unpleasant people—loud and arrogant men in expensive baggy gym clothes and silver jewelry, caught up in some football epic on TV and totally ignoring their ladyfriends who, I am sorry to report, were no less antisocial. Nor better dressed.

"Rock and roll trash," Mr. B. muttered to me, and though he was several generations off, his point was well made.

A little pink-cheeked, bespectacled matron in her fifties, her round body covered by a loud Hawaiian muumuu, navigated the crowd gracefully to greet us. "I'm Lulu Diamond," she told us, using a chubby finger to point to the glittering stones embedded in her eyeglass frames.

We exchanged introductions and she asked, "What can I getcha, kid? These bums B. A. calls his friends have cleaned out the portable bar, but I can order up room service."

"I'm fine," I told her.

"You, honey?" she asked Mr. B.

"I'm okay, too," he said, scanning the scene. "I don't see your client."

"He's, uh," she pointed to me and winked, "spending quality time with the missus in the bedroom."

The big detective winced. "Yeah, well, Ms. Diamond—"

"Make it Lulu, big guy."

"Lulu, you think you could pry him loose? We ought to get moving on this, assuming that we're dealing with a real situation."

Lulu frowned and suddenly didn't look so matronly. "B. A. Dawg, with three platinum CDs and the new one going gold after just two weeks, does not have to resort to fake death threats to make headlines."

"I hope not," Mr. Bloodworth said. "Because then we'd be wasting our time."

"I'll go get him," she said.

"There seems to be a lot of violence in the record business," I said, mainly to distract him from the ball game on TV.

"Yeah," he said absently, eyes glazing at the sight of pigskin. "Gangs. Drugs. Good old-fashioned business rivalry. I don't think we're dealing with that here. In fact, I don't know what we're dealing with here."

According to Lulu, Mr. Dawg had received one of those scary notes made up of pasted letters announcing that an organization called the Rap Tribunal had found him guilty of plagiarism. In his ultimate wisdom, he assumed the sender to be a crank, though he should have realized that anyone who went to all the trouble of clipping and pasting that sort of note surely would not go quietly away.

He'd no sooner disposed of the note when the Tribunal gentleman was on the phone, his voice electronically altered, offering Mr. Dawg a choice. He could donate a por-

tion of the profits from his most popular CD, "Smack At-
tack," to the poor street people from whom he stole most of
his lyrics. Or he could die. The amount requested was
$250,000 in $100 bills, to be placed in one of those aluminum suitcases.

He had twenty-four hours to get the money and stand by
for further instructions. But if he went to the police, he
might as well put a gun to his own head.

That's when Lulu dialed the Bloodworth Agency.

Mr. Bloodworth was falling under the spell of the ball game
when I spied Lulu waving to us from an open doorway.
"We're being summoned," I said.

Mr. Dawg, a man of thirty or so, was sitting on a rumpled
bed. He was wearing leather pants the color of brown mus-
tard. No shoes. No shirt. He was long and thin and very
black. His hair was dyed a bright orange. And there were
enough pieces of metal embedded in his ears and nose to
keep him off of planes for the rest of his life.

"You the fake fuzz?" he asked Mr. Bloodworth.

The sleuth allowed he was.

"Blood-worth. I like that. This your ladyfriend?" Mr.
Dawg asked, looking at me.

"Thrity-five years too late for that," Mr. B. said.

"She don't look so young," Mr. Dawg said. "Nasty's only
twenty. And she been Mrs. Dawg for two years."

His reference was to the woman seated at the dresser
combing her hair. She was nearly as tall as he, and as thin.
But there was a languid quality to her, as if she weren't fully
awake. I imagine it must have had quite an effect on sim-
pleminded men. She said, "I keep telling you, my name's
Nastasia. And it seems like I been with you an eternity, bro."

Mr. Dawg shrugged. "So, you gonna keep me in one
piece, Bloodworth?"

"I'll be honest with you, B. A. No one person can guarantee to do that."

"See," Nastasia said. "Told you, Dawgman. Get those cops from last year."

Mr. Bloodworth raised his eyebrows. "What cops would that be?"

"During the tour last year," Lulu said, "we had another little problem when we hit L.A.. One of the former members of the Dawg Posse, that's B. A.'s backup, went a little whacko and made some threats. So we called the cops and they sent us these detectives who specialize in dealing with celebrities."

"The Star Squad," Mr. B. said.

"Yeah. That's them," Nastasia said. "Headed up by this old guy and some young dude."

"Young dude was a little too fresh, you ask me," B. A. said.

"You just a crazy man," Nastasia said. "We oughta get those guys back. They didn't take more than a day to pick Walter up and toss his butt into jail."

"It's the way to go," Mr. Bloodworth said. "If you want me to duplicate the level of protection the cops can give you, I'll have to put on a bunch of other operatives. Could cost you as much as ten grand a day."

"That's no good," B. A. Dawg said. "But the man on the phone said no cops."

"They always say that. Cops know how to handle it."

Mr. Dawg snapped his fingers at Lulu and the two of them walked out onto the balcony to discuss the situation.

Nastasia looked me up and down. "What are you playin' at, girl?"

"Beg pardon?"

"What are you doing here?"

"I work with Mr. Bloodworth," I said.

"Yeah? Well, Mr. Blood, here, fits the private eye image, but you, I'd take you for some kinda Spice Girl wannabe."

"Then you'd be making a mistake," I said.

Mr. Dawg and his manager re-entered the room. He snapped his fingers at Mr. Bloodworth. "Cops are in. But I want you to handle it."

"How's that?" Mr. B. asked.

"The cops. I don't like 'em. So I'm payin' you to deal with 'em. Work everything out with them and then tell me."

"Mr. Dawg," I asked, "could it be your former employee, Walter, trying to get your attention again?"

He shrugged. "Walter's crazy enough to do it, I guess."

"Maybe the cops still have a line on him," Mr. Bloodworth said.

"C'mon, tall, blond and rugged," Lulu said to Mr. Bloodworth. "Let's go talk money."

Later, when he and I were driving downtown to Parker Center where the Star Squad offices are located, Mr. Bloodworth said, "Herm Gundersen and I go back a ways. This should be a snap; we'll just let him do all the work."

In point of fact, he and Detective Gundersen had gone through the police academy together. So there was none of the antagonism a private detective sometimes encounters when dealing with lawmen.

"The Dawgman again, huh?" Detective Gundersen said. "Hear that, Lucas?"

Detective Lucas looked up from his desk four feet away. "Who's he pissed off this time?"

"Maybe the same guy you arrested last year," Mr. B. suggested.

The handsome young detective picked up the phone and quickly ascertained that Walter Lipton, the recalcitrant ex-employee, had been released from prison only three weeks before.

"Talk about your likely suspects," Detective Gundersen said. "Well, we'll take over from here, Leo."

"That'd be fine with me, Herm, but Dawg said he'd like us to stick around."

Detective Gundersen hesitated, then smiled. "Sure, buddy. You and the kid are welcome to observe a crack team in action. Lucas, slap on that charming smile of yours and let's show 'em how we handle international celebrities in this man's town."

So we'd "observed" them shooing away the freeloaders at the hotel, setting up the phone taps, arranging for counterfeit bills to be placed in an aluminum suitcase along with a tracking device, and being generally obsequious in the presence of Mr. Dawg, his skinny sullen wife, and Lulu.

To give the Star Squad their due, when the representative of the Rap Tribunal finally called, they certainly leapt into action. Unfortunately, the call had been made on a cellular phone and was therefore untraceable. But at least we had a tape of the conversation and didn't have to rely on Mr. Dawg's rather short attention span.

The gentleman from the Rap Tribunal informed Mr. Dawg that he had thirty minutes to get into his Rolls Royce with the suitcase and drive to a public telephone at an address on Sunset Boulevard. Further instructions would be forthcoming.

So there we were, tagging along, being regaled by the so-called rapmaster's poetic but addled view of life. Suddenly, he stopped mid-rhyme to declare, "Mus' be the place."

He pulled to the curb at a bus stop in front of a sidewalk shop called Café Coffee and got out of the Rolls. The pay phone was just at the edge of the café's patio which was filled with folks satisfying their caffeine fix alfresco.

There were no other spaces, legal or illegal, for the van,

so Detective Lucas drove about a quarter of a block past the Rolls and double-parked. Up ahead was an unmarked sedan, stopped in a similar position. Its occupants were four other members of the Star Squad. They were a bit too far away to keep Mr. Dawg in view, but we could see him, resplendent in his powder blue leather jumpsuit, standing at the phone.

"Would you look at the hot babes at that coffee place?" Detective Lucas said. "Damn, I love L.A."

"Keep your roving eye on the Dawgman, huh?" his boss asked.

Thanks to the transmitter taped to Mr. Dawg's chest, we could hear sidewalk noises, the whistle of the wind and, eventually, a ringing phone. "Yeah, it's me," we heard him say. We could not hear the caller at all.

"Hold on," Mr. Dawg said. He reached under the ledge of the booth and removed a small object that had been taped there. "Got it." It was a cellular phone.

Detective Lucas said, "Check out that babe and the guy sitting at the second table over from B. A."

A young African-American couple seemed very interested in Mr. Dawg. In any other city in the free world, it would not seem unusual for people to be gawking at a blond African-American recording star wearing powder blue leather, tearing something from beneath a pay telephone ledge. But this was Hollywood. And none of the other patrons of Café Coffee was giving him a second's notice.

As he hopped back into his Rolls, the couple stood up from their table. The man tossed a few bills down and they both ran for their car.

"What now, Herm?" Detective Lucas asked.

"Wait and watch, lover boy."

Mr. Dawg pulled out into traffic. From our speakers, his voice blared, "Man said he'll call me on the phone, tell me where to go."

The couple got into a little red BMW. When they passed us, heading after Mr. Dawg, Detective Gundersen yelled, "Let's roll."

"I take it neither of those people are the guy who gave Dawg trouble last year," Mr. Bloodworth said.

"Lipton? Naw," Detective Gundersen said. "He's probably manning the phone."

"That's a heck of a bright red car they're using to collect loot," Mr. Bloodworth observed.

"Amateurs," Detective Gundersen sneered. "Mumms, run a check on that license, if you please."

It was blissfully quiet in the Rolls. Mr. Dawg evidently was too caught up in the moment to be thinking about rapping. But Detective Lucas took up the musical slack, humming nervously, oblivious to the scowls being sent his way by his boss.

Mr. Bloodworth picked up on the detective's melody. We listened to their duet for a few minutes, until Detective Gundersen growled, "Could we can the concert?"

Mr. Bloodworth looked at me and shook his head sadly. "You don't like that, you don't like good music," he muttered.

"Another of your Johnny Mercer songs?" I asked.

"Close. Bobby Troup. 'Route 66.' "

He started to recite the lyrics, which sounded to my ears almost like rap, except they were much more whimsical (rhyming "Arizona" with "Winona," for example). The ringing of Mr. Dawg's cellular interrupted him.

We heard the rapper say, "Okay. Make the next turn and head back to the ocean."

The unmarked sedan in the lead must've gotten the message because we saw it head into the left lane just in front of the Rolls. The red Beamer was directly behind Mr. Dawg.

We were several cars behind it. "How you doin' on that license check, Mumms?"

"We'll get it when we get it, Herm," she said.

Our little caravan made the turn and continued west on Sunset for about a mile when the cellular rang again. "Okay," Mr. Dawg said, "I turn down Doheny to Santa Monica Boulevard and keep going to the ocean." He was silent for a beat, then added, "Sure, I got the cash. I'm cooperatin'. No, sir, no cops nohow."

Officer Mumms emitted a little chuckle. "Isn't he somethin'?" she asked.

We moved along Santa Monica Boulevard, past the Century City shopping center and on under the San Diego Freeway. Past old movie houses, rows and rows of small businesses, restaurants.

The temperature dropped several degrees when we moved through the seacoast town of Santa Monica. I was starting to smell ocean salt in the air when the phone rang again.

"Right," Mr. Dawg said. "I turn right on Ocean, take the incline to the Coast Highway and keep goin' 'til I see the sign for Topanga Canyon. Then head up the Canyon. Why we going to all this trouble? Lemme jus' give you the damn money. I got me a concert tonight. I . . . Damn, he hung up on me."

Detective Gundersen scowled. "It would've been simpler to have us just stay on Sunset. Why the circle route?"

"Must be making sure the rapman is all by his lonesome," Detective Lucas said.

"Mumms, tell Maclin to press the pedal and go on up Topanga and wait." Detective Maclin was in the lead car. "Lucas, you'd better pull back as far as you can. We don't want to spook those folks in the red car. And, Mumms, can't we find out who the hell they are?"

"Searches take time," Officer Mumms said.

The couple in the red car didn't seem to care if we spooked them or not. They remained on Mr. Dawg's tail up into the Canyon.

My grandmother loves to tell horror stories about gruesome crimes that took place in Topanga back in the 1960s way before I was born, during that odd historic time of social unrest. As we drove through, it didn't look dangerous at all. Just another moderately populated rustic canyon.

Mr. Dawg's phone rang again. This time the instruction was to turn off into Calico Canyon.

Unfortunately, the instruction came too late for the lead car. The Rolls made the turn, followed by the red Beamer. Then, after a considerable distance, us. Detective Maclin and his men were now last in line as we climbed along a small road through the relatively uninhabited, tree-shaded canyon.

Higher and higher we went along the twisting macadam, barely keeping the little red car in sight and not seeing the Rolls at all.

The cellular rang and Mr. Dawg said, rather waspishly. "Okay. I'm stoppin'. And I'm tossin' the suitcase . . . Now what? . . . You sure I can get out of here goin' up? . . . Okay, you the man."

We rounded a curve and saw the Rolls pulling away.

But the red Beamer had stopped. The male, who'd been driving, got out and was at the side of the road, bending down to pick up the suitcase.

"It's a go-go-go," Detective Gundersen yelled.

"Book'em, Dano," Officer Mumms ordered Detective Maclin.

She, Mr. Bloodworth and I remained in the van. We watched as the six plainclothes policemen ran to the man holding the suitcase. The woman threw open her car door and got out, rushing to her companion.

"LAPD," Detective Gundersen growled, "Drop the money, boy."

"Boy?" the young man shouted back. "Who the hell . . . ?"

Then he made a big mistake. He threw the suitcase at the detective.

Suddenly the other three were on him, pounding him with their fists.

"Jee-zus," Officer Mumms said.

"This is bad news," Mr. Bloodworth said, getting out of the van. "Stay here, Sara."

As he ran toward the melee, Officer's Mumms's radio began to squawk and a static-y voice informed us that, according to its plates, the red BMW was licensed to a Mr. and Mrs. Joseph Laurence of Mill Valley.

"Where you goin' girl?" Officer Mumms asked me. "Your boss said stay."

"I took no vow of obedience to him," I told her.

Mr. Bloodworth had pulled one of the detectives off of the young man. And was getting a fist to the side of his head for his trouble.

Screaming at them, the young woman kicked another detective in the shin and received an elbow in the chest that sent her to the ground.

I ran to their car, looked in. Then I quickly opened the driver's door and kept pressing the horn until I had everybody's attention.

"They're tourists," I shouted.

"Huh?" Detective Gundersen said.

"Tourists. From Mill Valley. They've got luggage in the back of their car and highway maps in the front. Look," I held up a pair of Mickey Mouse ears. "They've been to Disneyland."

Office Mumms had left the van, too. She moved to Mrs. Laurence and was helping her from the ground.

The young man pulled away from Detective Lucas's grip, wiped his bloody nose on his shirt and staggered to his wife.

"You all right, baby?"

"Jus' got the wind knocked out of her," Officer Mumms said.

Mrs. Laurence nodded in agreement.

"You bastards are crazy," Joseph Laurence of Mill Valley said to all of them. "I'm gonna sue your ass off."

"Yeah?" Detective Gundersen said. "First you're gonna have to explain to us crazy bastards what the hell you *tourists* are doing out here with that metal suitcase?"

The young man lost just an inch of attitude. "My wife and I are having a cup of coffee wondering how to spend our last afternoon in L.A. when there's B. A. Dawg, himself, right there on the street. The rappin' rap master. So I figure, let's check out what the Dawgman's up to."

"That brings us to the suitcase."

"We're behind the man, see him toss something from his Rolls. I tell my wife, hell, B. A. Dawg may not want whatever that is, but for the rest of us, it's a solid gold souvenir."

Detective Gundersen looked dubious, but he said, "We'll check out your story."

"Check out my story? You sure as hell will. Right after I sue you and everybody else for beating on me and my wife."

The detective shifted his gaze from the battered Laurences and scanned the area. I wondered if he might be checking for a video camera. In a flat voice, he said, "We're pretty sensitive to stalking out here, pal. Got all kind of laws against it. So I'm giving you two choices—you can let us fix up your scrapes and bruises while we're checking out your story. Or you can keep mouthin' off about lawsuits and we'll throw you and the little lady into the tank for stalking and harassing Mr. Dawg."

I hit the horn again.

Everybody looked my way. Detective Gundersen seemed particularly peeved. "What now?" he shouted.

"Speaking of Mr. Dawg, aren't we forgetting something?"

In an absolutely horrific piece of bad timing, from the distance came the unmistakable sound of a gunshot.

Shouting orders for the others to stay with the Laurences, Detective Gundersen ran back to the van, followed by Detective Lucas. And me and Mr. Bloodworth.

Detective Lucas eased around the red BMW, slightly scraping the side of the van on the canyon wall before zooming up the road.

Half a mile or so later, we came upon the Rolls sitting still, its engine purring. I started to open the van door, but Mr. Bloodworth grabbed my arm. The two policemen had their pistols drawn and were searching the area through the van's windows.

Eventually, Detective Gundersen said, "The rest of you stay here."

He slipped from the van and, head moving from side to side like a radarscope, he approached the Rolls. He stopped, turned and stared up the canyon wall, then put his pistol back into its holster. He opened the Rolls's passenger door and bent into the vehicle. A few seconds later, the pale exhaust clouds ceased. Detective Gundersen backed out of the car and, looking at Detective Lucas, made a gun with this thumb and forefinger and pantomimed shooting himself in the temple.

Mr. Bloodworth felt it was his duty to notify the widow Dawg.

But by the time we got to the suite at the Beverly-Rodeo

Hotel, the news had already broken. The widow was in black—a lacy, sort of see-through outfit, but definitely black—holding a hankie to her red-rimmed eyes.

She thanked Mr. Bloodworth for doing his best to save her husband's life. Lulu Diamond wasn't quite so forgiving. "I hope you don't expect to get paid for letting poor B. A. take one in the head," she said. "You're lucky I don't sue. Maybe I will."

"You do what you want," he told her. He was feeling very low about the way things turned out.

As we started for the door, Mrs. Dawg called out, "Hey, Mr. Blood, don't listen to her. I'm grateful you did what you could for my husband. You'll get your money. It wasn't your fault the police panicked Walter into shooting B. A."

"It was his fault the bungling cops came into it," Lulu grumbled.

"No. That was my suggestion, Lulu," Mrs. Dawg said. "My fault."

"But when somebody doesn't deliver—"

"Pay the man, Lulu."

"Look, it's my opinion—"

"But it's my money."

Grumbling, Lulu Diamond went to the desk, opened a checkbook and began scribbling on it.

The phone rang and Mrs. Dawg said, "Could you get that, Mr. Blood? I'm not up to phone talk."

Mr. Bloodworth, looking even more uncomfortable than usual, lifted the receiver. "This is, ah, the Dawg suite . . . oh, hi, Herm."

The big detective listened a bit, then his face registered surprise. "Damn. That was fast . . . No kidding. Yeah, I'll tell her. Thanks."

He placed the phone back on its cradle and turned to Mrs.

Dawg. "That was the cops, ma'am," he said. "They found the guy who murdered your husband. Walter Lipton."

"Oh?" She said it as though it didn't matter much.

"He put up a fight and they had to shoot him."

"Is he dead?" she asked.

"Uh huh."

"Too damn bad, huh?" she said and went into the bedroom, closing the door behind her.

Lulu ripped the check from her book, waved it in the air and handed it to Mr. Bloodworth. "You oughta be ashamed to take this."

"Right," Mr. B. said, jerking the paper from her fingers and slipping it into his wallet.

"So they caught and killed the schlemiel who put an end to my meal ticket," Lulu said. "Big friggin' deal."

"Whew," Mr. Bloodworth said, when we were back in his car. "Tough racket."

As we drove toward the apartment I share with Grams, I opened his glove compartment and began digging through his music tapes. Finally, I found one titled "Kicks on 66, the songs of Bobby Troup."

I slipped it into his cassette player and heard a man with a very pleasant voice sing the title number. "You're right," I told Mr. B, "it's a neat song."

"Troup's a real talent. Used to be married to Julie London."

The name meant nothing to me. "According to the song, Route 66 runs from Chicago to L.A.," I said. "Where is it out here, exactly?"

The big detective scratched his head. "Darned if I know. I think they renamed it or something."

"I'll have to look it up," I said.

"The only thing I have to do is deposit this check," he said. "And hope it clears."

I imagine he must have spent some of it in his dim bars because he seemed a little slurry when he arrived at his apartment at ten that night. I'd been phoning him since four in the afternoon.

"Wha's so 'portant?" he wanted to know.

When I told him, he was silent for a few seconds. Then he said. "Could be a coinc'ence."

"A coincidence? Not likely."

"Hmmm. How can we be sure?"

I gave him a suggestion. I'd been thinking the problem through for five hours.

By the time the detectives, Gundersen and Lucas, arrived at the Beverly-Rodeo Hotel at shortly before eleven, Mr. Bloodworth seemed to have sobered up a bit. The lawmen were totally sober. And angry. "Leo, what the hell is this all about? We found the rifle that killed Dawg in Lipton's apartment. He's been IDed as the purchaser of the cell phone. All that was hanging fire was a checkup on the Laurences. That came in and we are now confident that Lipton was acting alone."

"He's dead," Detective Lucas added. "The case is closed."

"But Mr. Lipton wasn't acting alone," I said. "Someone was working with him, someone who could provide him with Mr. Dawg's suite telephone number, someone who knew that Mr. Dawg was familiar enough with Southern California streets and byways to follow rather cryptic directions."

Detective Gundersen shook his head and turned to Mr. Bloodworth. "Leo, I hope we're not here just because of this kid's fantasies."

"Serendipity's pretty good at this sort of thing," Mr. Bloodworth said. "Let's go on up to the suite. The ladies are waiting for us."

"You bothered that poor woman?" Detective Lucas said. "Interrupted her mourning?"

"She'll rest better when we clean this up," Mr. Bloodworth said, entering the hotel.

On the way up in the elevator, Detective Lucas asked me, "So, who do you think was helping Lipton?"

"Lulu Diamond, of course," I said.

The young policeman raised an eyebrow. "Why 'of course'?"

"She had a strong motive," Mr. Bloodworth said. "I checked in with this guy in New York who's on top of the music business. Says Dawg had feelers out for a new manager. Not only was Lulu going to lose her main client, the insurance policy she's been carrying on his life would be canceled."

"How big's the policy, Leo?"

"Half a mil," Mr. Bloodworth said.

Detective Gundersen let out a low whistle. Detective Lucas looked amazed.

The two women were waiting for us. Not cheerily. Nastasia Dawg sat on the sofa, a wine-colored robe wrapped over what appeared to be a satin nightgown. Lulu was dressed in yet another muumuu, this one with large blood-red flowers against a yellow background.

"Let's get this over with," she said waspishly. "I need my beauty sleep."

"Okay, Lulu," Mr. Bloodworth said, as planned, "these officers are here to arrest you in connection with the murder of B. A. Dawg."

Lulu's mouth dropped. And Nastasia Dawg seemed to shake off her languor for the first time, her eyes saucer-wide.

"You son of a buck," Lulu shouted at Detective Lucas. "You sold me out."

The handsome detective couldn't have been more surprised if Lulu's skin had peeled away exposing a Martian underneath. "Are you nuts?" he wailed.

"Yeah," Lulu said, advancing on him. "Nuts for thinking I could count on you."

"Hold on," Detective Gundersen shouted. "Mrs. Diamond, you're saying Lucas is involved in Dawg's murder?"

"Involved? He planned it."

"She's demented," Detective Lucas whined. "I don't even know her."

"You say that now, you bum," Lulu snarled. "But on the phone it was 'Lulu, honey, it's a perfect plan. I got this nut case Lipton all primed to pull the trigger. He's spent the last year getting crazier and crazier. All we've gotta do is get the rapmeister within fifty yards of him.'"

"This is insane," Detective Lucas protested.

"You located Lipton pretty quick today, Lucas," Detective Gundersen said. "And it was you shot him dead."

The young detective looked from his boss to Lulu to Nastasia.

"Stand up guy, huh?" Lulu said with contempt. She turned to us. "That's how he described himself last year when you cops took care of Walter Lipton the first time."

"You two have been planning this for a year?" Mr. Blood-worth asked.

"His plan," she said. "But I went along. I guess we can forget all about that insurance money now, huh, lover?"

Detective Lucas's hand went for his gun, but Mr. Bloodworth was too fast for him. One punch and the younger man was on the floor and Mr. B. was holding the weapon.

Detective Gundersen looked down at his partner and said, "You have the right to remain silent . . ."

As he worked his way through the Miranda litany, his young detective looked past him, staring at Nastasia Dawg. "Tell 'em," Detective Lucas shouted over the recitation of his rights. "Tell 'em, damnit."

"I don't know what you're talking about, mister," the sultry woman replied.

"I'm talking about *us*."

"You and Lulu?" Nastasia looked genuinely confused. But Mr. Bloodworth and I knew that to be a pose.

"Me and you," the no longer very handsome policeman screamed.

"Man's pathetic," Nastasia said, turning to leave the room.

"Yeah, I guess I am," Detective Lucas said bitterly. "I was dumb enough to fall for that, 'my husband beats me' routine. We had to kill him before he killed her. That's what she got me to believe. Then we'd be in velvet. All that loot. We'd live happily ever after. Just another goddamned pipe dream."

He grabbed Detective Gundersen's arm. "You know I'm not lying to you, Herm," he pleaded. "I wouldn't have done what I did for some ugly fat broad."

Lulu Diamond's eyes narrowed.

"I guess I do know that much about you, Lucas," the older detective said sadly. "Leo, you want to keep him and Mrs. Dawg covered while I phone for somebody to come take 'em away?"

Nastasia sneered at Detective Lucas. "It was a setup. Lulu's working with them, you vain jackass. Why is it I always wind up with fools?"

"Lulu, you were terrific," I said. "You should have been an actress."

"I tried that," she said. "But I never was much good. Guess I was waiting for that perfect role. Thanks for giving it to me, Bloodworth."

"Don't thank me," he said. "It was Sara who wrote the script."

Nastasia turned to me. "Of course, it was you. And tell me, little Spice girl, was it something I said?"

"No. Well, Mr. Dawg did indicate he was jealous of you and Detective Lucas. But, actually, it had more to do with our driving around today. Detective Lucas did something that indicated he knew where we were headed even before Mr. Lipton conveyed that information to Mr. Dawg."

"That's a lie," Detective Lucas said.

"I don't lie," I told him. "When we were traveling on Sunset Boulevard, you knew we would eventually drive out of our way to take Santa Monica Boulevard to the ocean."

"I knew that?" Detective Lucas said. "You need help, kid."

"One of us does. According to the Route 66 page on the Internet, the highway runs along Santa Monica Boulevard and ends at the ocean."

"Yeah. I know that. I once drove 66 all the way from Santa Monica to Albuquerque. So what?"

"So while we were still on Sunset, headed away from the ocean, you started humming Mr. Bobby Troup's famous song. You had Route 66 on your mind at a time when only those who planned Mr. Dawg's murder knew that's where we were headed."

"Another fool, just like B. A.," Nastasia said.

"But with better taste in music," I said. "Unfortunately for you both."

TOO MANY MIDNIGHTS

Carolyn Wheat

Carolyn Wheat has won the Agatha, Anthony, Macavity, and Shamus awards for her short stories. Of the six books in her Cass Jameson series, two were nominated for Edgar awards. She no longer lives along Route 66, but look for a collection of stories set along California's Pacific Coast Highway.

West Hollywood, California, 1985

How should a legend die?

As she had lived. With style and taste and that elusive quality called glamour.

There was no glamour anymore. Glamour was dead. When she'd worked in the Business, there were still women who exuded it like expensive perfume. They dressed to kill even for a trip to the Safeway; they always walked in a cloud of scent and wore hats tilted at rakish angles on perfectly coiffed heads, and their heels were never less than three inches.

Stockings had seams, and lipstick was bright red, and those women were bigger than life and so incredibly seductive that it made you feel more alive just to be near them. Bette Davis and Betty Bacall and that dear Missy Stanwyck and nice June Allyson—they'd been like friends, even if they were stars and she a lowly dresser at The Studio, which was always called just The Studio as if there were only one, and it was always referred to in capital letters.

Now they wanted her to die in a squalid nursing home, wearing some unspeakable hospital gown with a slit up the back and no makeup and mules instead of feather-trimmed slippers on feet without nail polish on the toes. They wanted her to die before she was dead, and this Gerri refused to do. She'd take matters into her own hands and do what she had to do in order to die in her own way.

The morning chat show had a feature on the closing of Route 66. Impossible, Gerri thought, a road that famous, in a song even, closed up like an old store put out of business by the new mall. This country had no heart, no sense of history. First they killed glamour, and now Route 66 was being put out to pasture. Wasn't it appropriate that she, too, should fade away?

But what to wear for her final appearance on this planet? The forties had been a nice period, if a trifle heavy in the shoulders for her taste. She had a lovely Balenciaga evening suit of black cashmere with embroidery around the neckline and rhinestone buttons. A small black hat with a veil and bright red lipstick and those suede pumps—dignified. Very dignified. But was it the right choice? Was it, perhaps, a trifle too Rosalind Russell?

Standing before the walk-in closet with the clothes organized according to period, she reached out a manicured hand and touched the fragile black chiffon number from the 1920s, laden with beads that twinkled in the strong California sunlight.

What stories that dress could tell!

Chicago, Illinois, 1928

"It's the most beautiful dress I've ever seen." Belinda Carlisle couldn't help crushing the crepe to her breast and burying her face in its sheer, bead-bedezened loveliness. "And you're a perfect darling for buying it."

It was her very first grown-up dress. The first dress in her life that would allow her legs, freshly shaved and encased in sheer silk stockings, to be the focus of male attention. The days of middy blouses and black lisle hose under demure long skirts was over.

"Oh, Daddy, thank you. Thank you so much." She gave the dress one more loving squeeze and turned toward her bedroom.

"Now, Belinda," her father said, raising his voice, "I want you to promise you won't do anything foolish tonight."

"Oh, no, Papa, I won't." The lie tripped lightly off her tongue, but the dress itself knew she was fibbing. How could anyone not act foolish wearing a cloud of crepe with beads that would gleam in the soft amber light and fringe that would tickle her rouged knees?

Oh, yes. The knees were rouged and so were her cheeks, and she pasted her hair into spit curls on either side of her face and one in the center of her forehead just like Clara Bow. She made a Clara Bow rosebud mouth at herself in the mirror, then broke into a wide innocent smile that showed the gap between her front teeth.

She clamped her lips shut; It Girls didn't have gaps in their teeth like farmer's daughters. They were cool and aloof and mysterious. And tonight she wasn't going to be Belinda Carlisle of the banking Carlisles. She was going to be a flapper, smoking a cigarette in an ivory holder, sipping gin from a silver flask, swearing and smelling of orchids and staying out all night with a college man. Talking of Paris and F. Scott

Fitzgerald and riding in an open roadster with the wind in her hair. She was going to be the kind of woman Daddy wouldn't want her to know.

She loved her father very much, but she wasn't a child anymore, and tonight she was going to prove it.

As she rubbed the rabbit's foot over her face one more time, adding a smidge more rouge, she hummed the new song that was all the rage:

You can bring Pearl,
She's a darned nice girl.
But don't bring LuLu.

LuLu always wants to do
What the boys all want her to.
You can bring Sal,
Or Dottie or Al,
But don't bring LuLu.

When Price introduced her to his friends from college, she said, with a toss of her newly-bobbed head, "Oh, don't bother with that old Belinda. Just call me LuLu."

And they did. As the night wore on, as they drove in Price's shiny new car with its leather seats from speakeasy to speakeasy, she gradually became LuLu, shedding bits and pieces of her old Belinda self along the way. The gin helped, of course, but it was the dress that transformed her, somehow permeating her very skin with its forbidden desires.

Finally Price's friend Mack said he knew a place that stayed open all night. A roadhouse. A real and true roadhouse, just like she'd heard about from the fast crowd at school. It was called Wicked Wanda's and it was out on the highway they'd just made a national road. Route 66 it was called, and the sound of it thrilled her because it was so strange and so filled with adventure. It went, or so they said, all the way to Los Angeles, California, and she wondered as they made their way to Joliet how it would feel to keep on going and going and wake up with orange trees all around you.

West Hollywood, California, 1985

Route 66. Nineteen and forty-four. The Texas panhandle; a town called McLean. Big army base and a POW camp to boot; Army shows with chorus girls from Vegas and a couple comics couldn't have played a full week in Jersey, they were so corny. But the boys ate that stuff up, and the biggest hand of all went to a bunch of soldiers in drag imitating the chorines. It was supposed to be funny, but to Private Gerald Tinsley, it was the thrill of a lifetime—dressing the way he'd always wanted to, and big macho men watching him perform without disgust.

Was it so much to ask? That he be allowed to die—to live until his death—wearing the clothes he loved? The clothes that transformed him from drab, uninteresting, flawed male to glorious, sexual, sensuous, enticing, fascinating She-male—Queen of all he surveyed?

He hated the term "transvestite." So clinical. And "cross-dresser." That sounded like one of those monks with a huge wooden cross dangling on his chest. No, the proper word for him and those like him was Queen. Regal, dignified, wearing only the richest fabrics, the best cut garments made by the foremost designers of the age.

He'd been lucky to own such luxurious gowns, lucky and of course blessed with a fabulous eye. Everyone said so. The movie stars he dressed for their roles all deferred to him (except Crawford, of course, but everyone knew how she was, never listened to anyone in her life, and my God, look at those lumberjack shoulders. Not a speck of femininity there, not like that sweet Loretta Young, who was happy to give him a castoff gown or two and never raised an eyebrow when he said it was for his sister in Duluth.).

He rambled nowadays. He was getting old. Not as old as he'd hoped to get, but, then, everyone had their cross to bear, and how did we get back to that anyway?

What friends he had left in the Industry said it was time for the nursing home. He couldn't live on his own any longer, not with his muscles failing and his eyesight going and even though the little fire in the kitchen could have happened to anybody—anybody!—the truth was plain.

But even in West Hollywood, there wasn't a nursing home that would allow him to take his true identity with him. Oh, they'd been very generous when it came to furniture. Bring your favorite chair, Mr. Tinsley. Bring photographs for your bedside table. And, since it was Hollywood and not, thank the Lord, Duluth, no one would raise an eyebrow if that special loved one's photograph was male instead of female.

But would they let him sit on the verandah in his favorite silk dressing gown with the breeze blowing the skirt about his knees, fur-trimmed mules on his feet? Would they let him come to dinner in his best Chanel cocktail dress, just the perfect basic black, worn with real matched pearls?

No, they wouldn't.

And so he would die. He would pack a little suitcase and check himself into that wonderful pink hotel in Santa Monica, at the very end of Route 66, and he would watch the sunset and sip mimosas until he fell at last into that long, long sleep. And he would wear his absolutely favorite frock while he waited for the pills to take effect.

When they found him the next morning, they would say, She was a Queen to the end.

But which dress? His closet spanned the decades, from his earliest youthful flings to his matronly years. Which dress would most fully express his inner self?

Perhaps the Thirties, the era of Harlow and Ginger Rogers, the sleek lingerie, the long, flowing lines and perfectly draped chiffon with—

Oh, yes. The pink-green fern print bias-cut cocktail frock that showed off his slender waist. The one in which he'd taught the Continental to a movie star no one ever could have imagined as an escort to not-quite-female beauties. He lay the beaded dress on his rose satin bedspread and paraded about the room with the fern print draped over his shoulders, moving slowly and sensuously to music only he could hear.

Ah, the Thirties. Hollywood before the Code, before the twin-bed hypocrisy of the Forties and Fifties. When no starlet worth the name owned a pair of step-ins, since underwear was guaranteed to ruin the perfect line of the gowns.

He'd worn lush honey-colored furs and carried an envelope clutch made of baby alligator, complete with head that still had little teeth like razors.

Perhaps this was the dress he should choose for his last appearance. If only he could find that alligator bag and the shoes that went with it. And the citrine earrings and the brooch with the filigree daffodils.

He sobered as he reflected that the Thirties hadn't been a terribly happy decade for everyone.

Goldroad, Arizona, 1938

"I do believe all the Okies in the world is on this road." Ma fanned herself with one of the paper fans they give out at church when Sister Hattie passed. It had a picture of Sister Hattie on it, wearing her big old black hat with white roses.

T'other side had a picture of Ransom's funeral home, big as life and twice as scary.

Pa grunted and shifted the tobacco to the other side of his mouth. "All the Okies in the world got car trouble, too, same as we'uns."

"What we gonna sell this time, Pa?"

I poked Bubba in the ribs. And I poked him hard. Ain't no call for a boy to be that stupid and him all of ten years old.

We was gonna sell whatever we had to. Whatever we had left.

Ma like to died when we sold Mawmaw's tablecloth, the one she embroidered with her own hands. It had flowers on it and birds and leaves and it was real pretty on the table back at the home place. When we done had a table.

Table went nigh onto a year ago. When the dust storms first hit our place.

Pa said we'd never leave. Said the folks sellin' up and headin' out west was traitors. Said the land wouldn't fail us. Said the Lord wouldn't fail us.

Now we're on the road, same as the others. Only we didn't sell up; we was pushed out by the bank. Lost the home place anyhow, and no money to show for it.

Only one thing left to sell. Ma knew it. I knew it.

But Pa didn't.

The car trouble was real bad, and that was on account of the road was real bad. We seen dust before, so bone-dry weren't nothing new, but this here Arizona dust was even drier and dustier than back home. I ain't never seen dry like this, dry and rocky like I pictured the moon.

And the hills. Lord, I done read about hills and mountains in McGuffey's reader, but living in Oklahoma, you don't hardly see none of 'em. The hill we climbed down to get to this here Goldroad town was so high and the road so snaky we had to come down backwards.

Bubba thought that was fun, but I could see the back of
Pa's neck getting all red and sweaty and I knew it was real
serious so I didn't laugh when we crept our way down like
an inchworm.

Along the way you could see cars that didn't make it.
Rusty old Model As like ourn and one or two newer models
with their hoods open and clouds of steam coming out of
them like dragons and the young'uns all scrambling around,
glad to be out of doors after all that riding.

The garage man told Pa he needed a new radiator and said
if he had a family to tote all the way to Californy, he'd get a
new set of tires. He said the desert was death on tires, and if
we thought we'd seen the worst of the 66 highway, well, we
were plumb wrong because the worst was yet to come in the
big hot desert that practically fried you like a hunk of bacon
and then froze you silly at night.

Bubba wanted an orange Nehi, but I gave him another
poke in the ribs on account of we didn't have no money for
such folderol and he could stick his head under the pump
and open his mouth if he was dry. Which we all was since
that hot Arizona air was half-dust and the sun like to pulled
all the water right out of a body, so that we hardly even went
to the privy the whole time we was driving.

The garage man had a little bitty old general store right
next to his car-fixing place. Inside it was filled with a lot of
things that made me homesick for Oklahoma. Quilts piled
on a wooden table and embroidered tablecloths like we used
to have. Family things people sold when times got hard and
they was out of gas and out of luck.

I knew what Ma was gonna sell, and I knew she was
gonna sneak it out of the cardboard suitcase when Pa wasn't
looking on account of he'd feel real bad if he knew, but we
had to have them tires. We had to.

"Earlie Sue," Ma said, her voice all sweet like molasses, which told me she was up to something, "Why'nt you take Bubba over to the shave ice stand and see if the man will give you a chunk without a flavor on it. He couldn't be so mean as to charge you if you didn't have no flavor."

Well, I wasn't so all-fired certain about that, since I didn't think we'd met with huge balls of kindness since we left Oklahoma, but I did take Bubba aside and tell him, "You look all nice and wistful, and be sure to call the man sir." He trotted off, happy at the thought of slippery cold ice between his fingers, running down his chin.

The ice sounded mighty fine to me, too, but I had to see what Ma was gonna do with Aunt Pearl's dress. See, that was what she was gonna sell, and that dress was meant to go to me when I got big enough. Pa always said so. Said I was the spit and image of Aunt Pearl, who was his baby sister and died young and tragic, and I wanted that dress ever since I first laid eyes on it, even if the little beads all over it was winking at me like nasty little crows eyes.

I wanted to be like Pearl and take the train up to Chicago and make me a new life. A new life without any chickens to feed or chickens to bury when the dust got 'em. And if I was goin' to Chicago, I was gonna need that there crow's eye dress so's I could pass for a city gal.

But on the other hand, if we never got those tires and never got to Californy, then I might just die out here in Goldroad, which sure as blazes didn't have no gold in it that I could see, and believe you me, I looked.

I stood just barely inside the general store, trying to grab onto a little bit of shade. Pa was kneeling on the griddle-hot hard ground, looking at them tires of ourn like he never seen them before. Ran his fingers over what was left of the tread and shook his head. I could almost see his thoughts over his head like Orphan Annie's. Them new tires were three dollar and fifty cent apiece, and we needed all four. I pulled the times tables out from the back of my brain and went to work a-calculating. Four times three makes twelve and four fifty-cent pieces makes two dollar and that was fourteen, which was about ten dollars more than we had left in the kick. Not to mention that we'd need gasoline and oil and bread to eat on the way.

That old dress wasn't gonna be worth ten dollars to the garage man, however much it might mean to Pa. Mawmaw's tablecloth was only good for a fillup of gas; the man at the Red Head gas station in Flagstaff wouldn't even give us an extra can to tote.

There was a sound inside the store; I turned and shaded my eyes and peered inside. A woman walked slow and swishy, like a move star, and the light glanced off the beads on Aunt Pearl's dress, but who—

Did the garage man's wife want to try it on before she bought it?

But then the light hit the woman's face, and I fell back with the biggest shock of my entire life. The woman was my ma, and the last time she tried to wear that dress, it wouldn't go over her big hips. Now it hung on her like she was a broomstick. But that weren't the real shocking part. My ma, chief deaconess of the Jesus Saves Through Faith Alone Baptist Church, had her face all painted like a Jezebel. Red lipstick and powder and black rims around her eyes. She looked spooky and pretty and scary and plumb straight-out determined all at the same time.

Well, we got the fourteen dollars and the tires and a can of gas to boot.

And when we needed more, Ma sent Bubba off some-wheres, which wasn't never too hard to do, and had Pa take the car over to a garage to check on something or other, and she came back with enough to keep us on the road.

I was in mortal fright the whole rest of the ride, all the way to Victorville, Californy, where Pa finally got some day work, figuring that if he found out what Ma was doing, I'd be a motherless child for certain sure. But as the years have rolled on and I look back on them days, I come to believe that my Pa knew but didn't know.

He didn't want to know, 'cause if he knew, he'd have to kill Ma. So they both kept the family together in their way: Ma by doing what she had to do, and Pa by not letting himself know what she was doing.

They was both heroes of Route 66, you ask me, which you did, come to think of it—but you hadn't better print any of it, because Ma died in the sanctity of her church and wouldn't want any of this told to strangers.

But I sure do wish I could have one more glimpse of her the way she looked in that there crow's eye dress that was meant to go to me but never did.

West Hollywood, California, 1985

The Forties wasn't his favorite decade. The women were too masculine for him all those suits and shoulders. And the shoes! He could weep for those shoes—although he had rather enjoyed the open-toe look, since it gave him a chance to paint his toenails bright red.

Come to think of it, the Forties hadn't been a bad time in which to grow mature. Which was to say, he'd lost his peachfuzz innocence and replaced it with a sophisticated woman-about-town look that suited his external rather than his internal age. Roz Russell with style, he called it.

The purple Chanel suit with the black velvet collar and the black buttons?

Too Eve Arden.

The copper crepe dress with the drop waist and the

beaded flower at the pleated fall? Lovely, but he wasn't at all certain he could still fasten that side zipper. His medication had added a spare tire around his middle even as the rest of him grew skeletonlike from the loss of flesh.

The Nile green shantung Anna May Wong number with the embroidered dragons and the slit up the sides? With real silk stockings like only whores could get during the war? Or should he wear nylon in memory of the war effort?

But did he really want to paint his toenails?

As he box-stepped his way back to the closet, the rose dress with the full, full skirt and no straps caught his eye. Oh, he'd been far too old to carry that one off, but he'd decided to ignore the mirror and dress to suit his inner self. He'd bought a blonde wig and pulled his face back with tape (a homemade facelift), and learned makeup tricks from his friends in the Business. Kim Novak was his ideal during this time, although he also loved dear Loretta. But the brunette wig added ten years to his face, so blonde and rose were the colors he chose for his Fifties look.

The long skirt covered bony knees, and the bare male shoulders could always be minimized by the furriest of angora sweater-tops, the ones that curved over the bustline and just barely reached to the waist. With pearls and beads in elaborate designs, made to match the little evening purse and shoes.

The Fifties had made him feel young again, after the business girl Forties.

He'd felt like a prom queen in that rose dress.

Elk City, Oklahoma, 1958

"If that isn't the ugliest dress I've ever seen in all my born days," the woman exclaimed in a loud hog-calling Oklahoma twang. "It's perfect. It's utterly and totally perfect."

She turned to the man in the ratty little shop. "How much do you want for me to take that old rag off your hands?"

"If it's such an old rag, why'd you want it in the first place?" The man shifted his pipe from one side of his mouth to the other; he didn't sound put out, just curious. And not a bit as if he intended to lower the price either.

"We're doing *Private Lives*," the woman replied. "That dress would be the absolute making of the production. It's so very Twenties. So dated. So passe. So gin and—"

"That there dress sells for fifteen dollars, ma'am. Fifteen and not a penny less."

"Oh, you can come down to ten, surely. It's for charity, after all. The Kiwanis donate all the proceeds to the Children's Hospital."

The Kiwanis of Elk City, Oklahoma, doing *Private Lives*? Taking dear Noel's words and twanging them to death with those god-awful accents?

It wasn't to be borne. So Gerald Tinsley stepped up to the man in the shop and said, "I'll pay twenty. Don't bother wrapping it."

The bulky little woman with the tight pincurled hair and the look of outrage on her Helen Hokinson face drew herself up and said, "You do realize you're taking this dress away from a charitable institution."

"Madame," he'd replied with an echo of dear Noel's charming hauteur, "I consider the rescue of this dress from the Elk City Kiwanis to be an act of charity unparalleled in the history of this squalid little town."

He left her standing open-mouthed as he carried the dress into the wide blue sky day and sped away in his Nash Rambler, heading straight for Hollywood. He felt so good that he raced the Rock Island train that ran parallel to Route 66. He was doing all right, too, until a huge truck pulled out ahead of him.

The dress would be perfect. A Hollywood song-and-dance man was about to hold his annual dress-up party, and Gerri would make a wonderful flapper. He wondered if dear Noel—whom he'd met only once—might deign to drop by.

Santa Monica, California, 1985

He smiled as he pulled the beaded flapper dress from its plastic casing and held it over his torso with hands that barely felt the tissue-thin fabric. He preened in front of the mirror, pantomiming an awkward, old man's version of the Charleston. In his mind, he was at the ball, his very first ball, where all the men wanted to dance with him, to take him into the gardenia-scented garden for a midnight kiss.

As he danced before the mirror, Gerald McEvoy Tinsley became once again, at least in his dreaming mind, the fabulous Gerri.

Joliet, Illinois, 1928

Oh, the music was hot at Wicked Wanda's, and she shimmied like Sister Kate and flirted like LuLu in the song she'd chosen for her anthem. She tossed back gin fizz like it was birch beer and inhaled cigarette smoke without coughing and she sat on a man's lap and let his hands slide up underneath the sheer crepe skirt of her beaded dress.

And the man wasn't her beau.

Price was disgusted with her, but she only laughed at the pinched look on his square-jawed face. He'd started out the evening with prissy little Belinda Carlisle and he was ending it with LuLu, who fascinated men and reveled in their frank admiration of her.

It was the dress that did the flirting, Belinda realized. The dress loved to be ogled and touched, liked the feel of rough masculine hands on its delicate, hand-beaded beauty. The dress wanted sex and gin and music and Life with a capital L. It wanted adventure, and as long as she wore the dress, she wanted it to.

If she stripped the dress off right here on the sawdust-strewn floor at Wicked Wanda's, would LuLu turn back into pumpkin Belinda, her Cinderella evening ending in the miserable realization that she'd lost Price and her own self-respect? Or would she laugh and throw her arms around the nearest man and beg him to do what she'd wanted a man to do since the night began? Was it the dress that was making her act this way, or had the dress only released an inner fire she'd kept banked since her girlhood's end?

She would never know.

Price brooded. She'd known that about him, but she'd thought it was essentially a bloodless habit of rumination and calculation. She'd seen him as a man wooing the boss's daughter in hopes of rising at the bank. She hadn't seen him as a passionate lover, hadn't realized he was keeping his own flame of desire under wraps for the sake of a girl he saw as a delicate virgin to be gradually initiated into the magic of physical love.

The delicate virgin lifted her skirts and showed her garters, shimmied her black-beaded bottom like a common tramp, and smiled the lusty smile of a girl just begging for it.

He couldn't stand it one minute longer. He jumped up and stepped into the dance floor, grabbing Belinda by the hand and twisting her toward him.

But was it Belinda or LuLu?

Which one did he want?

Was he enraged that his beloved Belinda had become the lusty LuLu—or was he jealous of the men who'd brought out the LuLu in her when all he'd been able to do was woo Belinda?

Thirty seconds later, it no longer mattered. His massive football-player's hands reached to her white neck and squeezed. She shook like a rag doll, her legs kicking so hard her shoes fell off. Men grabbed him from behind, but it was too late. He held on like a terrier, pushing his strong fingers into her vulnerable flesh, hating and enjoying the way her tongue popped out of her mouth and her eyes bulged red with blood.

Santa Monica, California, 1985

"Una momia, una momia," Lupe screamed, running into the hallway with her apron flapping like a crazy bird.

"What you talkin' about, girl?" That was Tasha, the head maid, who doesn't like to hear no Spanish on the job.

"She's says there's a mummy in there," I translated. Then I turned to Lupe and said in Spanish that she should stop talking crazy because there wasn't no mummy in that room and she knew it.

She pointed to the room with a shaky hand and I went inside, not being afraid of no mummies or anything else that you could find in the Surf Motel.

Well, I crossed myself right away when I seen it, but I knew it wasn't no mummy. It was just a dead lady was all, a lady in a black dress with lots of shiny beads all over it. An old lady, with big hands and feet like the gringos got, and too much makeup on her papery old face.

She had a glass of champagne next to her on the little table, and she looked to me like she went out happy.

It was a minute or two before I remembered that the party who checked into this room yesterday afternoon was a man instead of a woman. A man who gave me a nice tip and said to leave him alone.

I looked a little closer at those big hands and feet and understood. Then I reached out a hand and touched the dress, all filmy and heavy with the beads. It was a pretty dress, old-fashioned, and I wondered what it would feel like to put it on.

In a dress like that, I could get Roberto to look at me, even if it did make Carlos jealous.

I wondered if there was any way I could get the cops to let me have that dress when they finished with it.